THE ONE THAT I WANT

marilyn brant

Twelfth Night
Publishing

(Mirabelle Harbor, Book 2)

The One That I Want
(Mirabelle Harbor, Book 2)
Copyright © 2015 Marilyn B. Weigel
Twelfth Night Publishing

Cover Design © 2015 Sarah Hansen, Okay Creations
ISBN-13: 978-0-9961178-1-4

DEDICATION & THANKS

For my family, my good friends, and my amazing readers & early reviewers—I appreciate you all so much! And for Jeff, for endless reasons. Thank you to A.J. for your editorial eye—you have a true talent. And an extra-special thanks to Debbie Fortin, Gina Paulus & Ceri Tanti. Your insights on this book when it was in draft form were tremendously helpful!

OTHER BOOKS BY BESTSELLING AUTHOR MARILYN BRANT

According to Jane

Friday Mornings at Nine

A Summer in Europe

The Sweet Temptations Collection
~On Any Given Sundae
~Double Dipping
~Holiday Man

The Perfect Pair
~Pride, Prejudice and the Perfect Match
~Pride, Prejudice and the Perfect Bet

The Road to You
The Road and Beyond (expanded edition)

All About Us (novella)

The Mirabelle Harbor Series
~Take a Chance on Me
~The One That I Want
~You Give Love a Bad Name (coming soon)
~Stranger on the Shore (coming soon)

Wanderlust in Suburbia and Other Reflections on
Motherhood (nonfiction essays)

NOTE FROM THE AUTHOR

*THE ONE THAT I WANT is Book 2 in Marilyn Brant's
Mirabelle Harbor series, but this story and all of the
contemporary romances in this series can be enjoyed as
stand-alone novels.*

CHAPTER ONE

I could still remember how it felt to be a lonely teenager, sitting in the middle of another mind-numbing social studies class with old Mr. Tremain droning on and on about the political factors contributing to WWII...

As he jabbered, I'd drift off into my favorite, most often replayed romantic fantasy. The one where my high-school crush or my latest movie-star heartthrob—or, ideally, both—confessed their love for me. I'd mentally spool between their dramatic declarations of affection, like it was one of those cheesy film montages, complete with steamy love scenes and a hot musical soundtrack. And it always made me smile because it was *just so wonderful*.

But when you were two decades older than sixteen, the mother of a sensitive and depressed ten-year-old daughter, and a relatively new widow, you didn't expect fantasies like that to happen for real. Not anymore.

Then again, when you had the world's loveliest (but pushiest) best friend, you had to get used to expecting the unexpected.

Early in the summer, my best friend, Sharlene Michaelsen Boyd, said to me over the phone, "It's been

1

over six months since the car accident, Julia. You should come out for drinks with the Quest group. They did me a world of good after The Snake left, and I know you'll like them. It'll be fun. I promise."

I raised my eyebrows at this, glad Shar couldn't see me. The Quest group was a local singles' club she'd belonged to in the several years since her divorce from Stephen, aka "The Snake," Boyd. Once upon a time, Shar had been deeply in love with Stephen. He'd been her high-school sweetheart. Now, he was her ex-husband and ex-soulmate. Ex-mammal, too, if Shar had anything to say about it.

"We're trying out that new place in town—The Lounge. This Friday night. Seven o'clock. They're known for their merlots," she informed me. "And I hear they have wicked spicy chicken quesadillas, too."

"I'll think about it," I told her. My standard answer.

I heard a groan on the other end of the line. "Look, girlfriend, I'm serious. You're coming out with me this time. You have no more excuses. Summer vacation just started, so you can't bury yourself in teaching tasks, and Analise is leaving for camp in just a few weeks. You will not spend the entire two-and-a-half-month break at home reading Austen and the Brontës or watching *NCIS* reruns."

"*NCIS: Los Angeles*," I specified. "And what's wrong with that? The bromance between Chris O'Donnell and LL Cool J is—"

"Not the point," Shar interrupted. "I totally get that you're not yet ready to date again, and I don't blame you. I know you and Adam had a very happy marriage and that half a year of working through your grief might not be long enough. I'm not suggesting that you forget him or the life you all shared. But Julia—" She paused. Then her voice turned very serious. "How is Analise ever going to learn to move on if you won't? You need to model it for her."

I squeezed my eyes shut, feeling drenched in a wave of pain that came over me like a tsunami.

Dammit.

Despite all the months I'd already grieved and mourned, some days the loss hit me extra hard. I wanted to scream, "None of this was supposed to happen!" Losing Adam and becoming a single parent was nowhere in my well-structured plans. Or in my late husband's. But it had happened anyway, and now our once vibrant and joyful daughter was clinically depressed, seeing counselors, taking medications I could barely pronounce, and struggling to live without her dad in her life. Witnessing Analise's pain was far more gut-wrenching than even dealing with my own.

I bit my lip to keep a sob from escaping, but my silence had lasted too long for my good friend and teaching colleague.

"I'm so sorry," Shar whispered. "I didn't mean to upset you. I just want to help."

"I know you do," I said, trying to imagine myself going out with a group of strangers in just a few days, drinking wine, looking for new friendships or maybe love, and talking about...who knew what they all talked about during these outings? It had been a dozen years since I'd been on the dating scene. Music, movies, fashions, and pop culture had all changed. I didn't even know where to begin. Or how to start a conversation with a man. I told Shar this.

"Oh, c'mon. You're a better conversationalist than my brother Chance. The guy hardly speaks when there's a woman in the room, and not much when there isn't. Even *he* managed to meet someone and fall in love."

I rolled my eyes. Chance Michaelsen wasn't exactly your average guy. "Your brother is a dazzlingly good looking twenty-eight-year-old personal trainer. He has the body of an action-film star and the face of a Giorgio Armani model. He doesn't *have* to talk to a woman. He just needs to smolder at her."

My friend scoffed this off as "insignificant." Shar, who

was in her early thirties, was a classic middle child with excellent negotiation skills. She had two older brothers, Derek and Blake, and two younger ones—the twins, Chance and Chandler. In addition to being at the center of Mirabelle Harbor society, such that it was, every one of the Michaelsen siblings was strikingly and infuriatingly attractive. They never seemed to factor in that gift when talking to mere mortals like the rest of us.

"Just start with a glass of wine, Julia. That's all I'm asking. One hour. One glass. See how you feel after that and take it from there, okay?"

"Okay," I said, not wanting to keep fighting her on this. I knew my best friend. Very well. She was going to wear me down until I agreed anyway. "Friday night at The Lounge. See you then."

❀❀❀

My daughter literally stumbled into the house that afternoon.

"Ouch!" Analise howled, rubbing the knee she'd bashed into the doorframe. She bounced on one leg and, in the process, managed to bang her elbow on the inside doorknob as she twisted around to shut the heavy oak door.

She whimpered like an injured puppy, and I rushed to her, trying to soothe away the sting of both new bumps. If only all bruises could be tended to so easily. Sadly, I knew my daughter's deepest hurts were invisible to the eye.

"How was your play date with Brooke and Lindsay?" I asked. They were Yvette Hampton's daughters, our neighbors down the block. The girls were one year older and one year younger than mine, respectively. I'd known their mom ever since high school.

"Brooke got mad because Lindsay went into her room and borrowed her iPod without asking because she wanted to play me an Ariana Grande song. But then Lindsay got mad when Brooke took her phone and snapped pictures of us that she said she'd post on Instagram with the caption 'Annoying Aliens' if we didn't give her back the iPod." My daughter squinted at me and shook her head. "Whenever I'm with them, I'm always kinda glad I'm an only child."

I laughed, but I knew she was lying. I could see the wistfulness in her large gray eyes—the eyes she got from her father. Analise had always wanted a sibling, ever since she could point to her favorite doll and say, "Baby." Adam and I had tried to give her one. Halfheartedly at first. More intentionally in recent years. But he was busy with his medical practice, and I was only thirty-six. We thought we had time.

I made grilled cheese sandwiches and tomato soup for dinner—her favorite—and tried to get her to talk about her "everyday feelings," just like the grief counselor suggested. We were supposed to make a habit of discussing our emotions, not reserve such chats only for periods of stress and trauma. It was a routine we hadn't quite mastered yet, but we were both trying.

"Can you believe camp is coming up so soon?" I asked, injecting as much enthusiasm into my voice as humanly possible. "How are you feeling about that?"

"Brooke and Lindsay keep telling me I'm gonna love it," Analise stated in a tone that made me certain she wasn't a believer.

"Their mom said they both really did love it last summer. And they'll be there to show you around this year. You've got two friends as tour guides, which is pretty great!"

Analise cringed, the little cynic, and shrugged. "I liked what we did last summer better. Daddy and you and me and that trip to Florida." She sighed.

Yeah, well, it was hard to compete with the allure of Disney. Or with a living dad.

"I know. Me, too," I admitted. A part of me wanted to just cancel camp. Keep her home with me for the whole month of July instead. Cradle her in my arms where she would stay safe.

But the counselor had strongly suggested it was time for something like this. That, while some kids did better at home, clinging to memories and coming to terms with loss, Analise wasn't one of them. She was sinking deeper into depression. In order to break out of her shell again, the counselor felt my daughter needed a drastic change of environment, one that didn't constantly remind her of her dad. A place where she could "exercise her independence," do "high-interest activities" that she hadn't before tried, "feel empowered" as she "gently separated" from the past in a place where this was seen as a positive thing—not as a loss.

No one at the camp would have parents present. And though there were many kids, like Yvette's daughters, who had both parents still living in the same house, at least 65% of the children attending Camp Willowgreen this summer came from one-parent families, primarily because of death or divorce.

"Hey, what do you want for dessert?" I said enthusiastically. "We've got chocolate ice cream or those sugar cookies with sprinkles that you like or—"

"I'm not hungry now, Mommy."

"Not even for ice cream? Not even for cookies?"

She *never* used to turn down either treat, no matter how big the meal preceding it. And tonight she'd had only one cup of soup and three-fourths of her sandwich.

"Maybe later," she said, unable to disguise her apathy. "I'm gonna read." She meandered away. No bounce in her step. No spirit in her expression. Nothing.

Somehow I had to find a way to get her excited about life again. Even if I couldn't quite manage the same for myself.

Maybe Shar was right. Maybe, for Analise's sake, I needed to try harder. Set a better example of someone who still honored Adam's memory but was capable of moving on.

Even as impossible as that was to imagine.

CHAPTER TWO

Friday night, Shar was waiting for me at the entrance to The Lounge, arms crossed and tapping her long tapered fingers impatiently against her supremely toned biceps. She was a Pilates regular and had gotten tons of fitness tips from her brother Chance.

"What?" I said. "It's only 7:07. I'm not that late."

She waggled her brows at me. "You've missed seven minutes of fun already, and at least half of the club members have downed their first glass of merlot by now."

"Lushes," I joked.

My best friend chuckled. "You're going to love 'em. C'mon. I'll introduce you all around."

Inside the wine bar, it was dimly lit but pleasant. There were long tables, perfect for large parties, if not exactly conducive to intimate conversation.

The windows were open and without screens, like a café in Europe, so the warm summer breeze blew through the place and the laughing, chattering voices on the sidewalk outside filtered in without obstruction. It reminded me of the week-long trip to southern France that Adam took me on. A very belated honeymoon (five years late, to be exact) because we'd been so broke when we first got married. And, well, because I'd gotten pregnant with Analise just before the wedding, too.

I felt a sudden, sharp pang of loss at the memory.

Oh, Adam. Why did you have to drive so fast that early December night? Why couldn't you have worn a seatbelt like you'd always advised your patients at the clinic? Why...? There were still so many whys.

I couldn't keep straight the names of all of the Quest group members—there were more than a dozen of them—but they seemed nice enough, and Shar was right about my liking them. A few were inquisitive and asked me some personal questions, but they were still tactful and avoided inquiries about why I was currently single.

My guess was that Shar had already filled them in on the situation, no doubt issuing a direct command like, "Don't ask Julia about her husband's fatal accident." Mirabelle Harbor, despite being a suburb of a metropolis like Chicago, was as gossipy as one of those quaint small towns featured on every other nighttime TV dramedy. Even those residents who hadn't personally known the late Dr. Adam T. Crane would likely have heard something about that icy collision.

I had to admit, though, I was always a little surprised when I met people in town who *didn't* know Adam. He'd been so social, so talkative. How could anyone have missed out on meeting him? After all, he'd been at the center of my universe.

A younger woman named Vicky Bernier swigged half her glass of merlot and asked me about my job.

"I'm an English teacher at Mirabelle Harbor Junior High," I told her.

"Oh! Like Shar," the woman said, smiling warmly.

"Yes. That's where we met."

"I'm a teacher in town, too," replied Vicky. "High school French."

We talked about our two different schools for a while, since the K - 8 district was separate from the 9 - 12 one. Eventually, the topic rolled around to the universities we'd attended.

"I did my teacher training at Franklin College in the city," Vicky told me.

"Me, too! Small world," I said, and we launched into a long discussion about their secondary education program.

"So, will you be going to the reunion in July?" Vicky asked.

Something tugged at the edges of my mind. A letter I'd gotten from the university last month. I'd opened it only far enough to see that it had been addressed generally, to the "Graduate of the Franklin College School of Education." I figured it was another plea for alumni donations, and I'd set it aside for later. Then, of course, I'd forgotten about it. Until now.

"Was that the letter we got in the mail a few weeks ago?"

Vicky nodded.

I grimaced. "It's probably too late to attend. I'm sure I missed the RSVP deadline."

The other teacher regarded me thoughtfully and thumbed through a few screens on her iPhone. "Nope," she said brightly. "The RSVP deadline isn't until Tuesday." She flashed her phone calendar at me and grinned. "Register for it this weekend, and we can go together, if you'd like. It'll be more fun that way, don't you think?"

Her enthusiasm and warmth was infectious, and I found myself not only agreeing but, surprisingly, feeling a burst of happiness at the idea. There was a different energy here with this crowd than with most of my teaching colleagues (Shar excepted). I liked being seen in a new light, not as "poor Julia Meriwether Crane, whose husband crashed his car and died on impact." I liked that I'd just made a new friend, too.

Of course, I couldn't think about teacher training and my Franklin College days without thinking of Ben Saintsbury. I'd only dated a handful of guys as an undergrad, but my longest and most intense relationship had been with Ben. And it had ended badly. Like "Agony of Defeat" badly.

I cringed remembering. I wondered if he'd be there and, if so, how he'd react to seeing me again. Or how I'd react to seeing *him*.

But I decided not to think about it. Ben's potential presence aside, the reunion was scheduled for Saturday, July tenth—the first weekend after I had to take Analise to camp. I needed to plan activities for myself during her month away or I'd go batshit crazy.

The group's conversation turned to other things. A few of the guys brought up baseball, a topic that had many fervent fans, male and female alike. I listened, smiled a lot, and worked on finishing my one glass of merlot (it wasn't bad), as the discussion wove through other Chicagoland sports teams, sites to take in while down in the city, the horrors of home appliance breakdowns, and the best/worst of the summer movie flicks.

"Oh!" a well-dressed woman sitting near Shar exclaimed. I studied her casual but perfectly coordinated outfit and her gentle features, and found myself wishing I could project the kind of self-possessed, confident air she gave off. "That reminds me—"

"Billy?" a clear voice called from across the room, interrupting the lady and effectively halting conversation at half the tables in the wine bar. "Bill Dennon?"

"Hey, Kris!" the slightly balding Cubs fan across the table from me called back. "So good to see you, man. Heard you were back in town."

The guy was walking in from behind me, so I felt it would be rude to turn and look. It wasn't until Bill announced to the group, "Everyone, meet my old traveling soccer buddy, Kristopher Karlsen," that my head snapped around to stare.

Oh, hell, no!

It couldn't be. Not the same Kristopher Karlsen from high school. Not the hot, athletic senior who'd crushed my teenage heart when he graduated a year before I did and, immediately, broke up with me. Not—

"Who're you calling 'old,' Billy?" the man striding up to us said with a laugh. He and Bill shook hands.

Yep.

The *very same* Kristopher Karlsen.

My first outing with the Quest group and *this* was what I got, huh? Some kind of crazy walk down memory lane, just when I most desperately wanted to move forward... I felt a bubble of near-hysterical laughter rise up in my throat.

Kristopher waved in a friendly but somewhat unseeing way at the cluster of individuals in front of him. Not really focusing, I could tell, on any of our faces. His attention was on Bill and reminiscing about their old sports friends from the surrounding suburbs and a handful of their regional soccer tournaments, which was fine by me. It gave me a chance to study him.

Blue jeans. A perfect fit.

A Polo shirt and expensive leather loafers that contradicted his attempt at casualness. He was too studiously relaxed to be genuinely so.

His brown hair was shaved close, a militaristic buzz cut, so different from the longish look he'd favored during our high-school years.

Muscles that were weight-lifter toned. Not huge, but larger than I recalled.

His dark eyes—complete with those long, black eyelashes—fit my memory of him exactly, though.

It wasn't until Bill invited him to sit down with us that Kristopher's gaze locked on mine. He pulled up a chair directly across the table from me, those dark eyes never leaving my face.

"Jules?" he mouthed.

I nodded.

He scanned my eyes, my lips, my chest, then returned to my eyes again and broke into a warm smile. "What group is this, Billy?" he asked his friend. "Work colleagues?"

"Singles' group," Bill supplied.

Kristopher stared at me in shock. "Really? *You?*"

Half the table was now looking at us with speculation, but Shar was the first to speak. "How do you two know each other?" she asked.

"High school," Kristopher and I said together.

An amused smile played at the corners of Shar's mouth. "Did you two date or something?"

"Not seriously," I said.

"Oh, yes!" Kristopher said at the same time.

Shar's smile broadened. "I don't think I've heard this story," she told Kristopher then thumbed in my direction. "Julia and I only met about five years ago."

Kristopher beamed one of his gorgeous twinkly grins at my friend and then at me. "Julia and I dated for *months*. But then, well, I graduated, and she never wrote to me or anything. Forgot about me the second I left town." He gave a pitiable shrug.

"What?" I cried. "You broke up with *me*. You said you needed to 'focus on your sports.' That you had 'no time for girlfriends' when you had your 'true loves'—soccer and football."

He shook his head. "I didn't say that."

"You did!"

"No."

I crossed my arms, livid. *"Yes."*

"Really?" He squinted at me. "Was I that dumb?"

He caught me off guard and, in spite of myself, I

13

laughed. He laughed, too, and my indignation, along with about nineteen years of residual resentment, melted away in the span of just a few heartbeats. "Yep." I nodded.

He covered his face with his palms then peeked through his fingers at me. "What's the statute of limitations on stupid high-school jock behavior?"

I pondered. "Um...two decades?"

Kristopher feigned wiping his brow. "Whew. Got it in just under the wire. I probably owe you lunch or at least coffee and a muffin. Something to make up for being a dick when I was eighteen. How 'bout next week, if you've got a little time?"

Wow, that was skillfully done. *So. Smoooooth.* I was impressed. I'd had no intention of agreeing to a date with anyone, and yet...

Well, this was different. Kristopher was an old friend. It wasn't really a romantic type of engagement.

With the exception of Shar and Bill, the others had gone back to their conversations so, thankfully, I didn't have too many people witnessing my fumbles with setting up a (sort-of) date for the first time in twelve years. It was awkward, but I agreed to coffee and gave Kristopher my phone number, which he dutifully punched into his cell so we could arrange a time and day to meet later.

Shar nudged me when he wasn't looking and whispered, "See? Not so hard, is it?"

I made a face at her and shrugged.

Finally, the party was beginning to break up. I was mentally congratulating myself on making it through the evening when the very sweet, well-dressed woman—Elsie was her name—wolf whistled. "Wait, people!"

Everyone halted.

"I've been wanting to tell you this good news all night." She paused for effect. "You know my friend Rosemary, the one who works at the Knightsbridge Theater in the city, right?"

14

Most of the group nodded, seeming to have met Elsie's friend or, at least, heard about her.

"There's a dress rehearsal for their upcoming summer production, 'The Bachelor Pad,' this Thursday at six-thirty in the evening, in advance of next Friday's Opening Night," Elsie said. "And Rosemary reserved a block of seats for us."

Despite the noise in the wine bar, an audible spike in sound came on the heels of those words, and a couple of the women actually squealed.

I squinted at them. I mean, tickets to a play were always nice, but wasn't this taking theatrical enthusiasm a bit far?

"But that's not all," Elsie continued enthusiastically. "Rosemary also got us passes to meet the cast, just as she did for that steampunk musical last year—"

"Steampunk musical?" I hissed in Shar's ear.

She nodded. "It was bizarre. Tell you more about it later."

I grinned and brought my glass of wine to my lips, draining it of its final swallow.

"—including a special Q&A session with the director, Zachary Leeward," Elsie added, "and with the star of the show, Dane Tyler."

I choked on the last drops of merlot, coughing so hard that Bill reached across the table to hand me a fresh glass of ice water, Shar patted me on the back, and everyone else stared at me worriedly. Except for Kristopher. He shot me a knowing look.

Yeah, of course he'd remember *that*.

"Are you okay?" Elsie asked me.

I gulped down half the water. *Oh, God. Of all the actors on the planet—Dane Tyler. Here? REALLY?*

My teen world had just materialized out of thin air, like that freaky phantom ship that came from absolutely nowhere in *Pirates of the Caribbean*. My gut twisted weirdly, and I could barely breathe. "P-Please go on," I managed to whisper.

She smiled. "So, if any of you want to go to the performance, and I know you do, let me know now, and I'll email the list of names to Rosemary in the morning."

Elsie was right. With the exception of one accountant guy, who had an out-of-town business trip next week, and a very disappointed single mom, whose kid was playing in a baseball tournament Thursday night, everyone else signed up to go.

Including *me,* at Shar's insistence. And including Kristopher.

My old high-school boyfriend leaned over the table and said with a laugh, "Well, isn't that something? Maybe, if you ask him real nice, he'll recite your favorite lines from your favorite movie to you."

"Ha," I said weakly.

"Which lines? Which movie?" Shar asked.

Before I could reply, Elise jumped in and pointed to Shar and then me. "You two want to ride down with me?"

Shar answered for both of us. "Oh, yeah!"

Although I managed to stop tripping over my own tongue and was able to thank the kind woman, I didn't succeed in making more than a few last bits of small talk. All I could do was blush furiously and think to myself, in the fevered squeaking of an adolescent schoolgirl, *OMG, I'm finally going to see Dane Tyler in person! Maybe even talk to him!*

In just one evening, three distinct memories of men from my past played out like a warped summertime version of *A Christmas Carol* in my mind. Haunting memories of relationships that I'd had or had lost or had wanted—sometimes simultaneously and always more powerfully than I'd expected—were reeling through my brain on a continuous loop, braiding my emotions with the mental film footage.

Before my best friend could ask me any more questions

I didn't want to answer, I hugged her goodnight and raced into the evening, forgetting until my feet hit the pavement and I collapsed into the driver's seat of my car that I wasn't, in fact, lost in time.

That I wasn't living out some high-school fantasy.

That I wasn't a vulnerable young woman, helpless in the face of fate.

I started the engine, replayed those last three thoughts again, and shook my head.

Like hell I wasn't.

CHAPTER THREE

A few days later, Brooke and Lindsay were at our house, watching some Nickelodeon show with Analise in the family room while I was cleaning. I'd vacuumed. I'd dusted. And, now, I was flipping through a stack of papers and junk mail, preparing to de-clutter.

I'd unearthed the letter from the university after Friday night's wine-bar adventure. Read the whole thing this time. Couldn't miss seeing Ben's name on the bottom of it. If I'd had any question about whether or not he'd go to the reunion, reading his name alongside those of the rest of the planning committee confirmed the former. He'd be there.

I ripped the letter in half and tossed it out with a coupon for Steiger's Gas Station, which I knew I'd never remember to use, and the flyer about a local politician's booksigning, which I had no interest in attending.

Didn't matter in any case if I kept the Franklin College letter or not. I'd already RSVP'ed. Tempting as it was to back out of going, I'd promised Vicky I'd drive to the reunion with her. I didn't want to let her down.

As I sifted through some old magazines and a stack of paid utility bills, I could hear random but happy shrieks coming from down the hall. Some were eardrum piercing, but I didn't mind. Not the way I used to. Once upon a time, I might have gently reprimanded Analise for that, but not anymore. It happened so infrequently. Yvette's daughters brought out the silliness in her again, and Analise liked and trusted them. A lot. I was going to encourage their growing bond with all the strength I had.

Last fall, the other girls had lost their beloved grandfather, Yvette's dad. To their credit, they were somehow able to transfer their understanding of their grief to the way my daughter must have been feeling. Their empathy, in their youthful but fully honest way, helped pull Analise along through those very dark first months.

I couldn't help but feel eternally grateful to Yvette for that, too. She'd been particularly sensitive and supportive during the entire ordeal—not just to my daughter but, also, to me. Not a surprise, really. She'd been a sweet and compassionate person even in high school.

We'd been fringe friends at the time, not close ones, but I'd always considered her a good acquaintance. She'd preferred music to movies back then. Service projects over dating. So we'd had less in common as teens. Even so, I was pretty sure she'd shown up in my old diary entries. Among other people...

The giggles of the three girls receded as I raced down the hallway and slipped into our bedroom. Well, no. Now it was only *my* bedroom. Every time I remembered things like this I felt that familiar tear at the edges of my heart. Like a tugging at the borders of a scab. But, nevertheless, I slid the decorative cardboard box out from under my dresser, knowing that the memorabilia it contained predated my adult life or even my courtship with Adam.

I lifted the dusty lid and peered at the assortment of collectibles and sentimentalities inside. There were actual mix cassette tapes, filled with pop songs from a bygone era. There were pressed roses and a couple of corsages from dances that took place years ago. Homecoming. Prom. There were love letters—or what passed for love back in high school—from the boy who'd dominated my thoughts. And there were a handful of diaries, but there was only one of them that I reached for and pulled out of the box.

It was smallish. This light-blue relic of my adolescence had a soft leather cover, a small key attached and dangling from the front, and a broken lock refastened hastily with some crackled, ancient masking tape.

I brushed at the gaudy silver filigree with my thumb, tracing the scripty words: *"My First Diary."* Then I flipped to the first page of my old record of my high-school days, exhaling and counting to five. Did I really need to revisit this?

Yes.

Unfortunately, yes.

The first lines jumped out at me, dragging me back to another time and place: Mirabelle Harbor High School. Sophomore year. To a circle of friends: Megan Rhea. Debbie Brunmeier. Ashley Jennings. Cyndie Redding. Yvette Hampton, née Smythe. And let's not forget, Kristopher Karlsen, that tall, cute junior, who seemed to take up most of the space in my head when I was sixteen. Or Dane Tyler, the actor that made me wish I could be cast in my very own, real-life production of *Bye Bye Birdie*.

<u>*Saturday, January 14th*</u>

I can't believe I've been 16 for a whole week already! I love this diary that Aunt Barb sent me for my birthday—it's perfect. Now, when I don't want to tell any of my school friends about Kristopher Karlsen, I can still confide my private thoughts here.

Someday, he's going to like me. I can just feel it. Even Megan thinks so, and everybody knows how cynical she is. He smiled at me yesterday when I passed him going into the library for study hall. And he looked at me for longer than most people when he did. I think it's a sign.

*Anyway, next weekend Debbie, Ashley, and I are going out to see the new Dane Tyler movie—*Warriors of Warrenville High*. I can't wait!! Yvette and Cyndie might come, too. Maybe Kristopher and his friends will be at the theater as well... Wouldn't that be amazing?!*

I'll write all about it, and about everything else.

Oh, and I did. I wrote and wrote and wrote, ad nauseam.

Scores of pages of what Kristopher said, what he might have thought, what I think he did. And just as many pages devoted to Dane and the movies he was in, my interpretation of his acting, and the latest tabloid rumors about his love life. If I would've spent a fraction as much time and mental energy on my math homework, I might have gotten higher than a C- in geometry that semester.

I flipped through the next several pages, reading snippets of what I'd once thought were highly exciting details about my life.

Friday, January 20th

OMG! Warriors of Warrenville High was SO good! Dane Tyler is SO talented! He played Mark Adams, a quarterback who was struggling to lead his high-school football team to victory after several seasons of failure. Of course, there were all sorts of problems with his two-faced friend on the team, and then there was this girl he really liked, Alexa (played by Daphne Styles), and he was only able to convince her he loved her after he won the game and proved that the bad teammate was lying about him being a drug addict.

I thought Dane's acting was just amazing. And I guess he's even from around here! Can you imagine going to a real high school with guys like HIM in it? I'd love to know if he's got a girlfriend in real life. TeenLife Digest *said "sources" reported that he and Daphne were an item. I wonder if he liked kissing her, and if she liked kissing him. (Well, who wouldn't?!)*

This was clearly more important than any story on the national news involving such trivia as world hunger, genocide, or a multitude of natural disasters. I kept reading.

Tuesday, January 31st
There was a boys' basketball game tonight and guess who was playing? Kristopher, of course! So, Megan and I stayed after school to watch it and, then, she drove us to Pizza Palacio for dinner. (She's had her license for 2 months and is a great driver!) The best part, though, was that, after we'd been there for about a half hour, a few guys from the basketball team came in for pizza...and Kristopher was one of them! He actually WAVED at us!!! Megan said Kristopher Karlsen likes me FOR SURE, and that it would be really cool to go out with an upperclassman.

I cringed rereading all of this embarrassing dreck. Yeah. I'm not sure my adolescent self could imagine anything in the world to be as "cool" as dating a junior or senior. Except, maybe, dating a movie star.

Of course, the entries didn't stop after January. I scanned through fragments from the months that followed.

Saturday, March 4th
How does the name "Julia Karlsen" sound? What about "Julia Tyler"??!

Wednesday, April 26th
...and there was an issue of Totally Teen Magazine *that came out today with Dane on the cover, and it had a photograph in it with him standing next to an "Amy"-somebody with red hair. She's going to be in his new*

hockey movie. The reporter wrote that Dane was going out with her. (Ugh!!) But I guess that means he broke up with Daphne, huh?

<u>Friday, June 9th</u>
Last day of school, and Kristopher and I talked for 10 minutes—just us! He told me his family is driving to Maine for vacation. He'll be gone 2 weeks. At least I know not to bother going to the pool until July.

<u>Sunday, July 30th</u>
Tonight, one of my favorite Dane Tyler movies is on TV, though. The first one of his that I ever saw, Roberto & Julia—*a modern high-school version of* Romeo & Juliet *that actually ends happily. I love Dane's character, Mikey, who's one of Roberto's friends. He even quotes Shakespeare! He says, "We know what we are, but know not what we may be." (It's from* Hamlet, *I guess.) That's my favorite movie line EVER now.*

<u>Tuesday, August 1st</u>
Today is Dane's 20th birthday! Happy Birthday, Dane!! Wouldn't it be amazing to get to tell him that for real?

I had to give myself credit—I was impressive in my ability to over-focus. Kristopher and Dane...Dane and Kristopher. Hey, no one could claim I didn't know how to obsess with the best of them.

At least in Kristopher's case, I had some reality to back up the teen fantasizing. It took him until January of the following year before he finally asked me out, but he *did* do it, and our relationship lasted a whole four months, a near eternity at that age. Our first date, our first kiss, our first trip to second base (that was as far as I'd let him go) was somewhere in the journal, as was prom and the saga of our breakup. Oh, the drama.

Before I could flip to those key events, though, I came across a hard, flat piece of smooth plastic, like a library card but bright yellow and with the words "DANE TYLER FAN CLUB * Official Member" in black lettering across the top. I ran my fingers across my printed name and my special membership number: 49202. I'd mailed in my application for this card, not telling anyone else that I'd done it (not even my parents, my big sister, my friends, or Kristopher). And, when it arrived, I protected it like a valued possession. After all, it had Dane's signature on it. Copied from the original and printed about fifty thousand times, but still—

My cell phone rang. A number I didn't immediately recognize.

"Hello?"

"Uh, Jules?"

Kristopher. Ah, speak of the devil.

I greeted him and mumbled the usual "Hey, how are you?" chitchat. I already knew why he was calling.

"So, you said Wednesday afternoons might be good for you to meet for coffee. How's this week?" he asked. "Day after tomorrow?"

Too soon! I wanted to shout, but of course I didn't.

"I've already made some plans for the time when Analise is in her dance class," I told him, which was true. I'd planned to sit somewhere very quiet for that free hour on Wednesday afternoon and hyperventilate about the weirdness of suddenly having Ben Saintsbury, Kristopher Karlsen, and Dane Tyler reappear in my life. I would also probably eat about three double-chocolate brownies. By myself. Like an addict who was trying to hide her secret vice.

"How about next week instead?" I countered. "Besides, I think we'll get to see each other this week in any case. On Thursday night. You're still planning to go to the play at the Knightsbridge, aren't you?"

I heard him clear his throat on the other end of the line and chuckle. Sort of. "Yeah. I was always second to Dane Tyler when it came to you, wasn't I?" he said, but I wasn't sure if he was genuinely laughing. "So, wow. Your favorite actor is coming back to Chicago. First time seeing him in person?"

"It is," I admitted.

"Have you kept up with his career?"

"Not really." I fingered my official Dane Tyler Fan Club card. *Although, maybe a little more than your average person.*

"Well, it'll be interesting to see if he's any good onstage," Kristopher said, a surprising edge to his voice. "I was never quite the fan of his films that you were."

"Who was?"

He laughed, for real this time. "True." Then, after a beat, "But I still hope he can act in front of a live audience. Otherwise, it's gonna be a helluva long two and a half hours."

CHAPTER FOUR

The Knightsbridge Theater was a small but well-known venue on the north side of Chicago. It was, in my opinion, a magical place located less than forty minutes from my house. I'd enjoyed every show I'd ever seen there, and it had been host to a rotating cast of big stars, many who'd originally hailed from the Windy City and were hankering for a short-run theatrical stint back home and without the pressure or time commitment of Broadway.

Plus, the city got to welcome back one of its own and shower the actors involved with praise and admiration, which was a drug more powerful to some than heroin.

The fact that so many famous stars had been in town for lead performances over the years, combined with my own life's personal distractions, was the only excuse I could give for not knowing Dane Tyler was in the area.

Elsie's friend Rosemary—who, it turned out, was the stage manager for the production—stood at the door to the auditorium and ushered everyone into the building. Aside from those of us in the Quest group, there were a few classes of local university theater students, one cluster of lively senior citizens, and at least a dozen members of the press. For a dress rehearsal, we had nearly a full house.

Sharlene, who was sitting to my left with Elsie beside her, squeezed both of our hands in excitement. "Dane Tyler!" she half whispered, half squealed.

Kristopher was directly to my right with Bill next to him on the aisle. They seemed interested but far less enthusiastic. A college student handed Bill a stack of play programs, which he dutifully passed down the row. Written on the front in scripted gold lettering were the words: *The Knightsbridge Theater Presents "The Bachelor Pad"—a comedy in two acts by P.K. Lewis*. Inside, along with a list of scenes, a brief synopsis of the play, and information on a variety of cast and crew members was a lengthy profile on their Star in Residence.

From his start on the Chicago stage as a teen playing Willy Loman in "Death of a Salesman" to his Oscar nomination for his supporting role as Edward Bryant in The Journey: Crossing the Peaks *(ReelMax Pictures), Dane Tyler is a star who continues to rise...*

Well, I wasn't sure I'd say that.

Yes, Dane had been THE actor for a time, but that time was no longer. While he still got roles in some A-List projects, they were rarely as leads anymore. More often, he played well-drawn secondary characters or made a cameo appearance on one of the bigger flicks. And more time elapsed between completed projects. I'd Googled him last night and realized that his most recent film (a B-Lister, by the way, called *Midnight Alliance*), came out two years ago and had been a commercial bomb. There were no current projects slated as being in "post-production" either.

"So," Kristopher said, interrupting my thoughts, "are you nervous? Excited?"

"Curious," I replied.

Rosemary stepped onstage and waved at the lighting

guy in the back of the theater. Suddenly, the house lights dimmed and the exuberant chattering in the audience dissolved to a reverent hum.

"I can't tell you how thrilled we are to host 'The Bachelor Pad' here at the Knightsbridge, to have such a spectacular director, cast, and crew, and to welcome back to Chicago our very own Dane Tyler!"

She said a few more words, probably more than a few, but I tuned her out. My mind was fixating on the only important part of that sentence for me, especially when the curtain opened to reveal the cast in their starting positions onstage...and there he was at last. Dane Tyler.

I'd lied to Kristopher, maybe even to myself. I'd been waiting over twenty years for this experience. I was more than "curious."

Let me just put the magnitude of this moment into context, shall I? I took my every teen breath with Dane Tyler. I watched him with moony eyes as he kissed CoverGirl Amy Coleridge in *Center Ice Draw*, MTV darling Kendra Leigh in *Dorm Daze*, and that gorgeous Asian-American actress, Rumi Sakurai, who was the runner-up for Miss World one year, in *Chasing the Dragon*.

I tacked his poster to the wall above my bed, tilting it at a daring angle so he'd look even edgier than usual.

I kept his "Star Profile" from *Teen Explosion* magazine folded up and safely zipped in the secret compartment of my strappy teal purse for years.

I also memorized it.

I could recite it on command even now.

Name: Dane Tyler
Birthday: August 1st
Hair: Wavy dark blond
Eyes: Light blue
Height: 6'1"
Hometown: Chicago, Illinois

Acting Start: Spotted by an agent onstage at age 14 in a community theater production, etc., etc.

And, of course, I also joined the Official Dane Tyler Fan Club.

I wasn't merely curious about him. He wasn't part of some "adolescent phase" I had once gone through. No. He'd been my lifelong obsession.

Even Kristopher, who was surrealistically sitting next to me right now and who had been my prom date almost two decades ago, had to pledge back then to skip the midnight breakfast at Perkins so we could go to a late showing of Dane's just-released film, *Time Jumpers*, which also starred a model/actress from Ontario named Serena Bilogian. I remembered Dane's costars as well as my own extended family members.

But the guy who stood onstage before me now, nearly twenty years later, was no nineteen-year-old heartthrob. Our seats were close enough that I could see the expression etched on his still very handsome face, and it was one of exhaustion and world weariness. In those short seconds after Rosemary departed the stage to thunderous clapping for the players and before the action of the production began, I got the distinct sensation that my long-time movie-star idol didn't want to be back in the Windy City. That he didn't want to be up onstage or, indeed, anywhere near other people at all.

Huh.

All of that changed, however, the second the director pointed at the actors from his position stage left and, then, marched to the back of the theater to watch the dress rehearsal, clipboard in hand. Dane and the rest of the cast sprang into action, and the serious, intense, displeased-looking man transformed himself instantly into the charming, light-hearted bachelor who was the lead in this play.

I knew his work well—perhaps too well. I could pick out facets of his performance from films I'd seen years before. The way he delivered a humorous line to his acting pal, asking the other guy to keep one girlfriend busy while he dealt with another, reminded me of the way he'd handled a similar scene in *Dorm Daze*. And, oh, the short moment of sad introspection at the midpoint of the play called to mind immediately a poignant scene near the end of *Warriors of Warrenville High*. The words were different, of course, but I could track the facial expressions back to other performances. Was that simply his acting style? Or was it more deliberate? Maybe, on a subconscious level, he wanted his audience to make the connection. Wanted us to link his performance tonight to the familiarity of his glory days.

After the final curtain fell, the audience—me included—jumped to our feet to give the actors a standing ovation. The cast came forward, the house lights were turned back on, and the director strode to the middle of the stage. He spoke briefly with the actors, commenting on details involving a couple of scenes. Then he turned his attention to the audience and opened up the floor to questions.

"This is for Mr. Tyler," one of the male university students said. "Do you have any advice for aspiring actors?"

Dane smiled and cocked one eyebrow. "Consider changing your major to business."

The crowd laughed.

"Seriously," Dane continued. "If you want a long-lasting career in theater and film, you need to not only study the art of acting but the business of the stage and screen world. Plus, it helps to have some backup skills beside waiting tables, just in case it takes a while to land that first big role."

These seemed like reasonably wise words, if served,

perhaps, with a side dish of bitterness.

A young woman stood up and asked if Dane had ever been a struggling actor.

"Well, I started pretty young," he replied. "My mom didn't expect me to support myself when I was still in high school, so any income I earned from acting was a bonus. She set up a special saving account for me. But, yeah, even so, as an adult I've had some leaner years."

"So, about how much money do you make on your films?" a college guy sitting next to the young woman asked Dane.

My mouth fell open in shock. How rude!

I expected someone to tell the student that he was out of line or to let Dane know that he didn't have to answer that, but no one said anything. The crowd just waited expectantly for him to respond.

He seemed unfazed, as if he'd grown used to such inappropriateness and had been asked questions like these countless times. "A lot," Dane said simply and laughed in a way that dismissed the guy.

At this point, one of the members of the press stood up. An older gentleman. "Your role in this farce was that of a playboy who was stringing along multiple girlfriends. Being both a confirmed bachelor in real life, as well as a man who's known to be quite popular with the ladies, have you ever found yourself in a similar situation?"

Wow. I couldn't believe how personal some of these questions were getting. But, even though I was surprised, Dane didn't seem to be.

"You're asking if I'm actually an unfaithful, commitment-phobic manwhore?" Dane grinned and pulled out his smart phone. "Hmm. Not sure I can be objective. Just let me put out a quick poll on Twitter," he said, miming scrolling through a bunch of tweets and thumb-typing the question to his gazillion fans and followers. "I can get back to you with the results in fifteen minutes.

Twenty tops."

The reporter had the good sense to sit down with an embarrassed chuckle and let the subject drop.

A few of the acting students finally asked some respectful and relevant questions, but there were a couple members of the press who had a knack for being particularly invasive.

One lady reporter behind me called out to him, demanding to know about his long-term relationship with actress Emily Brennan. "Are the two of you still an item, or are the reports true that she left you for Jonathan Richie, the CEO of AlphaSig Technologies?"

For the first time, the laugh lines on either side of Dane's mouth seemed to tighten, and he stared hard in our direction. Not only at the press lady but, also, at everyone in our section. His gaze caught mine, and he looked at me for a long moment. Did he mistakenly think *I'd* asked that question?

Rosemary jumped in and belatedly reminded the crowd that we were to ask the cast members only about acting and the current production. "Please, let's stick to inquiries about the show."

"My apologies, Mr. Tyler," the reporter behind me said with an unmistakable edge of mocking in her voice. She stood up this time, resting her hands on the back of my seat, as if to include us all in this discussion. "Let me rephrase that. Will Emily Brennan be coming to see *the show?*"

"That would be a better query for her social secretary," Dane replied tartly. "I have my hands full just keeping track of my own engagements." He laughed it off, but there was a hard glint in his light-blue eyes. And, as he ran his fingers through his wavy blond hair, I saw him sneaking a glimpse at his watch. Couldn't say I blamed him for wanting this Q&A session to end.

If that was his wish, he got it after just a few more questions. The director gathered together some of the technical experts on the crew—particularly lighting and sound—to answer a few student questions specific to those specialties. Dane and the other actors slipped offstage.

"C'mon!" Elsie said to Sharlene and me. "Rosemary said she'd introduce us to Dane."

"What?!" I nearly shrieked, instinctively smoothing down my hair. "Oh, God, no. I can't actually *meet* Dane Tyler."

"Of course you can," Shar said.

Kristopher leaned past me to address the other two women. "It's always been her dream to meet him face to face. Make her go." Then, to me, he added, "Look, Jules, even *I* want to meet the guy, and he was my high-school rival for your attention." He winked.

Elsie raised her eyebrows at this and Shar broke into a wide grin. "Really?" both women said together as they all but pushed me out of the row and toward where Rosemary was standing. She was far off to the right side of the stage with Dane next to her. The two of them were speaking privately.

"We don't want to interrupt them," I murmured, trying to pull away.

"Nonsense," Elsie said. "Rosemary is expecting us."

"But—"

Before I could finish protesting, the stage manager in question spotted us and waved us closer.

"Dane, I'd like to take just a moment to introduce you to my good friend Elsie Whitcomb and her social group." Rosemary smiled warmly at all of us, even though she didn't yet know some of our names.

Dane, looking visibly drained but not irritated, reached out to shake hands with Elsie, who grasped his limb with exuberance.

"We're a singles' group!" she exclaimed. "Totally unattached."

He chuckled. "Excellent. Did you all want to get in on

my Twitter survey? Have any thoughts to share on the subject of my moral depravity or, perhaps, some words of wisdom on relationships going forward?"

Bill grimaced comically and shook the actor's hand. "Pretty sure you don't want relationship advice from *us*."

"Hey, you couldn't have crashed and burned more often than me," Dane said, his smile growing more genuine and his body language loosening a bit, too. He seemed to finally start to relax and realize he was among friends.

Bill introduced both himself and Kristopher, while Elsie made the official introductions between Dane and Shar. Then it was my turn.

"And this is our newest member, Julia Crane," Elsie said.

My hands, which were an embarrassingly clammy cold when I shook Dane's, began to tremble slightly under the scrutiny of his gaze. His hands were, by contrast, so steady, so smooth, and so warm. Initially, I thought, "Okay, I can do this. He's probably used to people being nervous around him all the time."

But once he took a good look at my face and my shaky hands, his expression changed. His eyes took on a wary cast and he gave me such an odd stare that I couldn't interpret it.

I managed to mumble something about what a pleasure it was to finally meet him but, unlike the way he'd been with the other members of our small group, he just nodded curtly at me and suddenly seemed to clam up. He didn't make any further jokes and he no longer looked as relaxed as when he'd greeted the others. I took a step away from him and let Elsie and Bill continue the discussion, which turned out to be very short anyway.

The director strode up to us and pulled Dane and Rosemary aside for a minute. While we were standing a couple of yards away from them, waiting to see if Dane would rejoin us for a few moments more, that obnoxious reporter lady, who'd been sitting directly behind me during the play, tapped me on my shoulder and pulled me away from my friends.

"How'd you score a private introduction to the hotshot?" she half hissed, half snickered in my ear.

I said simply that one of my friends knew the stage manager.

"Think she can swing me a few words alone with him, too?" the woman asked conspiratorially, leaning closer as if we were good friends.

I shrugged and leaned back. "I don't know."

Dane glanced over at us standing together, and his eyes narrowed. The director walked away after a minute more, but Dane bent toward Rosemary and whispered something to her. Both of their eyes turned toward me and the rude reporter woman.

"Look, I've got to go," I told the press lady, feeling self-conscious and judged for reasons I couldn't justify. I broke apart from her and told Shar and Elsie that I needed to use the restroom. Then I bolted away.

In the ladies' room, I tried to collect myself and get a handle on this strange nervousness. It wasn't so much the celebrity factor that had me feeling this awkward. Rather, it was that I'd felt appraised by him, and that I could tell the result of his observations had left me wanting in his eyes. Simply put, there was something about me that my movie-star idol just didn't like.

When I emerged from the restroom, the clusters of people in the auditorium area had shifted. Dane wasn't out there anymore and my friends were nowhere in sight.

One of the heavy dark-red curtains, which had been closed during the performance, was now pushed open, exposing a hallway with several doors on either side. I thought, perhaps, Shar and Elsie may have walked back there, especially if that was where Rosemary had her office.

A few of the actors who'd played in the smaller roles

came out of one of the doors, doubled over laughing about something and leaving the building quickly. Too fast for me to ask them if the stage manager and my friends might be back there.

So, I meandered a little farther down the hall, discovering a different passageway that broke off from the main one. It had doors, too, and some of them were labeled. "Dressing Room," said one. "Green Room," said another. There were voices within both, but none of those voices sounded like they belonged to my friends.

There was yet another door, this one without a label, and it was ajar by about three inches. I peered inside and was about to push it open a little more when I heard an angry voice behind me say, "What the hell are you doing back here?"

I swiveled around.

Dane Tyler.

"I—I'm sorry," I stammered. "I was just looking, um, for—"

"Looking for what?" he demanded. "Hmm? Messages? Information? Incriminating photo opportunities?"

I shook my head. *Incriminating photo ops—what?*

"Don't tell me you just happened to get lost backstage."

"Well, no. Not exactly. I was—"

"Snooping?" He crossed his lean, muscular arms and looked royally pissed off. "You're with the *Tinseltown Buzz*, aren't you?"

I shook my head again. "Um, no."

He shot me a disbelieving look. "I saw you talking with Caryn Dizinger, *Julia*—or whatever your name really is. Dizinger might not think I remember her, but I do. Painfully well. And Rosemary said she'd never seen you before. It wouldn't have been the first time that a pushy reporter wormed her way into a social club just so she could get an inside scoop."

"I'm not with the press. I've never talked to that

reporter before tonight. And I am here with the singles' group. I'm new, though—"

"Is that so?" He pointed at my left hand. "You joined a group for singles, but you're wearing a wedding ring? Not too good at subterfuge yet, are you?" He took a few menacing steps forward. "I'm sure you'll learn fast enough. Now, tell me, which fucking magazine or newspaper do you write for if, as you say, you're not with the *Tinseltown Buzz*?"

I just kept stupidly shaking my head, saying the same thing over and over again. "I'm *not* a reporter at *all*." I rubbed the gold band on my finger. Until he mentioned it, it hadn't occurred to me that I should have taken it off. In the months since Adam died, I'd thought about it a time or two, but I was never ready. I still wasn't.

Dane glowered at me, and all I could do was stare back, trying to reconcile the sexy fantasy hero I'd had in my mind all of these years with the man—the *very angry* man—who was standing right in front of me.

I noticed a few things:

His hairline was just starting to recede. It wasn't so noticeable yet, but it would be in a few years. Twenty years ago, gobs of moussed dark-blond hair was one of his hallmark features. Now, not so much.

His jaw was clenched tight in fury, an image I hadn't seen outside of a few onscreen moments in his more dramatic work. Twenty years ago, he'd sparkled with the good humor of youth. Now, not so much.

And then there were his eyes. In movies and in TV interviews they'd always mesmerized me. Twenty years ago, his penetrating light-blue eyes indicated a shrewd intelligence and a mind that was working overtime to figure out the world around him. Now...well, that was virtually unchanged.

He leaned very close to me, his eyes continuing to search and judge with an intensity that was both hypnotizing and paralyzing.

Finally, he blew out a long stream of air and asked, "What are you then?" with accusation coloring his tone. "An Actor's Equity rep? A wannabe actress? A closet playwright?" He paused. "No, I know—you're an Official Dane Tyler Fan Club member, right?"

He'd been speaking sarcastically, but my jaw dropped open nonetheless. I couldn't seem to speak or defend myself to save my life.

Suddenly he laughed and with no small degree of derision. "Too bad you're not. I can always tell who they are." He looked me up and down deliberately. "I usually reserve a kiss for card-carrying members."

As I looked into that knowing, mocking face that I'd once considered as dear to me as a family member's, I was consumed by a desire so powerful to slap him that I had to squeeze my palms closed to stop myself. And in that second, I got my voice back.

"My name is Julia Meriwether Crane, and I'm a junior-high English teacher," I informed him. "I threw out my Fan Club card at least a decade ago," I lied, "but my number was 49202. Should've burned it, right along with my high-school love letters and those rude notes from asshole guys at summer camp."

I began to walk away, but I made the mistake of glancing back. Just once.

It was only then—and only for an instant—but I suddenly saw Dane Tyler's defiant pride. The man who hadn't made much of a blip on *Entertainment Monthly*'s newsworthy-o-meter for the past couple of years (at least not for his acting, just for his personal life) was looking at me like a petulant, aging has-been, vying for a flicker of the fire he'd once ignited en masse from his fans. Perhaps he'd spotted it in me for a second, but then he doubted it, lost it, and refused to be pitied for its absence.

Oh, God. Dane Tyler was a human being after all.

He was also a callous, self-centered douche bag. Couldn't get away from him fast enough.

I stalked out into the open auditorium and, after a quick scan, found my friends at last. They had congregated by the entrance, and Shar waved as soon as she spotted me. Before I reached her, though, Kristopher jogged up alongside of me and said, "So, what'd'ya think? You finally met your teen fantasy." He grinned.

I did my best not to scowl. "It was...enlightening."

"Yeah? He was nicer than I thought. Still too much hair gel, but—"

I didn't want to talk any more about freakin' Dane Tyler. "Hey, I've got to leave immediately. I kept Elsie and Shar waiting for too long, but I'll look forward to seeing you this week for coffee. Maybe Wednesday?"

Kristopher looked pleased as we approached the other three people who'd been in our row. "Sounds great. I'll give you a call in a few days and we can set up a good time."

"Lovely. Thanks."

I waved him off and said goodbye to Bill as well, glad to at last be nearly out the door of the Knightsbridge Theater.

Then, turning to Shar and Elsie, I summoned up every bit of acting ability in my possession, plastered a delighted grin on my face, and said, "What an incredible night, ladies! Shall we go home?"

Never was I so happy to escape such a "magical" place.

CHAPTER FIVE

I had RSVP'ed via email to the Franklin College Educators Reunion the day after Vicky told me about it and had received an automated confirmation, so I hadn't expected any further communication until the event itself. But fourteen days before the reunion, my email pinged with a new message, and my heart skipped a beat when I saw Ben Saintsbury's name as the sender.

Analise was singing along with some Taylor Swift song on the radio. She seemed happy on this Friday morning. Her sleepover last night with Lindsay and Brooke had agreed with her, and Yvette's daughters had pumped her up—at least temporarily—with enthusiasm for summer camp. I prayed everyone was right about this thing being good for her.

In any case, while she was happily occupied, I clicked on Ben's message, subject line: *Franklin's Reunion*, to see what he'd written. Though it was addressed to me specifically, it soon became clear that it was an impersonally constructed thing. He wrote:

Dear Julia,

Our Reunion of Franklin College's Secondary Education graduates will be here in just a two weeks! What have you been doing in the years since you completed your coursework?

Like José Rodrigo, are you teaching at one of Chicago's finest magnet schools?

Working with gifted teens like our own Helena Kazuya?

Or maybe, like Natalia Ginsberg, you're globetrotting to Europe and Latin America with your high-school Spanish students?

I'm pleased to say that I've been busy with archeological digs in the Baja Peninsula and around Mexico with my honors students at Lincolnshire North Academy and couldn't be having a better time. Next year, we've got Ixtapa and the Xihuacan site on our agenda!

Hope you'll be ready to share all of YOUR exciting teaching adventures with your former classmates when we get together on July 10th. We've got a cash bar with cocktails, plus some appetizers, starting at 6:30pm. Dinner at 8:00pm. Bring your significant other and your best stories!

May the spirit of teaching touch your heart, as it has mine.

Warmly,

Benjamin J. Saintsbury

Associate Dean and History/Archaeology Instructor, Lincolnshire North Academy, a Blue Ribbon School

I tried to keep from scowling at the screen. Ben's tone, even in email form, irritated me. He'd always been hungry for love, for approval, for admiration, and even for envy. He *wanted* people to be jealous of him and never failed to slip in a boastful phrase when he could. I always suspected that was why our breakup had been so hard on him. It wasn't that he truly missed *me*. No. He was just afraid other students would find out that I'd left him. That they might feel sorry for him for something.

I clicked out of email and surfed the Internet for a while, looking up recent news stories on Dane Tyler.

What a disappointment meeting him had been! I still couldn't get over his jerky behavior. As my daughter transitioned to a song by Katy Perry, I read one of the *International Tattler* articles (I know, hardly a reputable source) on Dane's breakup with actress Emily Brennan.

Details divulged from "individuals close to the couple" included an impressive collection of action-packed verbs and descriptive adjectives that spoke of Emily's "agitation" and "despair" at the relationship's "fiery demise," and so on.

"It's been coming for months," one anonymous "friend" told the magazine.

"Emily was distraught because she was sure Dane was cheating on her with his longtime ex," confided yet another "close pal" of the couple. That "ex" being Kendra Leigh, with whom he'd had some *very* steamy love scenes about fifteen years ago in their Western romantic comedy *Love at Cedar Ranch.*

I didn't doubt the asshat slept around. It would serve him right if someone like me were to contact one of the tabloids and tell those paparazzi sleazebags about his lousy backstage behavior. After last night, I was sorely tempted.

But, of course, I refrained.

Much as I didn't appreciate Dane's accusations and his bad attitude, the guy probably had a right to be paranoid about reporters. From the looks of this latest article, they seemed overjoyed to have the opportunity to skewer him in their papers.

Having finally had my fill of sensationalism, I turned off the computer and asked Analise if she wanted me to take her to the pool.

She threw her arms around me. "Yes, if you'll come in the water with me! I'm going to miss you so much when

I'm away at camp, Mommy."

I was aware that she was trying to manipulate me. She knew I preferred to sit at the pool's edge and read rather than swim. But I didn't care. Her words hit me like a rock.

"I don't know how I'll be able to stand it for four whole weeks away," she added, a note of genuine melancholy finding its way into her voice.

Truth was, I didn't know how I'd be able to stand it either.

Despite the ultra-peppy teenybopper music still blaring in the background, her body grew still in my arms, as if the meaning of her own words suddenly dawned on her. My eyes filled with tears that I tried to blink away before she saw them. This upcoming separation was going to be torture.

"Don't worry, sweetheart. We'll be in contact the whole time," I reassured her, even though I knew this was only a half truth. The campers were able to bring up cell phones or tablets, but they were only allowed to use them for one hour each day, in the evening between the after-dinner group activity and bedtime. The rest of the day, the devices were kept locked up, except if one was needed in the event of an emergency.

At the pool, I played with my daughter in the shallow end—a task that used to always fall to Adam, since he was a lover of waterslides and pool games. She didn't ask me to do any of the things he used to do with her—she knew from experience that my skill level at such activities wasn't as high—but she seemed to delight in just being outside in the water and sunshine. In jumping, splashing, plunging, and even swimming a stroke or two. Anything to see my baby girl smile.

Because we were in the pool for two hours, I didn't get the text and voicemail messages on my phone until we were ready to leave. Both were from Kristopher.

Hmm. He didn't waste any time.

The voicemail said, "Hey, Jules! Great seeing you at the play last night. So, Wednesday? My work schedule is very flexible right now. I can meet almost anytime. Just let me know when!"

Then the text: "Me again. I *love* texting. So much easier than passing paper notes in social studies, LOL. Just wanted to let you know you can reach me this way, too, if you prefer."

I remembered those paper notes from high school. I'd even kept a few of them, slipped in between the pages of my journal. If we'd had text messages back then, I never would have had any record of our dating months... Did teenagers even write on paper much anymore? Even keep journals?

Then again, how much good did physical reminders of those old memories do for me now?

We returned home to find a Post-It note from Flowers4U stuck to the front glass door.

"Delivery attempt #1 at 2:07pm," it read. "Will return between 4:30 - 5:00pm."

"Flowers?" Analise read, sounding worried. "Who's sending you flowers?"

The last time we had floral deliveries, they came with condolence cards. I didn't blame my daughter for being apprehensive.

"I don't know," I told her honestly, "but my best guess is that they're from an old friend of mine from high school." I flashed my phone at her. "He's left me a couple of messages, too. He just got back into town and wants to get together to catch up over coffee this coming week. Probably on Wednesday when you're at your jazz dance class."

Analise visibly relaxed, but I could see that crease between her eyebrows and I knew she still had questions.

"Was he your boyfriend?"

I hesitated. "Yes," I said finally. "His name is

Kristopher Karlsen and we dated for a few months. But it was a *long* time ago. Years before I met your Daddy. Once I met him, there was no other man for me."

She smiled, if a little weakly. She was somewhat reassured, just not quite enough yet.

"Do you think your old boyfriend is someone you'll marry now?"

I swallowed. "I—I barely know him anymore," I told her, which was the God's honest truth. I wouldn't pretend that it was impossible for me to marry Kristopher—I'd very much wanted to at one time—but I was a teenager then. Sure, he was still very handsome and polite, but a lot had happened since the end of eleventh grade, and I still didn't know why he'd remained single all these years later.

Maybe he'd never found "The One" he'd been looking for.

Maybe he was secretly (or not so secretly) gay.

Maybe someone else had broken *his* heart and he'd never recovered.

Who knew?

When the doorbell rang an hour or so later, my daughter, who was faster and lighter on her feet than me, rushed to open the door for the flower delivery guy.

"Are you Ms. Julia Meriwether Crane?" the college kid carrying the (enormous!) floral arrangement asked my daughter sweetly.

Analise shook her head, staring in awe at the dozens of flowers pouring out of the delicate pink glass vase. She pointed at me, and the college guy said, "Somebody really likes your mom."

I was a bit speechless, actually. Kristopher had really outdone himself with this one.

After thanking the nice young man and bringing the arrangement into the kitchen, I pulled out my phone, preparing to text him or maybe even call.

Analise bounced around the kitchen table admiring the

flowers. "Oh, oh! Can I open the card?" she begged, picking up the small white envelope that had been decoratively placed into the center of the arrangement.

I laughed, pleased by her enthusiasm over such a small thing, and figured, hey, what could be the harm? Kristopher wasn't one to say anything too suggestive (I hoped!), and if he wrote in cursive, Analise wouldn't be able to decipher it anyway. Kids these days considered script akin to a foreign language.

So I told her, "Sure! Tell me what he says."

Then I hit Reply on Kristopher's last text and began to type, "Thanks so much for—" when my daughter started reading.

"Sorry for jumping to conclusions, Julia Meriwether Crane..." Analise paused and squinted at the writing.

I was more confused than she was, though. Kristopher knew my full name of course, but what had he been jumping to conclusions about?

"I didn't mean to take my bad mood out on you," Analise continued.

"What bad mood?" I actually said aloud. Kristopher had been in relatively high spirits last night—or so I'd thought. Had I misjudged him somehow? Been too concerned with my own feelings and completely misread his?

My daughter shrugged and finished reading he card. *"I hope you'll accept both my sincere apologies and these two tickets to Closing Night and the VIP party that follows."* She paused and pulled two smallish, golden colored tickets out of the envelope and handed them to me. Then my sweet little girl said, "Who's D.T., Mommy?"

I put down my cell phone. "No," I whispered. "It can't be."

"I thought you said your high-school boyfriend was called Kristopher."

"He—he...is," I stammered.

"So, this is another guy?"

I nodded. "Not an old boyfriend, though."

"Is *he* somebody you might marry?"

"What? No! God, no." I studied the card. It was carefully handwritten in very precise block print. Printing that I recognized immediately from signed movie posters I'd admired on eBay and would have loved to buy a decade or two ago, had they not been so expensive.

So I knew—Dane had written this note himself.

My daughter regarded me with all the skepticism her ten-year-old self could project before finally shrugging and skipping away to watch TV.

I was left to try to puzzle out what on earth could have induced Dane Tyler to send me this message, to say nothing of the gazillion flowers taking up half of our kitchen table. And how had he managed to find me?

The guy was insane if he thought I'd go to this VIP shindig of his, but I couldn't help but feel weirdly flattered by the invitation and, yes—I had to admit it—more than a little vindicated by the apology.

CHAPTER SIX

"So, what have you been doing since you returned home to Mirabelle Harbor?" I asked Kristopher over French vanilla lattés at Not The Same Old Grind on Wednesday afternoon.

The coffee shop in the middle of town was bustling, as usual, but we'd found a table in the back corner that was fairly quiet. It was comforting being here. Safe.

He blew on his coffee with lips I remembered thinking were so sensual back in high school. I still thought so, and was unable to keep from watching as he glanced around the shop and took a cautious sip. Lingering, in a way that left me convinced that he was stalling because he didn't want to answer my question.

"Uh, well...lately I've been the number one handyman for my mother," he joked. "She's got a to-do list twelve pages long. I don't think she's had any repairs done on the house in the three years or so since my dad died."

"I was sorry to hear about your father."

"Thanks," he said, but he flicked his hand as if brushing away the sentiment.

I knew Kristopher had always had an uneasy relationship with his dad, but I was sure it was still hard to lose him. My parents had relocated to South Carolina about six years ago for the warmer climate and the superior golf. And though they were both in good health, Mirabelle Harbor wasn't the same for me without them. Or without Adam.

"I was sorry to hear about your husband," Kristopher added. "Your friend Sharlene said it was a car accident."

I nodded and noticed he was staring at my wedding band. In the past week I'd suddenly become very self-conscious about it. I found myself reaching for it now, twisting it on my finger, recalling the quiet ceremony that had resulted in it being placed there.

It *had* been over seven months since Adam's passing. When he slipped the gold band on my finger those years ago, the reverend had said it was "until death do you part."

Well, I guess I could put a checkmark next to that requirement, huh? I was no longer obligated to wear the ring.

But until Dane called attention to it on Thursday night—and now Kristopher today—I hadn't considered separating myself from a symbolic piece of jewelry that had been on my hand 24/7 since my wedding day.

How long was a widow supposed to wait before pulling it off?

Kristopher cleared his throat. "Maybe we should talk about something other than the death of family members, eh?" He fiddled with his stirring stick. "Maybe a cheerier topic like the global recession...third world poverty...or the latest Ebola outbreaks."

I couldn't help but laugh. I'd forgotten about his sense of humor. How, when he wanted to, he could charm almost anyone.

"Yeah, that sounds like a much lighter discussion," I said. "Although it's hard to compete with funerals. It's got the word 'fun' right in there."

He threw his head back and laughed loudly, as if he'd

never heard that joke before. "Right you are. So, you're doing okay, Jules?"

"I am. At least as well as can be expected." I appreciated his asking, but I wasn't really in the mood to talk about *me* today. I remembered that about Kristopher, too—his gift for deflection. He always managed to turn a conversation away from himself if the topic was uncomfortable or too personal for his liking.

"But we were talking about you," I reminded him. "Aside from playing handyman, what brought you back here? You said you'd been working as a recruiter in Oklahoma. Did you transfer to the Chicagoland area?"

Kristopher had been in ROTC during high school and had served in the U.S. Navy for a few years. Then he went to college out of state, earning a degree in general business. I wasn't entirely clear on the timeline, but he'd somehow hooked back in with the military after that, and he'd become one of their recruiters.

"Yeah, I've been in Tulsa for the past eight years. I needed a change."

Why would he voluntarily leave a comfortable position in an area he'd lived in for that long only to return to a place where he'd been so anxious to escape at age eighteen? Why would anyone uproot themselves from a well-established lifestyle...unless there had been a big problem of some kind?

"You were bored with the position?" I asked.

Kristopher answered—reluctantly, I thought, "Not exactly. It was for personal reasons. Not job related. I just needed to get away."

"A broken heart?" I ventured.

"Something like that."

He was quick to move off that topic and return to our easy standby: High school.

"Sorry again for blowing you off after graduation," he said, a wry grin playing at the corners of those sexy lips. "I was in a weird head place then."

"Who isn't at that time of life? The transition between the last year of high school and the first year of anything else is always hard." I paused to take a couple of sips from my own coffee and broke off a piece of my peanut butter chocolate chunk cookie. This shop had the best cookies. "I'd probably have been more understanding of what you were going through that summer if I'd been a senior then, too. The following year was pretty stressful for me, and I wasn't moving nearly as far from home as you had."

He exhaled, long and slow. "Yeah, I needed to get out of here and go away. Start with a fresh slate. The navy was a good choice for that."

"Where were you stationed?"

"Mostly out in California. The San Diego area. For the first time in my life, I had a really deep tan."

We both laughed. Kristopher, like me, had very fair skin that burned easily.

"Bet you went through a lot of sunscreen," I said.

He nodded. "By the crateful. But that got old after a while, too, so when I started college, I chose somewhere different. Philadelphia."

I raised my eyebrows at this. "That is pretty different. Did you like it?"

He shrugged. "Sure, but I was itching for a new environment once I'd gotten my degree. Then the Tulsa job turned up, and off I went."

I was starting to see a pattern here. He'd move somewhere for a few years, become ensconced in the region, get bored with it for whatever reason (or maybe he'd cause some interpersonal turmoil that he needed to escape?), and then move somewhere new.

For the first time it occurred to me that Kristopher's return to Mirabelle Harbor might not be a complete move back home but, instead, just another landing spot for a few years until he got cabin fever again. And decided to move to Seattle. Or Juneau. Or somewhere just off the Florida Keys.

"Being there for eight years was a pretty long time for you then, wasn't it?" I asked.

He inclined his head in agreement but didn't offer up any additional details about his reasons for leaving Oklahoma.

Instead, he said, "Hey, do you remember that night we drove out to Barrett's Pier? The moon was almost full and we just sat there and talked for hours, holding hands—kissing a little, too—and listening to that Backstreet Boys CD of yours?"

I remembered. I could still recite the lyrics to every one of those Backstreet Boys songs. Particularly "I'll Never Break Your Heart," which held a certain degree of irony, given the company I was keeping. "Yeah."

He smiled and reached across the table to lightly grasp my hand. "It's memories like those that I missed most when I was away from home for all those years."

I didn't move or speak for a moment. I wasn't sure what to say or do. Couldn't guess what he expected, or even what I expected of myself. Finally, I smiled, squeezed the hand that held mine, and gently pulled away.

Looking into his warm brown eyes just then I saw something that reminded me of both Dane's facial expression from a few nights ago and Ben's recent reunion email. I realized Kristopher had a similar need to be regarded with the kind of admiration somebody like me had given him during his younger years. To be, once again, the center of someone else's world.

His seemingly open reminiscing about high school made it easy to get caught up in a fervor of adolescent love. But I couldn't escape the feeling that there were many things left unspoken. And that an intimate spring night almost two decades ago between two fairly chaste teens wasn't really the driving force behind all of this nostalgia. I enjoyed those sweet recollections from high school as much as anyone, but I didn't actively want to *relive* those years.

Kristopher pointed to my cookie. "Hey, I think I'm going to get one of those. Want another?"

I shook my head. "I'm good, thanks."

When he returned, it wasn't only with a bakery item but, also, with a bright, new tactic for steering our conversation in a different direction.

"What do you think of dinner?" he asked, motioning between him and me. "Just us. Are you still a fan of cheeseburgers and crispy fries?"

"Tonight?"

"Sure, if you're free," he said.

I checked my watch. "My daughter is going to be finished with her class soon, and I'd planned to spend the evening with her." I thought he'd understood that from the beginning but it seemed he didn't. "She's going to camp this coming weekend and will be gone for an entire month—"

"Ah," he said, interrupting me. "Say no more. These next few days will be busy and you'll want to maximize your time with her. I get it." He nodded in a show of understanding, but I strongly suspected he didn't *really* get it. He wasn't a parent, and there were some things you just couldn't explain.

Still, I appreciated his attempt at empathy. "Perhaps later next week, though?"

He jumped at this suggestion. "Perfect. You name the night, Jules. Coffee and cookies are great, but the truth is that I've enjoyed seeing you again so much, and I'd like to graduate to a real date."

Who could say no to that?

We'd just decided on next Thursday night for what appeared to me to be a recreation of our first date from high school—burgers at Sloppy Joe's and a movie at the

Mirabelle Harbor Cineplex (both Kristopher's idea)—when Analise pranced into the coffee shop, still flushed from dancing. Her jazz class was held across the street, and I'd told her I'd be here to meet her when she was done.

"Can I have a cookie, Mommy?"

"May I," I corrected, "and yes. Which kind would you like?"

"Sugar with sprinkles."

I handed her some money and followed her with my gaze as she went up to the counter. Kristopher glanced between the two of us.

"She's lovely," he said. "She looks like you."

"Thanks."

He turned to study Analise for a longer moment, his inquisitive expression reminding me of someone out birdwatching for the first time. He looked at her like she was an unusual species of egret. With her long legs and fair coloring, I supposed there was more than an average resemblance.

When my daughter came over to us again, I nodded at Kristopher and said, "Analise, I'd like you to meet my friend from high school, Mr. Karlsen."

She frowned slightly, but she shifted her cookie to her left hand so she could stick out her right. "Hi."

"Hi," Kristopher said, shaking her hand rather awkwardly. I got the sense that he didn't often interact with children. "It's very nice to finally meet you, Analise," he said, all politeness and formality.

"You, too," she replied, taking a step back as soon as she could. Then she squinted up at me. "He's the high-school boyfriend, isn't he? The one who *didn't* send the flowers, right?"

Kristopher looked confused. "What flowers? Should I have sent flowers?"

I stifled a laugh. "No, of course not," I reassured him, though it seemed clear to me that my daughter felt otherwise. That she didn't altogether approve of my high-school flame. "We should probably go." I gathered up my things and handed my keys to Analise. "Why don't you open up the car, sweetie?" When she was out the door, I turned to Kristopher, "Thank you so much for the coffee. See you next week?"

He nodded, still appearing more than a little bewildered. And he reached out to give me a quick hug and a peck on the cheek.

It felt...all right. Strange, but not entirely unwelcome. Maybe I was a little more prepared for dating again than I'd thought.

"Looking forward to it, Jules," he said.

Me, too, I added silently as I broke away.

CHAPTER SEVEN

The Fourth of July was on Saturday night, and we'd had longstanding plans to join Shar, her older brother Derek, Derek's wife Olivia, and their three boys for dinner and fireworks.

Analise had always been a girl's girl, one who kept to herself more often than not and, when seeking out friends, chose other girls as her companions. She rarely hung around boys if she could avoid it, so spending an evening with Shar's adorable but rambunctious nephews—ages eleven, nine, and five—always gave her a new perspective.

"C'mon, Analise," Riley, the middle son, urged. "We're gonna play Freeze Tag. James is it!"

James, the eldest, crossed his arms. "Yeah, that's right. I'm a ninja, you little brat. And you can bet I'm gonna get you first."

"Boys, be nice," Olivia called out to them then rolled her eyes at me. "And don't forget about Peter ." She patted her youngest son on the back and then began rubbing his shoulders like a coach readying a boxer for the big match. "Go chase your big brothers, honey. Go, go!"

"Okay!" Peter said, sprinting away, arms pumping, like

a mini superhero on the move.

Olivia and I laughed.

"You're lucky you have a girl," she said. "You can still have some breakables in your house."

I smiled. "Well, there was this one time when Analise decided to practice her *fouettés* in the living room. There was a vase and a couple of porcelain figurines that didn't survive the day."

The other mom grinned at me as Shar walked into the room.

"Hey, I just saw Chance's jeep pull up in the drive," Shar said. "Are he and Nia joining us?"

"They are," her sister-in-law said brightly. "It's been hard to nail those two down for many events this summer—"

"They're always 'working out' together," Shar said, using air quotes.

"Is that what all the kids are calling it these days?" Olivia quipped.

"Shh! They're coming," Shar said.

I couldn't help but smile at this. Chance and Nia had been an unlikely pair when they met at Harbor Fitness, the local gym, this spring, but they'd been inseparable from the moment they finally got together. Ahh, young love.

"Hey, everyone!" Nia said, entering the family room like a sprite emerging from the forest. She was a mass of long dark hair, sparkling eyes, and youthful femininity. I might only be ten years older than her, but it felt like four decades at least.

Chance Michaelsen trailed in after her, grinning but— as usual—silent. He offered a friendly wave to us all and took a moment to hug his sister and then his sister-in-law. To me, he just smiled and nodded, looking more like a marble Adonis than any living human had the right to.

"What do you have here?" Olivia said when Nia handed her a large foil-covered tray.

"Just a quick pan of *galaktoboureko*," she said. "My mom and I made extra."

I'd had this only a couple of times before, but it was delicious. Semolina custard in a phyllo pastry, covered with a sweet, lemony syrup. It was the signature dessert of The Gala, her family's Greek restaurant and bakery. Every dish they made was rich and mouthwatering.

"Yum," Olivia said, peeking under the foil. "Thank you. Derek has got hot dogs and brats grilling out back, and the boys—"

"Uncle Chance!" Riley shouted as he barreled toward the quiet man and attempted to tackle him.

Chance looked amused. His very buff body was hardly swayed by the nine year old's affectionate attack, but he pretended to cower in fear for a moment while his nephew boxed at him. Then he growled and grabbed for the kid, making Riley shriek with delight, and the chase was on.

"Wish I had his energy," Olivia said.

"Don't we all," Nia agreed.

Shar was unable to camouflage her smirk. "Well, from what I've heard about you from my brother—"

"Shut it, Sharlene!" Chance bellowed from down the hallway. He might not talk a lot, but he was direct when he did. And there was nothing wrong with his hearing.

Nia blushed.

My best friend just laughed.

Her oldest brother Derek strode into the room, grilling utensils in hand. "The dogs-n-brats are ready on the patio." Then, turning to Shar, "Behave yourself, Sis. We want these two to come to other family holidays, you know." He leaned in and pecked Nia on the cheek. "Happy Fourth, sweetie. Don't listen to my sister. I got stories about her that I'll tell ya later."

"Hey!" Shar said, fist on her hip.

I found myself giggling at this scene like a teenager, charmed by the warmth and fun of the Michaelsen clan. My friends didn't know how lucky they were to still be able to have family gatherings like this, and to enjoy the company of one another so much when they did. Not everyone had that gift in their lives.

But I appreciated the way they extended their hospitality to include Analise and me, even if tonight's memories would only serve as a reminder tomorrow of how alone we were at other times.

Out in the backyard, I handed a plate to my daughter, who piled it with food and was then quickly whisked away by James to a private "fort" he'd set up using old lawn chairs and ratty blankets he'd unearthed from their garage.

"Looks...interesting," I overheard my daughter say.

Analise sent me a backward glance as James tugged her along, but it was only a half worried look. The other half was pure curiosity.

I gave her a smile that I hoped would convey, "I'll be right here," and I pointed to the patio with my index finger.

She nodded and let herself get dragged away.

I exhaled in relief. I knew she was having fun in spite of herself. The young Michaelsens—much like their parents, their uncles, and their crazy aunt—had a way of getting a person's mind off any other concerns when in their presence.

Chance wandered over to me and motioned toward my plate and the square of Greek dessert I'd slid onto it already.

"The *galaktoboureko* is one of my favorites," he confided. "But don't tell that to my personal training clients at the gym. I've been warding them off of sugar."

I laughed. "Some sweets are fine in moderation, though, right?"

He raised a light-brown eyebrow, dubious.

"No?" I asked.

"Let's just say that a number of my clients are unfamiliar with the correct definition of 'moderate.'"

I laughed at that, too. "They're so fortunate to have you guiding them, Chance."

He inclined his head in thanks, but I meant the compliment sincerely. The guy came across as a bit firm and unyielding at first meeting, and he wasn't one for a lot of idle chatter, but there were very few people who were as softhearted and thoughtful deep down as he was.

After Adam's accident, and even though Chance only knew me as his sister's friend, he made a point to quietly check in on me whenever he saw me in downtown Mirabelle Harbor. Twice he scraped the ice and snow off my car when it was parked outside of the coffee shop—he didn't even know I'd seen him do it. And if he ever spotted me carrying anything heavier than one small bag of groceries, he'd insist on reducing my load by lugging the rest to wherever I was heading.

"I've got it," I'd tell him. Or, "You don't have to lift that. I can carry it."

Mostly, he'd just ignore me and do it anyway. Other times, he'd grin and say, "Look, Julia, it's my *job* to keep my muscles toned. You're the one helping *me* out here." And that would be the end of that.

Tonight, as we enjoyed the mid-summer sunshine and the array of delectable party foods, I watched Chance devour a piece of Nia's custard pastry, but he was looking at her as if *she* were the dessert for the evening. As if he'd rather devour her than any dish on the planet, no matter how scrumptious.

And when he was going back for seconds and exchanging a few words with Derek, I caught Nia gazing at him in much the same way. Whatever the differences that had initially kept them apart faded into nothingness in the heat of those passionate looks. And, furthermore, I could tell they knew they had something special.

I was delighted for them, but I envied them, too. There was no denying it. Once upon a time, I'd felt the same way about Adam. I missed the miraculous, wonderfulness of that feeling. But it couldn't be forced or manufactured. It didn't happen with just *anyone*.

"Oh, to be so young and high on pheromones," Shar whispered in my ear.

"They do look happy," I agreed.

"They look like they can't wait to get away from here and jump each other's bones," she said dryly. "Must be nice to start a relationship without much baggage. They're cute, but they're kids."

I snorted at this. "They're twenty-six and twenty-eight, and you're only thirty-two, Shar. You're hardly an old lady."

"But I'm divorced," she said simply and seriously. "It leaves a big, though invisible, scar, and it ages a person's soul."

I couldn't really argue with that. My own experience as a widow had aged my soul, too, and by many years.

"Do you think it's possible to love again?" I asked her. "Someone like you, who's been so hurt, and someone like me, who's lost so much?"

She studied my face. "Has spending time with Kristopher made you wonder?"

"It's crossed my mind. There's a stirring of...something in me, I guess. I'd been crazy about him once, although a lot has happened in both of our lives since then. It's just—"

"Just what?"

I swallowed. "Well, it's not that I want what's probably a little romantic fling to transition into a real relationship anytime soon, but it just didn't strike me as even possible until this week. I couldn't even imagine it before that."

"And now you can imagine?"

I nodded. "It's a pretty vague, faraway image, but it's not completely impossible now. Is it for you?"

Shar was unusually reflective tonight and took her time before answering. Finally, she said, "Yes. It may not be likely, but it's within the realm of possibility." She paused. "At least I hope so. But it'll be harder for me to fall in love again, I think, than for you."

"Why?"

She smiled sadly at me. "I don't mean to make light of your loss, Julia, but you, my sweet and lucky friend, at least had a happy love story once. For you, true love exists—not just in your imagination, but in your experience. That's no small thing. I'd need to be convinced first to trust again, and it would take an extremely unusual man to make me believe I could. I'm guessing he may need to be an alien life form, actually, because I don't know any Earthlings that come close to what I'm hoping to find."

"He's out there for you, Shar. I know he is."

She shrugged. "Maybe. We'll see."

As night fell, we relocated as a group to the openness of Eastman Field, where we'd get the best viewing of the fireworks.

Analise huddled with the boys while Shar and I propped each other up and turned our gazes to the heavens. The better to see the rockets' red glare light up the sky with a kaleidoscope of patterns...and, perhaps, to keep a look out for UFOs with potential romantic partners aboard.

The next morning, bright and early, Yvette and her daughters were waiting in our driveway—the trunk of their SUV stuffed with suitcases—ready to carpool together up to Camp Willowgreen.

My gut was churning as I boosted my daughter's bag into the back.

Analise seemed to be equal parts excited, nervous, and groggy, at least until Brooke and Lindsay started teaching her one of their favorite camp songs, "By the Light of the

Fire," the lyrics of which had elements that were reminiscent of that children's story, *I'm Going on a Bear Hunt*. Kept them occupied in the backseat for an hour and a half at least.

Meanwhile, Yvette and I chatted up front.

"So," she said, lowering her voice, "what was it like seeing Kristopher again after all this time? I remember how much you were crushing on him during our junior year."

I nodded. "Yeah, time is weird that way. He's an adult now, but a part of me still sees that shy, handsome teenage boy he once was. My eyes are looking at him through the lens of a high schooler."

"That's normal," Yvette said. "Though—" She paused.

"Though what?"

"Well, I'm not sure 'shy' is the right word to describe how he was in high school."

"You thought he was talkative?"

Yvette shook her head. "No, I wouldn't say that. But my brother Jim was a senior in the same graduating class as Kristopher. He had a different impression of him back then."

I raised my eyebrows and motioned for her to explain.

My friend checked her rearview mirror, changed lanes, and then snagged a quick glance at the still-singing girls in the backseat before continuing. "Jim said that Kristopher was athletic and good at just about every sport, which made him instantly popular. When the basketball or baseball team would go somewhere to hang out, he was always invited and he'd almost always go along."

"He was one of our high school's star players, Yvette. Everyone knew that."

"True. My brother said that as long as the conversation stayed on sports, Kristopher could hold his own. He was never quiet or shy during these outings—"

"Sports had always been his favorite topic, so I guess that doesn't surprise me," I said. "He had only so much enthusiasm for other things."

"Maybe," my friend said, but she was hedging, I could tell.

"Why the tone? What else did your brother say?"

She exhaled. "Jim said that he used to clam up only when talk turned personal—parents, siblings, girlfriends. That he didn't confide anything deep with anyone. He didn't have a best friend. He didn't even have an arch enemy." She shrugged. "My brother thought Kristopher wasn't shy so much as secretive. That he had something to hide."

I felt my jaw drop open, and I was conscious of wanting to contradict her but unsure how to do it. What she said rang true.

"Mom!" Brooke interrupted from the backseat. "Can we *pleeeease* put in the Owl City CD that Uncle Eddie gave us?"

Yvette sighed, rolled her eyes, and whispered something about having heard this particular album over three million times already. But she called back to the girls and said, "Sure." Then, under her breath to me, she added, "What's three million and one, right?"

The drop off at Camp Willowgreen went as smoothly as could be expected. On one hand, it was a stunningly quick procedure, designed to pull off the bandage of separation swiftly. On the other hand, the half hour transition felt to me like we were running in slow motion. A trick of real-life cinematography or something.

Analise was visibly shaken at the camp counselor's announcement that parents would need to leave. Her smiles from the moment before disappeared. She dropped the small tote bag she was carrying and clung to me, the way she had as a toddler before a "Mommy & Me" tumbling class.

The counselor for Analise's cabin—Shannon—tilted her head in concern and walked slowly toward us.

I was hugging my daughter and, at the same time, trying to detach from her. One of the hardest moments of my life.

"It'll be okay, sweetheart," I whispered. "Your friends are here, and I'm just a phone call away. Don't worry."

"I don't want you to go," my daughter murmured, her voice trembling.

I stroked her hair, giving in to the urge to pull her closer and let her bury her head against my chest. How did they expect me to let go when she was holding me so tight?

Shannon placed a soft hand on each of our shoulders. She smiled kindly at me and then, turning to Analise, she said, "I know you're going to miss your mom, but our cabin wouldn't be complete without you here. And we're going to need your help this afternoon with the scavenger hunt."

Analise lifted her head away from my body and glanced at the counselor, curious.

Shannon nodded. "The game is already set up, and your team won't do nearly as well without you." She reached down to grasp Analise's hand—just holding it for now, but poised to tenderly tug her away, if necessary. I could feel it.

"When can I talk to my Mommy?"

"Tonight," Shannon reassured her. "You can tell her all about the scavenger hunt, the opening feast, the dance party—"

"There's a dance party?"

"Yep. Tonight," the counselor said, tugging my daughter's hand ever so gently. "You can call or text her and tell your mom all about it afterward. Sound good?"

With her free hand, Analise squeezed me tight again and pressed her face even harder into my body. I squeezed my eyes shut, willing myself not to cry. Not to pull her away from camp and take her home with me right now.

But a second later, she pulled herself away and allowed Shannon to lead her across the cabin to where Brooke and Lindsay were waiting patiently. Yvette stood at the door.

"Don't worry," the counselor said to me this time. "I'll take good care of her."

I nodded and walked with Yvette out of the cabin and into the parking lot, where my friend let me sob in the car for several minutes before we began the long drive home.

When I finally got back into the house, I collapsed on the sofa and tried not to let the pervasive silence of my surroundings bother me. *Four weeks* of this, though! It already felt like an eternity, and it had just been a few hours.

I'd gotten a text from Shar on the way back that just said, "Call me when you get home," so I figured I'd better get my act together and do it. Shar wasn't as sweet or as patient as Yvette. Then again, as kind and responsible and caring as Yvette was, she'd never been my confidante. We were always casual, neighbor friends, even back in high school. Shar, on the other hand, was the sort of friend who was like a sister, and the rules were different with sister friends.

"Hey," I said to Shar when she answered her phone. "Got your text. What's up?"

"It's not about *me*, girlfriend. I wanted to know about *you*."

I couldn't help it. I started crying again.

"How many hours until you can talk to her?" my best friend whispered.

I checked my watched. "Not 'til eight tonight."

"Okay. I'm coming over. We're gonna watch a Ryan Reynolds movie. And there just may be some ice cream involved."

"Which one?" I asked.

"Which kind of ice cream? I was thinking, maybe, a tiramisu gelato—"

I laughed through my tears. "No, I meant which Ryan Reynolds movie?"

"Who cares?" Shar replied. "I just want to ogle his hot body for two hours. Those abs...mmm! He makes me wish I were Canadian."

Shar was good at distracting me and, as I brushed away the wet splotches on my cheeks and thought about something as frivolous as hot actors again, I was reminded of an event I'd neglected to mention to my best friend.

"Oh! By the way, are you free on the night of the eighteenth?"

There was a pause while Shar checked her calendar. "Sure. Why?"

"Because I've got two VIP tickets that I can't use for 'The Bachelor Pad'—the Closing Night performance that Saturday night and the private party afterward. I thought maybe you and Elsie might like—"

"How did you get those?" she interrupted.

"From Dane Tyler. It's, um, kind of a long story."

The shocked silence on the other end of the line let me know that my words hadn't gone unheard. Finally, Shar said, "I'm leaving now. There will be *no* Ryan Reynolds and *no* ice cream until I hear this story. In its entirety. That means Every. Flipping. Detail. Got it, girlfriend?"

"Yes."

"Good. See you in five minutes."

CHAPTER EIGHT

By the time Shar had finished grilling me on everything that had happened and every word that had been said between Dane Tyler and me the night of the dress rehearsal—and after we'd watched *The Proposal* for at least our tenth time each and devoured a pint of gelato straight from the container—the hour had finally come to talk to my daughter.

"How did the first day go?" I asked Analise.

She was almost gasping for air when she replied, as if she'd been running to keep up with a schedule that had left her breathless. "It was good, Mommy," she began, and then went on to list the stream of activities that started within moments of the parents' departure from camp earlier in the day.

I just listened and smiled—relieved and heartbroken at the same time that my baby girl had been forced to be so resilient. That such frenetic action was needed to break the pain of separation but, yet, that it could be done in the course of an afternoon and evening.

I told her enthusiastically, "Wow, you did a lot today! That sounds wonderful, honey."

While inside I whispered, if only to myself, "I miss you with my whole heart."

It was, perhaps, too much to expect that even the madcap daily routine of Camp Willowgreen would be enough to change the emotional circuits in my daughter's brain for an entire month. I wasn't, however, expecting her meltdown to come in the middle of my dinner date with Kristopher.

"I told them to bring us only the crispy fries," he informed me with a grin I recognized, almost as if it had come straight out of our high-school yearbook.

"Hope they follow orders," I replied, crossing my arms with mock severity. "Otherwise, we're out the door." I pointed to the exit of Sloppy Joe's threateningly, which made Kristopher burst out laughing.

"Yeah. Somehow, I don't think Joe is sweating in fear of losing our business," he said. A funny statement to us both because Joe Redland, the owner of Mirabelle Harbor's beloved burger joint, was one of Kristopher's second cousins.

Not only that, Sloppy Joe's was always packed—usually with repeat customers. We wouldn't be missed in this carnivorous crowd. They served the juiciest burgers, the sauciest wings, the tangiest barbecued pork, and the most succulent ribs on the North Shore. All that and they also had crispy fries.

"Hey, you brought back an old friend tonight!" Joe Redland himself said to Kristopher, as he did a proud walk-through of his restaurant.

"So nice to see you again," I told him, and I meant it. Joe was a good guy.

He clasped my hand and said warmly, "I've missed

seeing you, Julia. I'm so, so sorry about Adam."

A lump formed in my throat, so I just nodded. I hadn't been here since the accident. Had it really been that long?

The older man squeezed my hand tightly for a second before letting go and turning to his cousin again. "So, what's going on with your mom and that firecracker sister of yours?" he asked, grinning.

A look I couldn't interpret flashed across Kristopher's face. He looked—for want of a better word—*wary*. I thought about what Yvette had said on the drive up to the camp about him being secretive. My plan for tonight was to figure out more about him in the now. The adult Kristopher Karlsen. To see if I got the feeling that he was, indeed, hiding something.

"They're doing great," Kristopher said with an extra (pseudo?) burst of cheerfulness. "Haven't talked with Tricia in a couple of weeks but, last I heard, she was planning some sort of trek through Maine with a few fellow hiking enthusiasts." He laughed (forced?) and seemed to expect Joe to find it equally amusing.

The owner's smile broadened. "Yeah, we could always count on your big sister for adventure. But you're no slacker yourself, kiddo. How long are you gonna stay up in these parts, hmm? Planning the next big move or—" He shot a glance at me. "Ah. Maybe you'll stick around a little longer this time?"

"Maybe," Kristopher said quickly.

"Well, it's always nice to get together with old friends, isn't it?" Joe enthused, just as our server came rushing to the table with our order.

"Here you go," the college boy said. "Two cheeseburgers with the works and a double order of crispy fries."

"Thanks," Kristopher and I chorused.

"It looks heavenly," I added.

Joe beamed. He glanced at our table and called the boy

back. "You get them a refill on their sodas and, while you're back there, add on two chocolate-vanilla swirl milkshakes for them, my treat." Then he winked at us and said, "Enjoy your dinner, kids."

Before we could even thank him properly, he was gone, laughing with some customers half a room away.

"I swear that guy is, like, part leprechaun or something," Kristopher said.

I laughed. "He does seem a touch magical, and he moves faster than anyone I've ever met, especially for a man in his seventies."

"I know, right? My mom said he was like that, even when he was little."

"So," I said, between bites of my delectable cheeseburger, "how *is* your sister?" I knew Tricia was two years older than him and had been just as quick to blow out of town after high-school graduation as Kristopher did. "Did she ever get married? Start a family? I haven't heard news about her for ages."

He shifted awkwardly in his seat and fiddled with a couple of French fries before answering. "Uh, she's been in and out of a few relationships. Nothing sticking, though." He shrugged. "No children either, though it would be fun to be an uncle. I can just see the cute personalized mugs they'd give me for Christmas with 'World's Coolest Uncle' scripted on the side." He smiled.

I smiled in return, but I wasn't going to let him change the subject so easily.

"What about *you*, then? No desire to settle down and have kids of your own?"

"Oh, I'm not ruling anything out. But I do like that 'uncle' idea. All the enjoyment, almost none of the responsibility."

"Ha. Yeah, I can see where that would have its advantages, but what I meant was—"

"Oh, look!" He pointed out the window. There were a

bunch of teens driving by. So many that they were almost spilling out of a silver convertible. "Wonder where they're all headed."

Another change of subject, I thought. But I said, "They're kids on summer vacation. Wherever they go, they'll turn it into a party."

He nodded, watching them with a gaze I could only describe as one of deep yearning. "Wouldn't it be awesome to be that age again?"

No, a loud voice in my head yelled. But I said, "I don't know. I'm not sure I'd want to go back."

"What if you could go back to being eighteen, knowing then what you know now?" he asked.

"That would be a little different, I guess, but life doesn't work that way—at least outside of a time-travel movie. If you get all the youth, you also get all the uncertainty."

He grimaced. "When you put it like that, I'm not sure I'd want to go back either."

I laughed, but I was determined to get us back on a topic he kept avoiding: His family. "So, you and Tricia both left home really young. Was it hard for you to leave Mirabelle Harbor? Or were you glad to have escaped?"

He shot me an odd, anxious look. "What do you mean...escaped?"

"Oh, you know, getting away from the suburbs. The Midwest. The familiar."

Some of the tightness in his shoulders seemed to fall away when he shrugged, almost as if he was trying to get rid of it faster. "There was a lot of, um, *tension,* I guess you could say, in my house when Tricia and I were growing up. I think we both needed to put a little distance between ourselves and that...atmosphere."

This was the first I'd ever heard Kristopher speak of that. Although, thinking back, I remembered with a flood of recognition how he and I always went out for our dates or, on the few nights we stayed in to study, how we met at *my* house, not his. In fact, I remember only going into his room one time, and it was on a weekend when his parents were out of town and his sister was already living in another state. We made out on his bed for almost two hours that night. I blushed, remembering.

"What?" he asked me. "Are you okay? You look a little flushed. Too warm in here?"

"It's fine. I'm good," I said with a laugh.

I was about to ask a few follow-up questions about his parents, but I was mentally tripping over how to word it. No one just wanted to blurt right out and ask about the source of that kind of tension. Were his mom and dad always fighting?

I wasn't given the chance to figure out the best phrasing, though, because my cell phone rang. Analise's ringtone.

"Hello, sweetheart," I said, delighted to hear from her, although it was a tad early. Her nightly calls didn't usually come for another hour or so.

"Mommmmmy!" she cried. "Oh, Mommy, I want to go home." There was a pause on the other end of the line and I heard my daughter's big gulping sobs.

My pulse kicked into high gear. I jumped up and excused myself from the table, telling Kristopher to wait there. Then I raced out the front door and away from the noise inside the burger place. Before I could even ask her what was wrong, I was reaching for my car keys, ready to drive up to Camp Willowgreen with only a split second's notice, if necessary.

"Talk to me, honey. Please. Tell me what's wrong. Are you hurt?"

She sniffled and gasped for air. "I—I—"

I was aware there was another conversation going on between Analise and someone else who was next to her. As my heart continued to pound, I could hear an adult voice asking her, "Do you want me to talk to your mom for you?"

Analise mumbled something to that person and then said, "Mommy, here's Shannon."

"Mrs. Crane?" the young camp counselor said.

"Yes, yes! What's going on up there, Shannon? Please tell me what happened. I'm so worried."

"Everything's okay. Analise isn't sick or hurt, just very sad. She really wanted to talk with you, and even though it's before our regular cell-phone time, I thought it would be a good idea to let her call you. We were just starting an evening art project, when Analise panicked. She realized what we were doing and started weeping."

"Because of an art project?"

"Yes. It involved wrapping silver-colored thread around nails that had been hammered into a piece of wood. If the campers followed the directions exactly, it would make a pattern. A pretty design. But Analise got very upset with this activity."

And suddenly I knew exactly what had gone wrong. "It's string art," I told her, feeling the tears beginning to pool in my eyes.

"That's right," Shannon said, surprised. "You're familiar with it?"

"I am." I swallowed. "Analise's father had a number of string art designs hanging up in the patient rooms of his doctor's office. He always—" My voice broke and I had to stop for a moment. "He'd promised her that they'd make a few pieces together sometime, when she was on vacation. But they never got the chance because...well..."

"Oh, I'm so sorry," Shannon whispered. "We had no idea."

"I know. I know. There's no way you could have known." My heart was bleeding for my sweet, sensitive daughter, having to deal with the onslaught of such memories alone, hours from home. And it was aching even for me. Having to be so far away from her. "Please let me talk with her again."

"Of course," the counselor said, giving the phone back to Analise.

"I just couldn't do it, Mommy," she told me. "I just couldn't make that project."

"I don't blame you, my love. I couldn't have done it either."

And the two of us spent the next few minutes on the phone, crying together.

Finally, I said, "Do you want me to come up and get you tonight? Was everything else okay today?"

She sniffled a few times and blew her nose. "We did some fun things today. Before *that* project." She sighed. "Tomorrow, there's supposed to be a play. I'm in it."

"Really? What's your part?"

"I'm the sun." She sniffled again. "It's kind of important. There are only three characters. Me, the wind, and this guy with a jacket."

The storyline rang a bell. "One of Aesop's fables?"

"Yeah."

I wasn't sure if I felt more relieved that she seemed to be looking forward to the next day at camp or disappointed for myself that I couldn't rescue her from the land of rolling hills, quaint cabins, and sparkling waters, if only so I could have her back with me again. But I was the grown up here. I had to ask the big questions. Do whatever was in her best interests, not mine.

"So, you probably don't want to miss that, huh? I mean, how would they put on the play without you?"

"Right. I suppose I should stay here for that, but—" She paused. "It was a tough day for missing Daddy."

"Oh, Analise. I've had those, too."

Shannon got back on the phone a minute later and told me that my daughter seemed pretty tuckered out. "She's yawning, her eyelids are drooping, and she looks like she needs a good night's sleep. I think we could relax the rules again and have her call you in the morning. Would that help, Mrs. Crane? To see how things feel for her when it's a new day?"

I agreed that this was a good idea. After talking with Analise one more time and telling her that I loved her, I reluctantly hung up, feeling every single mile of distance that separated us tonight.

Finally, once I'd gotten myself together, I returned to Kristopher, who was still sitting contentedly at the table, playing with the last of his crispy fries.

"Everything okay?" he asked.

I briefly told him about my conversation with Analise and her counselor. How I was glad she was, more or less, all right, but how the worry had left me feeling drained. Sad. A little helpless.

Kristopher said, "Well, I'm glad you don't have to drive up to the camp tonight. That would've been a tragic end to our dinner and movie date."

I squinted at him and forced a slight smile, but his reaction puzzled me. I knew he was trying to make light of the situation (maybe a misguided attempt to cheer me up?), but it was a self-centered comment. Not the kind of thing another parent would have said in this situation.

"You know, Kristopher, I'm really not in the best mindset for a movie after that phone call. Maybe we can skip that for tonight and just talk a while over coffee?"

He looked crestfallen. "That's not quite what we did on our first date, though."

"Well, we're not quite high schoolers anymore, are we?" I said, a little too fast and with a little more of an edge than I'd intended. I hadn't wanted to insult him, but my irritation with his inflexibility and his persistence in pushing this "recreated date" on me, given what had just happened, was rising.

He seemed to sense that something was amiss and backpedaled a bit. "I've heard lots of great things about

Camp Willowgreen. Neither Tricia nor I ever went there, but it always sounded like heaven with that big lake and all the games the campers got to play during the day."

"It's a very scenic environment, yes, and they do have—"

"Plus, the routine has to be a good thing for the children. You know, it's kind of like the military. Everyone knows when to wake up. When to eat. When to play or to talk to friends or to go to sleep. There's no time for wallowing. Kids need structure and rules or they'll stay too soft."

Wallowing?

"Perhaps," I said slowly. "I have the highest respect for the military but, remember, my daughter is ten. I'm not worried about her being *too soft*."

I wasn't liking the turn the conversation had taken. Not at all. It was almost as if Kristopher was suggesting that Analise lacked discipline, and that I should be taking a harder line with her. He wasn't acknowledging the depth of her loss—or mine, for that matter. It was as if he expected me to forget that I'd experienced nearly two decades of life without him in it. He seemed to assume that we could just pick up where we left off as teenagers.

"Did you want to finish your burger?" he asked me.

I shook my head. I'd made a serious dent in my meal, but I knew I wasn't going to be able to eat another bite. My stomach was roiling uncomfortably. "It was delicious, though. Thanks."

We stayed at Sloppy Joe's for only a few minutes longer then strolled around Harbor Square, window shopping and chatting about light, superficial things. It was pleasant enough, all things considered, but I couldn't say I felt bonded to Kristopher as a result. And when he walked me back to my car and asked me out for another date this weekend, "So we can finally see a movie together," I found myself making excuses. Delaying.

"I'll call or text you next week, then," he said, undaunted. "I'm going to be doing some recruitment work in the city, but I'm sure we can find a time that suits us both. You can't be busy every night, right?" He chuckled at the improbability of that.

I was decidedly noncommittal in my response.

And this time when he moved in to hug me, it was a tighter and more insistent gesture than the one after our coffee date. I could tell he wanted a kiss on the lips, too, not just a peck on the cheek. I turned my head away before he succeeded at either and stepped back immediately, breaking the connection between us.

"Sorry, Jules. Maybe I'm moving too fast, but I'm a passionate guy, and I've missed being with someone like you," he said, beaming at me. "We can take things slow." With a wink, he waved and backed away, utterly confident that I saw our burgeoning relationship as he did.

Someone *like* me?

The phrase struck me as odd...and not complimentary. As I got in my car and drove home from downtown Mirabelle Harbor, I couldn't help but think that Kristopher had mixed up his words, not merely the signals I'd been trying to send him. His behavior felt less to me like *passion* and more like *possession*.

Worrisome that he didn't seem to know the difference.

CHAPTER NINE

The next night, ten seconds after walking into the reception room where the Franklin College reunion was being held, I knew I shouldn't have come.

Vicky Bernier, the young high-school French teacher I'd met during the Quest group's wine outing, wasn't the problem. We'd driven down to the event together and had a fabulous time singing along with the radio in the car. She was friendly, very smart, and had a great voice—not to mention some hysterically funny dance moves to accompany the songs we were listening to. If I'd known what was ahead of us for the evening, I would have insisted that we just stay in the car and drive around Chicago, blasting Maroon 5 and Fall Out Boy.

Vicky squinted as we entered the dimly lit room, glanced around, and then pointed to a table weighed down with drinks, appetizers, and some sweets. "Punch?" she asked me.

I began to nod, but then I saw a distinctive figure standing by the table and staring right at us.

Ben Saintsbury, of course.

"Um—" I said to Vicky.

"What?"

A leggy blonde joined Ben by the refreshments table. She invaded his personal space with the cool assurance that this would be welcome. From what I witnessed of Ben's reaction, she was more than correct in her assumption. He splayed both of his hands across her ass and pulled her closer than the skin-tight spandex she was wearing.

I winced.

"You go ahead, Vicky. I have to use the ladies' room." I raced out of there, puzzled at the oddities of my own reaction.

I'd been the one to break up with Ben. I'd felt guilty about disappointing him, but I'd never *missed* him and I'd never had any interest in getting back together with him once we were apart. So, I knew what I felt wasn't jealousy. But, in a strange way, perhaps it was longing. Like when I watched Chance and Nia together.

I sighed, adjusted my makeup, and smoothed down a few stray hairs, studying my reflection critically in the bathroom mirror. Not terrible, considering I was now thirty-six and the mother of a pre-teen. Not a young sexpot either, though.

Just as I was thinking these very thoughts, who should walk in?

The blonde, of course, in her body-hugging blue...er, dress? (Not quite sure what to call her attire. It was part skirt, part scuba-wear.) With her spiked heels, she was at least five inches taller than me in my old black flats and, up close, I could tell she was at least ten years younger.

I hastily slipped out of the ladies' room, but who was waiting just outside the door?

Ben, naturally. I should have guessed.

Cursing my lack of premonition, I was reminded of that classic saying, *"You often meet your fate on the path you take to avoid it."*

He looked at me expectantly. He knew he had me

trapped.

"Hi, Ben," I said weakly. "How have you been doing?"

"Great!" he exclaimed. And, indeed, even up this close and in brighter lighting, he *looked* great.

"Glad to hear it. Well, you have fun. Enjoy the reunion." I took a few steps away.

He laughed. "What? Wait! You can't just run away like that, Julia. I need a moment of glory here." He angled his torso and puffed his chest out in the direction of the bathroom door. "I'm fit. I've still got all my hair. And I'm here with a hot babe. You're supposed to be impressed, dammit." He crossed his arms and grinned.

In spite of myself, I grinned back at him. "Okay, yes. I'm very impressed, Ben. Well done."

He bowed slightly. "Thank you. I finally feel vindicated. All you need to do now to complete my sense of victory is admit that you're sorry you ever broke up with me during college and that your husband can't compare to my awesomeness in any way. Although, I noticed you didn't bring him tonight. So, maybe that means you're on the market again, hmm?"

I knew he was being flippant—that was just Ben's particular style of humor—but I pressed my lips together to keep them from quivering. Even though I'd come a long way toward the acceptance stage when it came to Adam's death, the jab of pain that accompanied the memory of losing him still hurt like hell. But there was no way I'd let myself get all teary-eyed in front of Ben.

"That's, um, an interesting theory," I said, weighing whether or not to tell him the truth. Not only would it lessen his sense of triumph, which he was clearly reveling in, but I didn't want to be Julia Crane the Sad Widow tonight. Not in his eyes or in anyone else's. I'd had more than seven months of that already, and it had grown tiresome. I always appreciated empathy and even sympathy, when genuine. Pity, however, I didn't need.

"Alrighty then. So, what's the *real* reason?" he urged, the slightest bit of something feral in his smile, which reminded me anew of why his behavior had turned me off in college. He was razor sharp, no doubt about it, and witty when he wanted to be, but he was always on the edge of being cruel. Never quite able to disguise his contempt for anyone who couldn't—or wouldn't—play along with his little mind games.

After the frustration of being with Kristopher last night and his clueless remarks about parenthood, not to mention Dane's snappish accusations after his play rehearsal, I'd had just about enough of men leveling their judgments at me. I'd given Ben his "big moment," but one was all I could spare.

"I'm not on the market, Ben, but I appreciate your interest," I said dryly. "I do have a friend here who's waiting for me, though, and I need to find her now. It's been good seeing you again, and I'm glad to know you're doing so well. Have a wonderful time with your *hot babe* tonight."

He stared at me with a slightly deflated look on his face, shrugged in a show of indifference, and waved me away. I went. Quickly.

Before I returned to the dim lighting and the cacophony of the reception area, I checked my phone for texts or missed calls from Analise. We'd spoken again this morning and, as the camp counselor had predicted, things looked brighter for my daughter on a new day and after a restful night's sleep.

But, still, she was my priority. And if she needed me for any reason, even before our scheduled chat time, I wanted to be there for her without a second's delay.

However, there were no messages, and I had no excuse to postpone my return to the reunion festivities.

Vicky immediately introduced me to some old friends of hers—a small group of jovial people, huddled at one circular table in the corner of the room. They were, each and every one of them, as friendly and kind as Vicky herself. And, for over an hour, we sat together, making small talk, snacking on appetizers, reminiscing about former professors that we'd loved and a few that we'd despised, and comparing notes on our various school districts.

It was, in a word, nice. But *just* nice.

I found my mind drifting back to the people who'd inhabited my past. To Ben, of course, who was making a show of nibbling on the ear of his blond bombshell across the room. I remembered him doing that to me a few times when we were together. It felt oddly animalistic. Such a public display of affection. I also remembered that I'd rather liked it back then. I'd liked being with someone who openly showed his attachment to me. Who was proud of our physical connection.

And Ben, to his credit, had actually been pretty good in bed. He'd been my first...and he'd managed to make the experience funny and sweet, which was more than many of my friends had reported about their first times having sex. I was always grateful to him for that.

But he was so insecure during college and, given what I was witnessing tonight, that didn't seem to have changed much. Ben still wanted to win me over. I would have thought he wouldn't care about my opinion by now, but he was still so desperate to impress me. To impress *everyone*.

On the other hand, there was Kristopher. I suspected he *had* changed in some key ways but that he wished he hadn't. He came across as longing for those old days. Trying to recreate them. Willing to force them into reality, if necessary. But life just didn't work that way.

Come to think of it, Ben, Kristopher, and even Dane seemed to want the same thing: To go back in time and reclaim some aspect of their younger selves. Were all men in their late thirties like that? Unsure of themselves, wistful, battling regret over the passing of their youth? Or were these three guys just hitting their midlife crisis a decade too soon?

I wondered about Adam. He'd been confident, I always thought. Secure in his professional choices, his family life, his overall accomplishments. Had he lived longer, might he have changed in a few years' time? Become disillusioned in some way? Gotten bored, even with the happy life we'd created together? Would I?

Perhaps everything would have been different if Adam and I hadn't met when we did. Add a string of unfulfilling relationships, a broken engagement or two, a failed marriage to someone else...and maybe both of us would have been left wishing we could go back to our high-school or college selves again. As it was, I'd been second guessing my every reaction over the past several months. Without Adam around, I wasn't sure who I was anymore, or who I wished I could be.

"Another cocktail before they serve dinner, Julia?" Vicky asked me. "I'm going to get myself a strawberry margarita this time."

"Oh, that's too tempting," I said, jumping up from the table. "I'll go with you."

As we walked to get our drinks, I knew that from the perspective of anyone looking in on me—and I'd caught Ben glancing curiously in my direction more than once in the past hour—I appeared to be calm, contented, and having a lovely time.

But I was acting, just as much as a professional actor like Dane Tyler might act when putting on a live performance. I knew no one around me, however friendly or nice, could see into my heart.

I missed my daughter.

And I missed my late husband.

But, surprisingly, what I missed most of all was being fully myself.

CHAPTER TEN

One of the downsides of living in a small suburb was that the people in it knew where to find you, even when you didn't want to be found.

Especially then.

Which was how it came to pass that, despite my better judgment and my vow never to lay eyes on the popular Dane Tyler in person again (I could hardly avoid seeing him onscreen), I got talked into attending a radio interview and an afternoon tea reception for the asshat.

"But you *have* to come to the radio station," my best friend informed me Monday morning. Shar knew I'd be grocery shopping at Mirabelle Market then, as was my habit during vacations, and she cornered me in the middle of the produce section. "My brother is doing the on-air interview!"

In my opinion, Shar had too many brothers. Not that I was going to tell her that. The one she was referring to today, Blake, happened to be a DJ at 102.5 LOVE FM, Mirabelle Harbor's only local radio station.

"No," I said to her for the second (third?) time, pretty sure I couldn't have been clearer in my enunciation.

"Julia—"

"I told you how badly things went with Dane after the dress rehearsal. I don't want to be in the same room with him ever again. Period."

"But he apologized to you. He sent you flowers. You can put your differences aside for Blake's sake. He needs a healthy listening audience at the reception. His job depends on whether or not the bosses think he's making a good impression on station's fans and is drumming up more community interaction. If Blake can get enough people to show up and be excited, the head guys will be pleased. And if the bosses are pleased, he'll be able to keep doing his show. He was the last DJ hired, and he'll be the first person they let go if the listenership is down." Shar took a couple of deep breaths before continuing.

"Look, Julia, I love my brother, but you know how impulsive Blake can be. This is the only occupation that has held his interest in years, and he was the one who suggested the Dane Tyler interview to the upper management. He really does need for this to work." Her vocal tone, facial expression, and body language were all pleading with me to go along with her plan.

Usually, I would do whatever she asked without question. But this?

I groaned.

All I knew for sure about Blake Michaelsen was that he was as talkative as his kid brother Chance was quiet. He had a snarkiness about him that made him stand out among the Michaelsen siblings. And, as his younger sister had said, he tended to be more shoot-from-the-hip impulsive than all of them, with the possible exception of Chance's twin, Chandler, who lived somewhere in Virginia. Or was it Georgia. I couldn't remember. That guy just kept moving.

So, I understood Shar's fears. She wanted Blake to be successful and contended or he might leave the area. And Shar was extremely clannish when it came to her brothers.

She was determined to keep them nearby.

I sighed. "I'd like to help, but it would be far worse if there was a scene. What if the awkwardness and antagonism between Dane and me reappeared today? That would be the worst thing that could happen for your brother."

"Let me say this again—Dane Tyler, Mega Star of the Silver Screen, apologized to *you*. I read the note he sent you. I saw the flower arrangement. It was as big as Nebraska. He *wants* to see you again. He gave you VIP tickets to his post-play party—"

"Which, as you'll recall, I gave to you and Elsie. Why? Because I don't want to see him again. It would just be too weird."

Shar mumbled something that sounded like "hopeless case" and crossed her arms. I thought this meant I'd managed to get off the hook.

I should have known better.

"Listen up, girlfriend, you are my best friend. When you need my help, I'm there for you, right? And when I need your help—"

"Seriously? You're really gonna play the best friend card on this one? It's *that* important to you?"

Shar grinned in victory. She knew she had me. I knew it, too.

"It is," she said. "You know that expression, 'to kill two birds with one stone,' yes?"

"Yeah?"

"Well, this event is the equivalent of killing the whole flock with a really big teacake."

"That's one dangerous dessert."

She laughed. "All I'm saying is that a lot of good things will happen if you're there this afternoon. We'll get to help Blake out. We'll show community spirit to the organizers on all sides of the event. We'll keep the balance of levelheadedness intact." She raised a meaningful eyebrow.

There were, we both knew, some community members who could be kind of inappropriate and tactless.

"You and Dane will get some closure, and he'll have a chance to apologize to you in person," she continued. When I began to protest, she cut me off. "I know he won't pick a fight with you, Julia. You'll be able to part as friends. Plus, you'll get to see inside the radio station, which is a cool place to visit, and we'll all get to eat teacakes and pastries from The Gala, so we'll be supporting Nia's family business. There is literally no downside." And she held up a warning finger to keep me from arguing back.

When Shar put it that way, it was nearly impossible to disagree.

"Besides all that," she added, "we'll have an excuse to go get manicures before the event. C'mon! I'll help you with these groceries.."

After I'd gotten the few food items I needed and dropped them off at home, Shar and I went to the salon for manicures and then changed quickly for the radio interview-slash-afternoon tea reception.

Shar was right about the station being an interesting place to visit. I'd seen a few larger broadcasting buildings in Chicago, mostly for television news, and one other radio station in the city, years ago. But I'd never gone into Mirabelle Harbor's own small station before.

There was just one soundproof booth, filled with equipment that I had no idea how to operate. Blake, however, looked comfortable with the various buttons and levers, and we could see him through the clear glass from the hallway outside of the booth.

He waved to his sister and to me when he spotted us, but he had his headphones on and looked pretty busy getting things organized. It reminded me of the small radio station that Minnie Driver's character worked at in the film *Grosse Pointe Blank*—only without John Cusask and a bunch of hitmen running around.

Thankfully, Dane Tyler didn't seem to be inside the radio station yet. I figured we might miss running into him altogether, especially once I realized that the listening/reception area was in a different part of the building from Blake's booth. We would only be able to hear them talk during the interview, not actually see them.

The room that the bosses had approved for the various newspaper people to congregate in was swarming with live bodies, though. Nia's parents, Mr. and Mrs. Pappayiannis, and her brother Dimitri were busily setting up all of the desserts at a long table—a veritable feast of Greek pastries, English teacakes, chocolate confections, and a range of hot and cold beverages. I spotted dueling trays of *baklava* and *galaktoboureko* from across the room and my mouth began to water.

Nia waved to us when she saw us walk in.

"Where's Chance?" Shar demanded.

His young girlfriend flashed a grin. "Don't be mad at him. He has a client for the next hour, but he's planning to pop in as soon as he can get here."

"Okay then," Shar said. "Do you need any help?"

Nia shook her head. "We've got it under control. Maybe just tell some of your friends not to be shy. They can come over and get a dessert plate or a drink anytime."

"Will do." Shar blew her an air kiss and the two of us began spreading the word about the refreshments. It gave me an opportunity to praise the bakery publicly, which I hoped would lead to even more business for Nia's family. They were good, hardworking people. They deserved it.

In our rounds, Shar and I got to chat with Elsie, Vicky, and a few other members of the Quest group. Shar had put out the word to all of them about the event, of course. And even though several couldn't come because of work, vacations, or other commitments, I could tell that Shar had singlehandedly been responsible for at least half of the attendees.

The other half consisted of media people. There were local photographers and a few reporters, including that obnoxious woman from the dress rehearsal night. This afternoon, I spotted her relentlessly pushing her business cards on people and trying to dig for more information on Dane Tyler. She even approached me once, but I slid away from her as fast as I could. I didn't want her trying to trap me into saying anything or misquoting me on something. People like her scared me.

Blake's bosses from the station—Leonard and Doug— were also there, and Shar and I were both relieved to see how delighted they looked with the size and enthusiasm of the crowd. Shar had been right about that, and I was glad we could be present to help out her brother.

I made a point of saying to Vicky, within Doug's hearing, "Wasn't Blake clever to think of doing a celebrity interview like this here in Mirabelle Harbor?"

She readily agreed. Although, later, once the boss guy moved away, she whispered, "Have you ever even met Shar's brother?"

"A few times. You?"

She shook her head. "He has a sexy voice, though."

I laughed. "That he does."

Blake epitomized the modern radio personality in that way. Not only was he more loquacious than most people, his voice was incredibly resonant. At Michaelsen family gatherings, I could tell instantly if Blake was in the house, long before I ever saw him.

But, as good looking as he was, I knew I'd never be able to think of him romantically. And all of Shar's brothers, Blake included, always treated me like just another sister. Even Shar knew better than to speculate about matching me up with one of them.

Up until the time of the actual live interview, the station's typical playlist was being broadcast. The music was piped into most of the rooms in the building, including our reception area. Given that it was "LOVE" FM, the songs on rotation on this afternoon's playlist were a compilation of romantic hits through the decades. I'd already heard a smattering of eighties hair-band ballads— Poison belting out "Every Rose Has Its Thorn" and Whitesnake's "Here I Go Again"—along with a few delightfully sappy Air Supply hits, some seventies-era Bread and Kansas, more recent Elton John tunes, and a handful of really modern power love songs, including Jason Mraz's "I'm Yours."

"Nothing but love, 24/7," or so said the 102.5 slogan.

But promptly on the hour, Blake announced that, after the next commercial break, he'd have "the guest we'd all been waiting for." And he urged us to "stay tuned for Dane Tyler," who was apparently "already in the house."

My pulse kicked it up a couple of notches. Dane wasn't in the reception room now, but that wasn't too surprising, given the crush of people and the immediacy of his interview ahead. But would he be able to avoid coming in here afterward? With so many reporters present, I seriously doubted it. Talking to the press after events like this was part of his job.

Everyone in the room paused in both their conversation and their afternoon tea treats when Blake's voice came back on the air.

"Today," he said, "we're fortunate to have a guest from Hollywood that you all know and love, Dane Tyler. Welcome to LOVE FM."

"Thanks, Blake," we heard Dane reply. "It's a pleasure to be here in beautiful Mirabelle Harbor."

I snuck a glance around the room as Shar's brother asked Dane a series of questions about "The Bachelor Pad" and what it was like to be back in the Midwest again. Every person I could see—male or female, young or old—was listening with rapt attention.

After chatting about the play and its run for several minutes, Blake said, "Have you reconnected with any old friends in the area during the past month?"

"You mean beside the mosquitoes?" Dane quipped.

Those of us in the room laughed, a very encouraging reaction for the bosses in attendance, even if Dane couldn't see or hear us. Shar's brother chuckled into his mic.

"Most of my family has moved away from here, either because of work or to head into warmer climates," Dane admitted. "Although, yes, I've seen a few old friends from when I was in high school. And I've even met a couple of new people that I'd like to get to know better."

The collective sound of "ooooooh" echoed through the reception room.

"Ah," Blake said, amusement vibrating through his voice as it piped down to us from the overhead speakers. "I'll bet you've set some hearts on fire since your return to Chicago this summer. And, since this is the station of LOVE, after all, perhaps you could offer our listeners some advice on how to get that special someone to notice them."

The sound Dane made was suspiciously like a snort. "Neon clothing, dangerous looking tattoos, and a few unusual piercings usually do the trick. If all else fails, just take a trip to L.A. and tell everyone you're a director."

Blake chuckled loudly. The guys were having fun in there.

"I may have to try that, Dane, especially if my love life in the Windy City doesn't improve soon. But seriously now," he said, although I more than suspected that Blake wished he could just go with Dane's irreverence and take the jokes to a slightly racier place. "Got any wisdom to give us regular single guys—or gals? Our listening audience is hopeful you might."

"Hmm," Dane said. "The truth is that I consider honesty a big turn on. And kindness. And authenticity. There's not enough of that out there." A long, nearly uncomfortable moment of dead air followed, and I was worried there might have been a technical malfunction. But then Dane cleared his throat and the joking tone returned. "I'm not much of an expert on long-lasting love, although I seem to be asked about it fairly frequently. I can, however, suggest some romantic movies, starring yours truly, of course, that should set the scene for love in anyone's bedroom, family room, or den."

"Do tell," Blake encouraged.

"Trust me on this, all of you in radioland," Dane said. "Just put on *Love at Cedar Ranch* or *Weekend in Maui,* pour some wine for yourself and your significant other, and let the love flow."

I had to admit, both of those films had some incredibly steamy scenes in them. They'd probably have an aphrodisiac effect on many. Once upon a time (until I met Dane in person), they turned me on, too.

"Or, better yet," Dane continued, "recreate that scene from *A Private Obsession* where my character filmed his love interest for three years through that small opening in the wall separating their townhouses. Just turn off the lights, turn on the camera—with mutual consent, of course—and I'll *guarantee* you'll get some action."

This made Blake, all the afternoon tea attendees, the bosses, and probably most of the 102.5 listeners burst out laughing. The guy Dane had played in that latter movie was a stalker—non-violent, but still very creepy, and pretty much the polar opposite of "romantic." The "lights, camera, action" bit was a cheesy play on words, but Dane knew how to sell it.

The men bantered back and forth for a few minutes more in the booth before the DJ paused for a commercial with many thanks to the actor for visiting and the promise of a John Legend tune coming up after the break.

And then bedlam overtook the reception room as Dane Tyler entered it.

Everyone cheered. The bosses beamed. The reporters swooped in. And I backed away toward the only side exit.

I didn't quite reach it, though, before Elsie sought me out. Then Chance stopped me. He'd slipped in toward the end of the interview and wanted to make sure his sister caught a glimpse of him. "I don't want her to hound me later. You know how she gets."

I assured him that, yes, I knew.

He winked at me then dove into the heart of the crowd to find Shar and, then, Nia.

At one point, Dane himself caught my eye, but he was trapped in an onslaught of questions by press people. I made sure to slide out of his view before he could get any closer.

Hiding out for a while in the far back corner of the room, I checked my phone for voicemails and messages. Nothing from Analise or the camp, but there was one email that surprised me. Sender? Ben Saintsbury.

Curiosity had me clicking on it.

"Hey, Julia!" Ben wrote. "It was great seeing you in person at the reunion. Sorry we didn't have a chance to chat more on Saturday night, but...well, I've just been thinking about you a lot since then."

It was fascinating the way Ben tried to reel people in and convince them he cared. He'd thought about me "a lot" in the past day and a half? Great. That was a true sign of interest and commitment. There was more to his message, though.

"I spoke with a couple of old friends who knew a few of your old friends, and I just wanted to say how sorry I was to hear about your husband's death last year. I hope you're doing okay, and that my comments to you weren't TOO tactless."

At this, I actually laughed aloud. A group of women nearby turned to glance at me. I smiled and pointed to my phone. "Funny Facebook joke," I explained. They nodded and looked away.

Ben's email ended with a pair of "XO"s and a plea to get together for drinks sometime soon. Yeah, that would be happening—not.

Still, it was thoughtful (maybe?) that he'd thought to email me. Insecurity made people act like jerks more often than any of us probably wanted to admit. And I knew he hadn't known about Adam's accident when he'd made those insensitive comments at the party. It would be fair to give him the benefit of the doubt with that at least.

So, I clicked Reply and typed, "Thanks for the condolences and the invitation, Ben. Now's not the best time for me to get together with anyone, but I appreciated hearing from you. Hope you'll have a fun summer."

I signed it, hit Send, and exhaled. I'd had my fill of men behaving foolishly for a while, midlife crisis or not. I needed a break from them all.

A moment later, Shar came over with a plate piled with desserts. "Help me eat these," she demanded. "It's in celebration, so they have no calories." She glanced approvingly at the management heads who couldn't have looked happier.

As I gave in to my temptation for Greek pastries, Blake himself approached us. His shift had just ended and he'd turned over the reins, with the help of REO Speedwagon's "Keep on Lovin' You," to Amelia, the next DJ on the station's schedule.

"Thank you, ladies," he said warmly to both his sister and me. He kissed Shar on the cheek. "I know what you did. I owe ya."

"Oh, don't worry. I'll collect on that later." She grinned at him, but Blake and I both knew she wasn't entirely joking. Shar was a loving sister, but she didn't let her brothers off the hook when it came to an unpaid debt.

"No doubt," he countered.

We talked for a few minutes before he nudged Shar and motioned subtly toward Vicky, who was across the room chatting with one of the bosses.

"Who's the babe talking to Leonard?"

"She's a friend of ours, and her name is Vicky. Do not call her 'the babe,' that's insulting," Shar retorted. "She's a high school French teacher. Lives in town."

"Really..." Blake raised his eyebrows. "When did foreign language teachers become so hot? Is she single?"

"Behave yourself, Bro. She's currently unattached, but she's looking for a *nice* guy."

"What? I'm nice. Mostly." Blake paused. "Well, okay, not *that* nice but—"

Shar slugged him not very gently in the bicep, but she couldn't hide her laughter.

I excused myself, congratulating Blake on a very successful event and edging even closer to the exit. I figured I could probably slip away now without anyone else caring.

I got as far as the hallway when a voice behind me said, "Excuse me, Julia Crane?"

I swiveled around and Dane Tyler himself had materialized by the door, as if he'd been teleported there, just like his character in that one sci-fi thriller, *Time Jumpers*.

"So, I was surprised to see you here, but very glad. I've been trying to talk with you since I got done with the interview," he said, smiling at me but looking wary, as if he was afraid I might snap at him and bolt without warning. It wasn't without precedent.

"Oh? Um, I—well, you've been very busy," I managed. "T-Thanks for the flowers you sent me, by the way. They were lovely."

He looked mildly reassured but still glanced anxiously

over his shoulder and down the hall. "They were just a little token." He paused. "Look, I can do small talk for hours, but I'd rather not. Most likely we'll get interrupted in a minute or two, though, so I'll cut to the chase. Do you accept my apology for my idiotic behavior at the play that night, or do I need to grovel a little longer?"

In spite of myself, I grinned at him. "Well, I'm not sure. I still have a few unanswered questions."

"Shoot."

"How did you get my address?"

"You're in the book. Well, you know, the online book. They've got you listed in the White Pages. It doesn't take a detective."

I considered this. "But how did you know which suburb I lived in? Julia Crane isn't exactly an unusual name, especially not in a metropolis like Greater Chicago."

He exhaled. "Okay, you caught me. After everyone else left the Knightsbridge that night, I asked Rosemary which town her friends were from. She said Mirabelle Harbor. You told me you were a junior high English teacher. On a hunch, I thought you might work in the town, so I looked up the school's website. And there you were." He bowed his head. "I pretty much wanted to crawl under a rock."

He glanced up at me—his expression sheepish and embarrassed, yes, but his eyes told me more of the story. He looked pained. Truly disappointed in himself. I could tell he was genuinely sorry for having hurt me. He wasn't just going through the motions of an apology. At least I didn't think so. The guy was an actor, after all.

When I didn't immediately reply, he swallowed and said, "That's when I looked up your address. And, uh, when I contacted my agent."

"Your agent?"

"Yeah. See, there's a database for the Dane Tyler Fan Club members. A record of all the people who've ever joined. And there was a Julia Meriwether on that list.

Number 49202, just like you'd said." He rubbed his forehead and I could see a thin sheen of sweat forming. He was actually...nervous. "So, then I Googled you, and—"

"Wait, what? You Googled *me?*"

He nodded. "I came across your husband's obituary. I read it. All of it." He paused and swiped at his forehead again. "Julia, truly, I'm so sorry. I was incredibly out of line at the theater. When I think about what I'd said to you—"

"Dane?"

"Yeah?"

"You've groveled enough. Really. Your apology is accepted."

I don't know why I did this next thing, but I reached out and gently touched his arm—an added gesture of reassurance. He seemed to need it, and I wanted him to believe what I was telling him.

He lightly covered my hand with his. Just briefly. Just long enough only for me to feel the warmth of his palm on my knuckles.

"Thanks," he whispered, pulling his hand away. I did the same.

In the silence that followed, I heard a few people talking and some footsteps from down the hall, moving leisurely toward us.

"So, who are you bringing to the Closing Night party on Saturday? A friend? A boyfriend?" he asked, a glint of pure curiosity in those blue, blue eyes.

"Neither," I was forced to admit. "I'm not coming. I gave the tickets away to two of my friends. Sharlene and Elsie."

"W-Why? Are you busy that night? Out of town?"

I shook my head. "No. I just hadn't really thought it would be a good idea after...um, well, after last time. I wasn't sure you really wanted me there, so—"

"They're *VIP* tickets," he sputtered, half laughing and

half indignant. "We only give those out to family members, *very close* personal friends, or huge theater donors."

"Then I guess you should've given them to someone like that," I retorted, "since I don't fit any of those categories, do I?"

He leveled a speculative gaze at me, his jaw dropping open and then closing again. "Okay," he said finally. "I misjudged you when we met. You misjudged *me* when I sent the flowers and the tickets. No more assumptions, Julia Meriwether Crane."

The voices and footsteps behind us were closing in now.

Dane leaned toward me, tugged at my sleeve, and motioned toward the red EXIT sign at the other end of the hall, which led to the back door of the radio station. "Meet me at the corner of Western and Spring in ten minutes. Look for a dark-blue Lexus. It's my rent-a-car for the month."

"What? No. We're not leaving here together—"

"You're right. We're leaving *here* separately." He pointed to the speckled floor tiles we were standing on. "But, I'm picking you up and taking you back to my old neighborhood, just for a couple of hours, I promise, so we can talk uninterrupted. I know a great place."

My head swirled with a funnel cloud of thoughts that both conflicted and were just plain confusing. "But why would you want to—"

"A million reasons. The question you should be asking is why *wouldn't* you want to go to a place that has the most amazing brownies in North America."

"Brownies?" I squinted at him. Was this about food? Because it seemed to be about a whole lot more, but I couldn't quite wrap my mind around it.

"See," he said with the unmistakable tone of triumph. "You're intrigued, aren't you?"

More like speechless. I stared at him, mute for a

moment but, yes...undeniably, intrigued. I nodded, but I also said, "Dane, there have to be scores of people here who—"

"Want to talk to me?" he said, finishing my sentence. "Maybe. But I'm done talking to most of them for today. We, however, are not done with this conversation yet." He motioned between us with his fingers. "I said no more assumptions. I'm a man of my word, no matter what that skanky chick from the *Tinseltown Buzz* said about me or whatever fiction about my life they'll run next week in that crappy little tabloid everyone knows as the *Hollywood Kerfuffle*." He grimaced. "Ten minutes. Will you meet me, Julia? Please?"

"Don't you have to perform tonight?"

"Nope. The theater's dark on Monday."

"I'm told getting into cars with strange men is dangerous."

"True," he agreed. "And I may be a strange man, but I'm not a *stranger* to you anymore, am I?"

I didn't answer this. I thought I'd had enough of dealing with men for a while. All of them, with all of their issues. But this was a pretty unusual circumstance. It also wasn't a "date" or anything. It was just a conversation. With the movie star I'd always dreamed of talking to in person. And though I wasn't going to admit it to Dane, no, I didn't think of him as a stranger.

The people behind us were talking loudly, probably trying to get Dane to turn around and chat with them. The door back into the reception room suddenly swung open and a reporter lady I hadn't seen earlier said, "Oh, good! Mr. Tyler, I've been looking everywhere for you. I had a few more questions about—"

"Just a moment, please," he told her, never looking away from my face. Waiting for my response.

I bit my lip and nodded. "Fine," I whispered. "But you'd better not be exaggerating about those brownies."

He laughed. "I'm not." And then turned back to his adoring public and the always insatiable members of the press.

I walked down the hallway in a daze and pushed open the door leading to the stairs and the street below. Was I really going to go somewhere and have a private conversation with my film idol? I never would have imagined—

"Jules," a voice behind me called.

Kristopher. Oh, damn.

Walking past Dane Tyler and the crowd in the hall, Kristopher shot the actor a distrustful look and trailed me to the exit door. "Leaving already?" he asked, blocking my retreat.

"I've been here for a couple of hours," I informed him. "It's time for me to go."

"Saw you talking with the big movie star," he said with fake jollity. "Looked real...*friendly* between you two."

To me, his words had the uncomfortable ring of an accusation. My defensiveness rose in response.

"Yes, well, it was pretty loud in the reception room. Were you in there?"

"For a bit," he said. Then he glanced at his watch. "Hey, got any plans for dinner? I was thinking of grabbing a couple of sandwiches at the deli, or maybe going somewhere more romantic, and—"

"I'm sorry, Kristopher. I *do* have plans. I need to meet someone in just a few minutes actually." I noticed Dane had disappeared from the crowd down the hall. He did say he was a man of his word. If he told me to be ready in ten minutes, I was guessing that wasn't just an estimate on his part. "I have to get going now. Perhaps another time?"

Kristopher crossed his arms. "What are you doing?"

Jeez! *None of your damned business.*

"Getting dessert," I said simply.

He snickered in apparent disbelief. "After all of The

Gala pastries in there?" He pointed in the direction of the reception room. "Why?"

"Because I want to," I said with finality, realizing the instant the words were out of my mouth that they were one hundred percent true. I did want to talk with Dane for a little longer—brownies or no. "See you later," I said to Kristopher.

I pushed my way past him to the landing, headed down the stairs, and exited onto Western.

My ex-high-school boyfriend wasn't quite as easy to shake as I'd hoped, though.

"I'll walk you to your car," he said, his long legs having no trouble catching up with me and matching my stride.

The parking lot for the radio station and for several of the local businesses skirted the sidewalk next to us. At the corner of the lot was the intersection of Western Way and Spring Street.

"Where are you going?" he asked me as I race walked right past my vehicle.

I didn't have to give him an answer, though, because just then a speedy dark-blue Lexus zipped out of the parking lot and idled at the corner. Dane was in the driver's seat. He revved the engine impatiently— just for effect, I more than suspected—and motioned for me to hurry.

A little laugh escaped my lips as I skipped toward the car.

Kristopher did not look remotely amused but, then, he wasn't in on the joke.

I waved him off with a pleasant, "Gotta go! Talk to you soon," and hopped into the passenger seat of Dane's rented car.

Kristopher squinted after me and got as far as saying, "Is that Dane T—?" before Dane hit the gas and we sped away.

Literally.

The guy was driving at least twenty miles above the

posted speed limit.

I glanced over at him, his eyes crinkled in good humor. "So, did I interrupt an important conversation back there?" he asked lightly.

"No. To be honest, I was glad to get away."

He grinned. "Thought so. The look on your face was one I recognized. I've been there. Often." He slowed down for a stop sign, almost deigning to actually stop. "Now, we need to get you a taste of these brownies. They're orgasmic."

Over the sound of the car stereo, which was, interestingly enough, set to 102.5 LOVE FM, I wasn't sure if I'd misheard his comment. "They're, um, *organic?*"

His grin broadened. "That, too."

CHAPTER ELEVEN

He wasn't lying about the brownies.

"Oh. My. God," I murmured after taking my first bite. The burst of buttery batter plus real milk chocolate, which played hide and seek with thin ribbons of caramel, melted together on my tongue, creating a sensation that fit my notion of Nirvana.

"I told you I was a man of my word." Dane looked smug, but deservedly so. "Best in North America, right?"

"I've never tasted better," I admitted.

The Lovin' Spoonful Bakery, located in an unfashionable section of Highbury Park, matched the picture-perfect definition of a hole-in-the-wall joint. The brick veneer looked hastily constructed. The stone steps were crumbling. The paint had begun chipping on the walls and door. Everything about the place should have said "dilapidated"...except that, on the inside, it wasn't.

The shop was absolutely teeming with customers. All locals, from what I could tell. And they'd packed the place until it was standing-room only.

It provided an interesting contrast to our afternoon tea at the radio station. The reception room had been sardine-packed as well, but the vibe was entirely different. I realized why after only a few moments: No one was pestering Dane or trying to get his attention in any way. No one asked for an autograph or the answer to any personal questions. Considering the number of individuals per square foot, there was no invasion of privacy. None at all.

In fact, the only person who approached us was the owner—an elderly gentleman with a silver afro, smooth dark skin, and the warmest smile I'd ever seen in my life. When he walked up to us, huddling as we were in a corner of the shop and devouring our brownies, he brought such pure energy with him that it felt as though the room actually got brighter.

"Julia, this is my man Samuel," Dane said, introducing the two of us. "He's the creator of the best brownie in North America—quite possibly the world."

The man's smile grew even warmer as he grasped my hand in his. "Ahhh, don't believe him. Our young Mr. Tyler is exaggerating again."

I shook my head. "No, sir, he's not."

Dane nodded his approval at me, and the man just threw his head back and laughed. "I like her, Dane. You showin' her the old neighborhood today?"

"Yeah. Thought we might swing by the park, check out the school, maybe bum around for a while in Liam's apartment."

"Then you'll need some extra treats for the road." Samuel took a step back toward the bakery counter with eager customers crowded all around it. He had a couple of assistants packaging orders and ringing up the totals, but they were clearly struggling to keep up with demand.

"Step over here," he told Dane. Then the older man winked at me and disappeared behind the counter.

"I love him like a father," Dane whispered. "More, actually."

There was no trace of humor in his voice when he said

this, and I remembered reading in several articles over the years that Dane's dad had left the family when he was little. His mom had raised him and his brother alone.

"Have you known him for a long time?" I noticed a familiarity in the interactions between the two men that was hard to fake.

"Since I was a kid."

Samuel suddenly reappeared, holding out a large white paper sack that was stuffed with treats unseen. My mouth watered at the delicious mystery within.

Dane took the bag with a bow at the baking master and pulled out his wallet.

"No, no," Samuel said. "It's on the house."

Dane reached around the counter and man-hugged the guy. Then he slipped a one-hundred-dollar bill into the tip jar before parting the sea of customers so we could reach the door.

I couldn't help but observe that, while a number of people appeared to recognize Dane, no one—right through to the end—did anything more than nod kindly in greeting. Not even the slightest breach. It was uncanny. I asked Dane about it as soon as we got outside.

"Samuel runs an interference-free zone," he explained. "He doesn't tolerate drama of any kind or the disturbance of one of his customers, whether that customer is a popular school-board candidate, an off-duty cop, a troubled teen who just needs some down time, or—"

"Or a famous actor who'd like to avoid being hounded by the press?"

He smiled. "You nailed it. Samuel's done some great business over the years and he could easily snazzy up the place, but he's not a greedy man. He wants the bakery to be for locals. He figures if it looks too appealing on the outside, the snootiest and most demanding of the North Shore types might start swarming in. He wants the people who walk into his shop to be the kind who believe that what's on the inside is what matters most."

"That's got to be an unusual philosophy compared to your Hollywood crowd, living most of the year, as you do, in the land of liposuction, Botox, and plastic surgery."

He laughed. "True, though I like to think I haven't completely bought into that philosophy myself, even though I've spent so much time in L.A." He ran his fingers through his dark-blond hair. Still thick and kissed with gold as he neared forty, even if it wasn't quite as abundant as when he was just starting out in show business.

"I do have one confession," he said. "I've gotten highlights these past ten years."

"Really?"

"They're supposed to look natural." He fingered his sun-streaked hair a bit more. "I paid my stylist a fortune for it. How'd he do?"

"I'm in awe."

He arched a brow at me. "Your sarcasm is showing. But, you know, it gets harder and harder to maintain the illusion of youth in a field like mine."

I wasn't joking with him when I replied, "I don't doubt it, and I don't envy you having to deal with that." Aging in Hollywood had to be hell for anyone who stepped in front of a camera, male or female.

He shrugged. "It's part of the game." Then he pointed at a forested bike path that looked all but deserted. "That's the shortcut to my high school. Wanna see it?"

"Sure."

We meandered down the path, a canopy of trees separating us from our view of the sky and blanketing us in a leafy cocoon. I realized it had been a very long time since I'd gone on a nature walk. During the past school year, I'd kept myself busy out of necessity and in an attempt at maintaining my own sanity. I wouldn't allow myself to have time for much beyond my classroom and my life at home with Analise.

But, even last summer—even when Adam was still alive—I didn't do much out of doors. I'd forgotten about the restorative powers of Mother Nature. About the peacefulness I felt in her bountiful presence.

"This is really a pretty walk," I told Dane.

"Glad you like it. It's still a favorite of mine. Although, every time I pass through here, I'm rocketed back to high school."

"Good memories or bad?" I asked, just as we came to a railroad crossing.

The bike path opened up onto a two-lane street. There was a large park to the right—Highbury Park, the namesake of the town—and then farther ahead was the high school.

I couldn't quite decipher the expression on Dane's face as he considered my question.

"Let's just say I was from the wrong side of the tracks." He pointed toward the park and the school as we crossed the very tracks that separated the unruly, overgrown bike path from the well-manicured parcels of land ahead. "The people who live to the east of this line tend to have enormous houses. Those to the west of it," he thumbed behind us, "are often 'the help.' I used to mow lawns for the rich families out here during the summer and shovel their long driveways in winter. Plenty of snow in these parts."

I nodded. "I grew up in Mirabelle Harbor, so I know all about those snowy winters."

We saw a few kids playing soccer in the park and a lady walking a pair of white poodles. Dane and I stopped and watched them for a while.

"The upside of living in a town with lots of disposable income was that the families on the east side financed a kick-ass high school. We had one of the best secondary school theaters in the area," he said proudly. "And an Olympic-sized indoor swimming pool, a state-of-the-art foreign language lab, and tennis courts that were maintained as well as the ones at the local country club. My big brother practically drooled when he saw the chem lab. All those rows of glass beakers and Bunsen burners." He laughed, remembering.

"How much older is he than you?" I knew he had a brother, but there hadn't been many details about Dane's immediate family in the tabloids. The stories mostly just focused on his love interests over the years.

"Three years older," he said, but he didn't share any more than that, and I didn't want to pry. What if they had a bad relationship and still didn't get along as adults?

We stood in front of the high school, admiring it. The building was in perfect condition. Impressive. Stately. Reminded me of the one they'd featured in the movie *The Breakfast Club*.

"It wasn't that the additional money flow evened the playing field for all of the kids in town," Dane said, "but I think those of us on the west side got a few extra opportunities we might not have had otherwise." He paused. "Can't say it made me any more attractive to high-school girls on either side of the tracks, though. At least not until I scored my first film role. I could never get a date with 'the girl next door'—not any of them."

"I'm sure they gravely regretted their oversight later."

He grinned. "Well, later was too late, unfortunately. Hollywood had already messed me up by then, and I wasn't normal anymore."

"But you come across as pretty down to earth. At least you do today." It was true. He hadn't behaved like an entitled movie star at the radio station or at the bakery or during our walk. Even when he was answering questions during the theater Q&A he hadn't been too high and mighty. He only got temperamental when he thought I was some tabloid snitch.

"I know how to *act* well balanced, Julia. That's different from actually *being* that way."

I shrugged. "Say what you will, but I'm not sure I believe you. You seem much more normal than I'd have expected."

He rolled his eyes.

"I remember reading about you also doing community theater during high school. You did that in addition to performing at your school, right?" We walked the length of the building and started to circle it.

He cleared his throat. "Yeah. There were seasonal auditions just down the road at the community college campus. It was a pretty big deal for a high schooler of any background to get a part. After the cast list was posted, word spread like a brush fire. We'd come to school the next day and feel like a celebrity."

"Ah! So you had some practice with that, long before Hollywood came calling."

He chuckled. "The star treatment usually only lasted through third or fourth period, Julia, but, yes, it was an adrenaline rush. No doubt about it. A person who craved attention could get addicted to that."

"And need more?"

"Yep. Like a narcotic."

I glanced over at him. His eyes were facing the school building but his gaze was a million light years away.

"Ever take any of those?" I asked lightly.

He turned toward me and tilted his head, as if weighing whether to tell me the truth or a give me a canned, media-ready response.

Finally, he exhaled and said, "Yeah, a few times. It was a mistake. They made the highs higher for a while, but they also made the lows much lower. And, once you lose a friend or three to OD'ing, it's enough to make a guy reconsider his choice of vices." He held up the bag with Samuel's brownies. "I choose more wisely now."

I smiled at him. He was making a joke, of course, and, yet, he'd told me a hell of a lot about himself that we both knew wasn't funny at all. I appreciated his openness, his honesty, but I was, admittedly, most surprised by his willingness to trust me.

"What makes you so sure I won't go blabbing your secrets, Dane? I mean, I *won't*, but you couldn't possibly know that for sure."

"Couldn't I?" he said. "Look, I've been watching for signs of potential betrayal every moment of my life for the past twenty-five years. I have a long history of my privacy being invaded and people trying to siphon from me what they hope will be incriminating information."

I felt myself blush a little, remembering Dane's accusations when he thought I was a reporter, and I also remembered the rude questions some of the students in the audience and members of the press asked him at the theater. I mentioned this.

"Oh, that was nothing," he said. "Believe me. When I was a kid and less guarded, I made a few slips that I lived to regret deeply. Since then, I study everyone's non-verbal behavior, looking for tells. And as an actor, this also has the benefit of giving me a range of facial expressions I can channel—to help me mimic character ticks and emotions. But, when I was younger, it was purely so I could avoid getting myself in trouble." He looked closely at my face, as if analyzing every contour and crease. "You're a puzzle to me in a number of ways, but you're not *trouble*, Julia Meriwether Crane."

"Thanks," I said. "That was a compliment, I think."

He laughed. "We've officially talked enough about me for a while. I'd like to know a few things about you."

"Okay. Like what?"

We'd finished our rotation around the high school and began heading back, through the park, and soon met up with the bike path again.

"Tell me something important about you," he said. "I can Google basic details—"

I grimaced.

"Don't look at me like that. Almost everyone has a digital footprint these days, even if it's not a mile long, like mine." He nudged me with his elbow. "And don't forget, I can ask people in Mirabelle Harbor questions about you, too. After that radio station visit today, I know *lots* of people that you know."

"That sounds suspiciously like blackmail, Dane."

"Hey, just keeping you honest. But I'm serious. What I'd really like to know is what *you* think is something real about you. Something about you beyond the researchable facts."

I stopped mid-stride to think about this. "That might just be the hardest question anyone has ever asked me. But, also, one of the most thoughtful."

"Well, I've been interviewed a lot in my life." He shrugged, feigning modesty. "Guess I picked up a few things."

I laughed. "I'll bet."

But I hadn't been entirely joking. It was a hard question. One I had to consider more deeply than the usual. I'd often felt very few people really knew me, but what would I have wanted them to know? Not the superficial details. Living where I did, in the kind of suburb that felt like a small town, everyone thought they knew those things about me already. But how much of the real me did I actually want to share with them? With anyone?

"What I'm telling you right now isn't something I've told to anybody—at least not anybody still living." I paused. I had told Adam, but not my parents or the rest of my family. Not even Shar. "I secretly wanted to be a poet when I was a kid," I told Dane. "I loved to read, but I couldn't imagine writing anything as long as a novel. Poems, though, could be short, intense, and packed with meaning. In just a few well-selected phrases, a good poet could describe an entire world."

Dane nodded, taking this in thoughtfully, as if matching my words with what he knew about me so far to see if all the pieces fit together.

"Why didn't you?" he asked. "Become a poet, that is. I think you'd have made an excellent one. You have an eye for things. For places and people."

"I went part of the way there. I was an English major in college. But I hadn't really lived long enough to have much to write about, and I knew it. So I got my teaching certification and started the adventure of working with kids. It turned out I liked it. Then I met Adam, my late husband. He was in med school, and we were in love. I needed to do practical, income-generating things with my degree, especially since I got pregnant right away." I smiled, replaying in my mental viewfinder the day Adam and I found out that amazing, life-altering news. "We'd already planned our small wedding, but I was two months into my first trimester during the ceremony, and our daughter Analise was born seven month later."

He grinned. "So you had family and friends counting back on their fingers?"

"Exactly."

"How old is your little girl now?"

"She's ten," I said. "And spending this month at Camp Willowgreen."

He studied my face again as we neared the end of the bike path. "Sounds like you have quite a few things you could write about now."

"I hadn't thought about it that way but, yes, you're right. I'm not that sheltered suburban girl anymore who only shops at the mall with her friends, talks about dating cute guys, and watches her favorite actors in the movies."

He shot me one of his mega-watt grins, the kind he probably reserved for high-profile photo shoots. "Please tell me I'm still one of your faves."

I considered messing with him, but something in his

tone told me that he cared a little more about my answer than he wanted to admit. And I remembered the look he gave me as I turned away that night at the Knightsbridge. Defiant. Hurt. Wanting to still be the idol of his youth and knowing those days were gone.

So, I told him the truth. "You're the only actor whose fan club I joined in my entire life, Dane. And I don't think I've ever missed one of your films."

"Not even *Dorm Daze*? That one was terrible."

"Not even *Dorm Daze*. Your performance as an irresponsible and frequently drunk college student was strikingly believable."

"Oh, God, kill me now," he deadpanned.

We laughed and found ourselves back in front of The Lovin' Spoonful Bakery.

"I'd suggest stocking up on more of Samuel's brownies," I said, "but we still haven't eaten the extra ones he packed up for us."

"I know. I'm dying for another. C'mon."

"Where are we going?"

He was walking toward a green door just to the right of the bakery. I initially thought it was an entrance to another shop—a dry cleaner's—but when he opened the door I saw it led to a staircase.

"To the apartments upstairs," he explained, holding the green door for me and ushering me inside.

I shot him an apprehensive look. "Do I need to be worried about this?"

He shook his head. "Trust me, the walls and doors are very thin. One squeak out of you, and the other residents will come running. Also—" He paused. "If I laid a hand on you and Samuel got wind of it, he'd flatten me. You'll be safe."

"Well, all right then."

Like the bakery, there was chipped paint and an air of disarray, but the stairs were sturdy and the few apartments at the top looked to be occupied by responsible residents.

Dane stopped in front of apartment 2B.

"To be or not to be..." he mused.

"Whose apartment is that?"

"My brother's," he said and immediately produced the key from his pocket.

"Wait! Don't we have to knock or something? What if we're interrupting him?"

Dane laughed. "Liam's not here. He and his wife and their two very adorable kids live in Massachusetts. He's a thoracic surgeon and owns a couple of houses, a smattering of condos, and a few rental properties around the country. Including this place, which he keeps for sentimental reasons." He pushed the door open and invited me inside. "Welcome to my childhood home."

I couldn't entirely hide my surprise. "This is where you, your mom, and your brother all lived when you were in school?"

It wasn't a tiny place, per se, but it was definitely on the smallish side for a two-bedroom apartment that once housed three people. Not many frills. Well kept, but minimalist in every way.

It reminded me a bit of a budget motel room, only with a small kitchen included and a couple of extra doors to section off the bedrooms.

We walked in and Dane pointed to the smallest of the rooms, which had bunk beds against one wall. "My brother and I shared this one. It got trickier once we both sprouted over six feet. I fought him endlessly about being the one who'd gotten stuck with the top bunk." He rubbed his head. "I think I still have the scars from bumping against the ceiling so many times."

I laughed. "Well, he probably hit the six-foot mark first."

"Only a year before I did. And I'm half an inch taller now, which still pleases the competitive younger brother in me."

I hadn't wanted to pry into his relationship with his brother earlier, but now I felt justified in asking a few questions.

"So, were you close as kids? And are you two friends now?"

Dane looked at the bunk beds, wistfully, I thought. "When we both lived at home, Liam and I fought like a pair of demons, but the arguments never lasted beyond a day. After he left to college in Boston and I left to California, we lived very different lives, but we always stayed in touch. He's still my best friend in the whole world."

"You're lucky," I whispered.

"You have siblings?"

I nodded. "A sister who's four years older than me. Katia. We're very polite to each other on the rare holiday that we get together. She's not that far away—Michigan— but it's a big deal if we see each other once or twice a year. And we were never best friends. Not when we were kids. And not now."

"Sometimes we have to make our own family," Dane said.

I thought of Shar, who was the closest I had to a sister, and the whole Michaelsen clan that had adopted me as one of their own. "That's true."

Dane set the white paper bag on the small Formica table and pulled out a couple of cream-colored plates from one of the cabinets. He added forks, two napkins, and a pair of empty glasses.

"What can I get you to drink? A soda? Sparkling water? Wine?" He swung open the refrigerator door and held it to show me an extensive collection of beverages.

I burst out laughing. I couldn't help it. "You keep it extremely well stocked."

"Yeah, well, this is my private escape pod when I'm in the Midwest. The Knightsbridge people very kindly set me up in a gorgeous suite at the Hotel Royale nearest the theater. It's spacious, beautifully appointed, spotless, and bright...but it's not home."

"So you sneak away whenever you can to your childhood apartment above the bakery that serves the best brownies in North America?"

"You got it. Samuel and his wife have lived across the hall in apartment 4B since before I was born. I consider them family."

"I got the sense that Samuel feels the same about you, Dane. I only just met him, but I think he's a wonderful man."

"They don't come better."

I chose a diet Sprite and he unloaded the contents of the bag. In addition to several brownies, Samuel had packed for us a selection of cookies, scones, and a couple of oversized muffins.

"I suddenly know how Hansel and Gretel must have felt, walking up to that candy house," I said.

He groaned, staring at the array of baked goods. "I'm going to have to work out in the hotel gym for about three hours tonight, but it'll be worth it." He handed me a fork. "Dig in."

By the time we'd made a modest dent in the desserts, I learned a few other things about Dane Tyler:

He was here in Chicago just for this limited engagement and would only be staying for about a week after the play closed.

He was flying to New York City for a few days after that, before finally returning to L.A.

He had a film that was set to start shooting in early August but, once that wrapped, he didn't have any projects on his schedule for a while.

He planned to take time then to seriously consider what his next steps should be professionally. Maybe directing, although he admitted his insecurities there. Would he be able to pull it off? Get the right people behind it? Work well with all the actors?

And whenever his mom, who now lived in Florida, got sick of hearing him complain, she'd tell him to drop the Hollywood scene entirely and just do theater for the senior citizens in her retirement community.

"That," he said with a grin, "is usually enough to get me to shut up."

He asked me a bunch of questions, too.

About Adam and Analise.

About my friends and what it was like teaching junior high kids.

About growing up as a "normal" teen in Illinois.

I laughed at that. "Dull," I said, remembering my pages upon pages of inane journal entries from high school. "There was never much in my life that any gossip rag would've swooned over," I told him. "Even if I'd turned out to be a talented actor like you."

I caught him glancing at my wedding band, and I twisted it on my finger. I still couldn't quite bring myself to pull it off.

"Honestly, Dane, aside from losing Adam so early and having to consult counselors on how to help my daughter work through her grief, there's very little that's unusual about the way my world operates. Nothing I've done that could be considered exceptional by anyone." I shrugged. "*Normal* can be pretty boring."

"I don't find you boring, Julia. And, don't take this the wrong way, but you aren't exactly my idea of 'normal' either. You might have been as a teen—I didn't know you then—but you grew up into someone with an exceptional soul."

It was the kind of compliment that would have been jarring coming from most men, but it didn't seem fake when Dane said it. Maybe he was just *that good* when it came to acting. But I couldn't detect any motivation he'd have for needing to flatter me.

And I soon lost track of how long we spent just talking at that little kitchen table.

At one point, Dane pulled out some whole-wheat crackers, cheese slices, and cold cuts, and we nibbled on those for dinner or, as Dane called it, "the antidote to Samuel's sugar bombs."

"Everyone should eat dessert first sometimes, though," I stated, and he readily agreed.

It was nearly dark by the time he drove me back to Mirabelle Harbor and to my car, parked in the lot by the radio station.

"I'm still pissed that you gave away those tickets to the VIP party Saturday night." He pulled into the empty space next to my car and fished his cell phone out of his pocket.

"Sorry," I said. "I would have kept one of them if I'd have known you better before today." I meant that.

"Good. 'Cuz I'm not letting you off the hook." He swiped at his phone, his thumb poised over the keypad. "What's your number?"

I recited my cell to him and, a second later, my phone beeped.

"That's a text from me," he said. "From my *private* cell phone. Let me make this perfectly clear to you. This is a number I give out *only* to family members, very close friends—"

"And big theater donors?" I joked.

He glanced heavenward in a show of exasperation, but his lips quirked upward. "Actually, no. Not even them. My mother, my brother, my agent, my PR reps, and my lawyer all have it. And some friends. But if you give it away to anyone, I swear I won't be responsible for my actions. Got it?"

"Yeah, yeah. Idle threats."

"You think I'm kidding, Little Miss 49202. I will find you, and you will be sorry."

119

We both laughed at that.

Dane Tyler.

I was sitting in a car, joking around with Dane Tyler.

My sixteen-year-old self would be squealing uncontrollably if she knew.

"I'll protect your privacy with my life," I said, in a tone of mock reverence.

"You'd better. Now, I don't have any other tickets on hand, but that's okay. I've got a new and improved plan," he informed me. "The gold VIP tickets let the guests come in at the theater door and are necessary for entry into the Carmody Room at the hotel for the party after the show. But you won't need that if you meet me at the Knightsbridge earlier."

"How much earlier?"

He squinted into the distance, calculating. "Couple of hours. You can sit in the auditorium for the final performance or, if you'd prefer, you can be backstage with me and the cast. Then we can go to the party."

"As a group, you mean? With the other actors?"

He shook his head. Then, because I must have looked confused, he said, "Julia Meriwether Crane, will you be my date on Saturday night?"

CHAPTER TWELVE

Kristopher Karlsen showed up on my doorstep Wednesday morning. He wasn't smiling.

I was tempted not to answer when he knocked, but that would have been cowardly and, besides, my car was in the driveway. He would have guessed that I was most likely at home and avoiding him.

"Hi," I said, trying to infuse a little more enthusiasm than I felt into the greeting. "What a surprise."

"Hopefully not an unwelcome one," he said, though he didn't wait for my response. "Can I come in?"

"Of course." I opened the door wider and he marched into my foyer. "Would you like some coffee or something else to drink? Tea, lemonade, bottled water?" The list of beverages reminded me of being at Dane's place on Monday, and I found myself smiling at the memory.

Kristopher shot me an odd look. "Uh, the lemonade would be great, thanks."

I poured him a glass and set it on our kitchen table, inviting him to sit down. I'd thrown out most of the flowers from Dane's beautiful arrangement, but there were still a handful of persistent ones that had held their bloom, even a few weeks later.

Kristopher eyed the flowers suspiciously, disapprovingly, but he said nothing about them. In fact, for several moments, he said nothing at all.

"So, what brought you by this morning?" I prompted. "Just happened to be in the neighborhood?"

He took a sip of lemonade and shook his head. "I think we have to talk, Jules."

"About?" A feeling of dread slid down to my stomach and lingered there.

"Seeing you leave the radio station with Dane Tyler on Monday really upset me," he said. "I mean, we're dating now and I just—I just don't think it's appropriate for you to hang around lots of other guys, especially someone as ridiculously unsuitable for you as *him*. He's a stupid movie star—a player, if you read anything written about him in the paper—and he doesn't even know you."

I inhaled sharply, needing the oxygen to reach my head fast since all of my blood had drained from it and rushed to my hands, both of which were itching to throw something breakable at him.

There were so many things wrong with what he'd just said, I needed to list them in order to keep them straight:

"...we're dating now..."

"...don't think it's appropriate for you..."

"...lots of other guys..."

"...someone as ridiculously unsuitable..."

"...he's a stupid movie star—a player..."

"...he doesn't even know you..."

I wasn't sure where to start my rebuttal. I wanted to argue against all of these charges simultaneously.

"Kristopher—I...we...the two of us, you and I, got together once for coffee and once for dinner. They were very nice, and it was fun to catch up on the nineteen years since we'd last spoken. But two get togethers does not mean we're *dating*, certainly not exclusively."

He crossed his arms. "They were dates, Jules. I think you're playing with semantics—"

"I don't," I said, cutting him off. "Because I'm *telling* you, we are *not* dating. Also, I'm not hanging around 'lots' of guys. But, even if I were, it's not up to you to tell me what's 'appropriate' or not for me. Last I checked, you weren't my father."

He scoffed. "I just meant that it looked—"

"I don't give a damn what you think you meant or how you thought it looked. You have no right to try to tell me what to do. Ever. *That* is my definition of inappropriate, and you can be sure that I'm not going to listen to you."

"So what then? You plan to run around with some loser actor who probably has a bunch of bimbo groupies in every city he—"

"Stop it, Kristopher," I snapped. "You don't know Dane. And the degree to which he and I know each other— or don't—is none of your business."

My cell phone was resting on the table, face up. I caught myself glancing at it, wondering if Dane would text again, as he had a few times in the past couple of days. No major messages. Just a few funny follow-up comments about my response to his invitation for Saturday night. But it would only antagonize Kristopher further if he saw one of them.

I reached for my phone, brought it closer to me, and turned it face side down on my side of the table.

Kristopher narrowed his eyes. "What? Expecting a call from your *buddy* Dane? You think he considers you a close personal friend now?" He snickered. "You're just as silly as you were in high school, Jules. Still daydreaming about your teen heartthrob. What a joke."

I replayed Dane's parting words Monday night. He'd specifically asked if I'd be his "date" to the VIP party. The high school girl still living inside of me practically keeled over in shock.

But the adult I'd become—the same adult who'd spent several very pleasurable hours with Dane Tyler talking openly—well, she merely blinked a few times before replying, "Sure. I'd love to."

And when my teen heartthrob smiled so charmingly at me and whispered, "Excellent. Now I have something to look forward to on Saturday," even my adult self turned into melted brownie batter and caramel. I was riding high on that sweet sensation all night. And the next day, too.

"I'm not claiming to be special to Dane," I told Kristopher on a sigh. "But the one thing I can tell you is that he's not ridiculous, unsuitable, or stupid. He's a hardworking actor, and I consider him a friend. And since I don't talk trash about my friends, particularly not behind their backs, this conversation needs to end. Now."

I stood up from the table and waited for Kristopher to do the same.

There was frustration—no, more like fury—emanating from every pore of his body. To be honest, I felt a bolt of fear as he glared at me, his hands fisted at his sides, his jaw tense with barely restrained aggression.

"You're making a huge mistake," he ground out. "That fucker is gonna screw you over, and you'll have no one to blame but yourself."

I nodded at him and pointed toward the door. "I'll take my chances."

He pushed his chair back so hard as he stormed away from the table that I flinched at the scraping sound it made.

And then he was gone.

When I saw Kristopher's car zoom away from my home, I let out a breath I hadn't realized I'd been holding.

I inhaled freshly, trying to slow my racing pulse. Then I reached out to touch one of the blossoms left from Dane's big bouquet. A dark-red carnation with its edges tinged white. It had to be both delicate and hardy at the same time to have lasted so long and, yet, still look this beautiful.

In a surprising way, the carnation reminded me of Dane himself. He'd always been talented and attractive but, with greater age and acquaintanceship, he'd only improved.

He deserved to be recognized for his long career and his contributions to his art—more so than he had been, in my opinion. But maybe I was blinded by my own enchantment with him. My cumulative years of admiration toward him.

Only...that wasn't how I'd felt after our brownie excursion this week.

If anything, Dane had done everything in his power to drop whatever remained of the veil of enchantment from my eyes and help me to see him clearly. Flaws and all.

Paradoxically, my appreciation for the man and his gifts were only magnified as a result. Turned out, Dane Tyler was *real*, not merely a phantasm on the screen.

And try as Kristopher might, I wouldn't let him succeed in tarnishing my opinion of the guy.

If I dug deeper and Dane ended up being just an illusion after all, so be it.

The only thing I felt positive about was that spending time with him on Monday had flipped back on a switch inside of me. One I'd feared would forever stay off. There had been a moment—a few of them, really—when we were in Dane's childhood kitchen. When I'd felt fully alive and filled with a sense of promise for the first time since Adam died.

For that alone, I was grateful to Dane Tyler, and I was resolved to enjoy his company for however long it lasted.

CHAPTER THIRTEEN

Aside from a handful of additional texts, I didn't have any other contact with Dane until early evening Saturday at the theater.

Shar, however, was a different story. She was omnipresent, like a swarm of mosquitoes on a damp summer night.

"When are you meeting him?"

"Is he sending a special car to pick you up?"

"What did he tell you about his family? Ooooh! Any secrets?"

"He said this was a *date,* right? Do you think he's gonna kiss you at the end of it?"

There may have only been one of her, but she asked enough questions for ten friends at least.

I'd finally had enough of the interrogation. "Dear God, Shar. If you don't stop grilling me, I swear I'll have to tape your mouth shut."

She paused for a second, raised her eyebrows in a sudden jerky motion, and then asked, "Do you think he'll take selfies of you two at the party and post them on social media?"

"Ahhhh!" I screeched at her. I marched toward the kitchen and left my best friend sitting in the living room. "I know I have some duct tape in one of these utility drawers," I threatened, yanking a couple of those drawers open.

She followed me, pointing at me in this insistent, menacing way. "You're not seeing the big picture. I'm being serious here. Do you think Dane will go public with your relationship? I'm not saying it would be a bad thing—I actually think it would be freaking fantastic! But people will *know* about you then. Everyone will see you two together, and you need to be aware of that." She stopped jabbering at me for one blissful moment before gasping, clapping wildly, and saying, "Oh, Julia—there might even be paparazzi!"

"Stop sounding so gleeful." But her comment made me pause.

I sure hoped that the paparazzi wasn't something I'd have to worry about. Dane's star wasn't quite as big and bright as it used to be, but he was still very popular in some circles. Perhaps not the current generation's "It" man—one who inspired hordes of squealing fans to follow him around, chant his name, live and breathe based on his Twitter feed, or demand a constant stream of tabloid photos featuring him. But, like Kristopher had implied, there were still "silly" women like me, in my age group, who would be highly interested in news about him. But probably not enough for actually paparazzi, though...right?

"I don't think this event is that big of a deal," I told Shar. "It's not as though Dane and I are going out on the town or anything. I'll just be watching the play again, like you and Elsie and the rest of the audience. Then, afterward, we'll all be at a private reception a few blocks away. Everyone in attendance will have a reason to be there. It's just for the Knightsbridge Theater VIPs, along with friends and family of the cast and crew."

Shar opened her mouth to speak, but I cut her off before she could ask another question. "Dane said there wouldn't be more than a couple of reporters admitted to the After Party. Only highly vetted ones that the theater knows and trusts. So, it won't be the obnoxious free-for-all press experience like it was during the dress rehearsal."

This information was still not quite enough to pacify my best friend, who seemed convinced that my life was going to change drastically before the end of the weekend. She was positively determined to make sure I was ready for it.

"Don't you think you should get a little touch up on your manicure?" she asked, scrutinizing my fingernails. "If you did, you'd be right next to the hair salon. What do you say I make you an appointment for both places?" She looked me up and down, considering my attire. "And, um, what were you planning to wear to the party?"

I sighed as Shar buzzed around me, making beauty arrangements, speculating on my future, and reminding me of why it was sometimes easier to share secrets with only a journal, for instance, rather than loving but nosy friends.

For the record, Dane did not send a "special car" to pick me up because one wasn't needed.

I drove myself to the Knightsbridge and parked in the lot Dane had told me was reserved for the cast and crew. He also instructed me to text him when I got to the theater, so he could meet me, give me an official parking sticker— "Hey, you could stay here all night if you wanted to now," he joked—and let me into the building from one of the side doors.

"There'll be lots of food at the party," he told me as we walked to his private dressing room, "but it's not a sit-down dinner, and it's still hours away. So, I ordered in some sandwiches for us." He pointed to a plastic-covered tray, piled with enough sandwiches for at least half a dozen people. There were also several bags of chips and cans of soda. "Anything we don't eat, I can put in the green room for the other actors." He paused and met my gaze directly. "And you look stunning, by the way."

"Thank you," I murmured, silently thanking Shar for insisting that I wear my most elegant dress—white with gold accents. It had a very silky and flowing fabric. Always made me feel just a bit princess-like, but I hadn't worn it since before Adam's accident. I put my hand behind my back and rubbed my wedding band. It spun around my finger, not quite ready to twist off but no longer as natural feeling as it had once been.

"Oh." He held up a white paper bag and handed it over to me. "I saw Samuel this morning and he sent these for *you*. I'll be strung up by my thumbs if I horde them and he finds out, so you'd better take 'em now."

I opened the bag to find about three thousand calories worth of brownies and these little cake balls rolled in shredded coconut. They smelled very strongly of...what was it? "Rum?"

He nodded. "Samuel's famous rum balls. Potent enough to give someone a hangover, so be forewarned."

I laughed. "Well, you'll have to help me eat them." I set the bag down. "Maybe we should wait until after your performance, though. Don't want you getting tipsy and slipping off the stage."

"The press would have a field day with that."

I glanced around the room. "I'm guessing not everyone has a private dressing area, huh?"

He shook his head. "There are just a few private ones. A perk of being the headlining actor in this production and the special guest of the theater company. But I mostly hang out with the rest of the cast in the green room or in the wings. They're a good bunch overall."

After having spent so much time with Dane on Monday, I had to admit that it wasn't nearly as awkward between us as it might have been—a gift for which I was grateful. But, likewise, it wasn't as easy between us either as it had been in his childhood apartment a few towns away. There was an unexpected fission in the air tonight that I couldn't account for, except that it seemed in some way connected to being at the theater itself, on the verge of a show.

"Have a seat, if you'd like," he said, nodding in the direction of the only comfortable-looking armchair in the room. The rest of the seats were short wooden stools.

"I will in a minute. I, um, just want to look around." There were costumes laid out for the different scenes of the play, and a smattering of props. One of them—a pair of handcuffs, used in Act II—was sitting on top of his dressing table, inches from the mirror. I smiled remembering Dane's part in that scene, which involved a lady in a cop outfit trying to "arrest" him, and how sexually suggestive that whole onstage interaction was.

He caught me staring at them and picked them up. "Did you want a closer look?" he asked, grinning.

"Oh, no, that's not necessary." I felt myself blush. "I'm just surprised to see the cuffs here with your props. I would have thought the actress who played the phony cop would've needed them instead."

"Nah. We tried it that way a few times but, because Lana has to do that somersault-ninja move first, we ran into the problem of the handcuffs falling out of her pocket and clanking onto the middle of the stage. Zach, our director, thought it would work better to have me carry them in my jacket and then secretly slip them to her after that gymnastic bit."

I hadn't really put much thought into the details of the choreography, but it occurred to me just then that Dane must be an exceptionally good dancer. Anyone who could remember all of those steps from dozens of scenes and execute them so flawlessly in front of a live audience had to be amazing on the dance floor, too.

"Was it difficult to learn to do that?" I asked. "To remember all of the actions that accompany the dialogue and where, exactly, you need to be at every moment during the play?"

"The blocking?" He shook his head. "Not if you're into the scene deeply enough. I mean, that's why we practice so many times, to make sure it feels completely natural. Once it does, then our bodies seem to remember how to pair the words with the movements. Like the way our fingers know which notes to play on a musical instrument, even when we may not consciously recall the specific fingering that comes next. If we stopped to think about it, we might get confused and second guess ourselves. But if we just let our fingers go where they were taught to go...well..." He shrugged.

"Then it's kinesthetic memory," I said.

"Right." He flicked a small latch on the cuffs and they sprung open. "I can show you. Here, take these."

And before I had a chance to protest or even step back, he thrust the handcuffs at me, twirled me in the same move he used on the actress ("Lana," apparently), and turned himself in front of me so that his hands were crossed behind his back. To an outsider, it would look as though I'd neatly trapped him and was ready to slap cuffs on his wrists.

"You can put them on me, Julia. Don't worry." He laughed. "They're props. They don't really lock."

"Would serve you right if they did." I tried to make a joke of it and just play along but, as I snapped the handcuffs on Dane Tyler's strong wrists and swiveled him around to face me, I couldn't ignore a spark of something sizzling between us. Something that wasn't either humorous or a mere game.

His blue eyes regarded me seriously for a moment before his lips curved into another smile. "Just because they don't lock doesn't mean I can get them off easily." He tugged at the silver restraints.

I swallowed and walked toward the table with the food, needing to take a few steps away from the man—both literally and figuratively. "Bet this would be a great time to have a sandwich," I said, lifting the plastic wrap off the tray. "Mmm. Too bad you're otherwise occupied, huh? They're all mine now."

He snorted and leaned back, less gracefully than usual, against the corner of his dressing table until he'd finally managed to rub the cuffs against something jagged enough to flip the latch. He set the cuffs down with an air of deliberation and massaged his wrists. "That was a little tighter than I'd expected. You have some background with S&M or something?"

"Okay, whose idea was it to have me put them on you?" I pointed an accusatory index finger at him, which made him snort again. Then I reached for one of the sandwiches, more as my own personal prop than as any form of sustenance.

He approached me, slow and panther like.

I inhaled quickly and held the sandwich out to him like a shield. "Egg salad?"

He shook his head.

I scanned the sandwich tray and blindly grabbed another offering. "Ham and cheese?"

He just laughed and kept walking toward me.

"Um, I'm not sure, but it looks like there might also be chicken—"

"Julia?"

"Yeah?"

"I'm not hungry—for sandwiches." His gaze hovered at my lips and then rose upward.

My heart was sprinting against itself, as if trying to

break a world's record. Could Shar have been right? Would he really try to kiss me? "I see," I said.

"I don't think you do." He tilted his head and studied me. "We were almost neighbors growing up, you know? You were very nearly the girl next door." Again with the head tilting and the long analytical look. "We didn't go to the same high school, and I would have been a few years older than you if we had, but we were probably close to running into each other a hundred times. We lived just a few suburbs apart during our childhoods. And, yet, we never met until three weeks ago." He exhaled slowly. "I'm so damned glad."

His words began to sink in. I wasn't sure I'd heard them correctly. "You're *glad?* Glad we didn't meet earlier?"

"Yes. Trust me on this, you would've hated me in high school." He ran both sets of fingers and palms through his professionally highlighted hair. "I would've had some crazy-ass crush on you that would've only ticked you off. You'd have thought I was an arrogant prick with a chip on my shoulder. It would've been bad."

"And how was that so different from three weeks ago?"

"Ouch!" He clutched at his heart, pretending to be struck.

I burst out laughing. "C'mon, Dane. You know I'm kidding. I got over the shock of our disastrous first meeting at least—oh—four days ago."

"Thank God." His blue eyes twinkled at me. "Did you really throw away your Fan Club card? Wish you'd burned it?"

I began to nod, just to tease him, but then shook my head. "Would you believe that I still know where it is?"

"Really?"

"Really. I kept it with my favorite high-school mementos."

I noticed his gaze dropped for a split second and I caught the briefest glimpse of pride in his expression.

"Thanks for saying that."

"It's true." I shrugged, trying to appear less affected by him than I clearly was. Just below the surface of my skin, my pulse was doing some kind of syncopated dance that felt suspiciously like the flamenco.

He cleared his throat and took another step forward. "Uh, Julia—"

A knock on the door interrupted us.

"Yes?" he called.

"Makeup in five minutes," a woman's voice called back.

"Gotcha. Thanks." Then, to me, he said, "The next few hours are going to be a circus back here. You're welcome to watch the play from the auditorium, if you'd like. Or, if you'd rather not see it again—one viewing of 'The Bachelor Pad' was probably plenty—you can make yourself at home in my dressing room or in the green room. Your choice."

"Actually, I'd really love to watch the play again. I can sit in the back, though, if seats are scarce."

He smiled. "No worries. We'll find you a good one." He paused and cleared his throat again. "What I was going to say earlier, Julia, was thanks. If, somehow, I forget to tell you later, I'm really glad you came tonight. You've already made this a great evening."

Dane got me a premier seat. Of course. Third row center, and a few rows closer to the stage than the VIP tickets would have placed me, had I kept them.

I knew this for a fact because Elsie and Shar were sitting in those very seats. I spoke with them a few minutes before the curtain was slated to go up.

"Oh, honey, you look like a vision!" Elsie gushed.

I thanked her and pointed at Shar with my play program. She was grinning at me like a sweet but slightly egotistical little sister. Then again, she'd known what she was doing. "I wouldn't have managed to wear anything but jeans and a pullover without Shar's help," I told Elsie.

My best friend rolled her eyes. "Wasn't much of a trick, girlfriend. You looked fabulous before, but now you're glowing." And when Elsie wasn't looking, Shar leaned close to me and whispered, "Did he make a pass at you backstage? Try to feel you up? You've gotta give me something juicy here."

"No, he didn't. And, no, I don't."

She frowned. "Spoilsport."

Then we both started giggling until the lights blinked three times and Elsie said, "It's showtime!" She patted my arm and added, "See you at intermission, dearie."

Shar just fist-bumped me and winked. "Later, Gator."

As I settled into my seat and the house lights darkened, I couldn't help but compare this viewing of "The Bachelor Pad" to the one back in June. My stomach had been fluttering with excitement that night, too, but the cause was different this time. Well, everything was different this time. I got to watch Dane Tyler—my *friend*—onstage tonight, rather than just getting a voyeuristic viewing of the dream man from my teen years.

When I saw Dane step into the spotlight, my pulse began to hopscotch, and I was filled with an emotion that was as complicated as it was wholly unexpected: Pride.

I was *proud* of Dane.

Watching him perform Act I so cleanly. The way he held the audience in the palm of his hand so expertly and charmingly. I appreciated his efforts like an impressed critic, rather than merely a longtime fan. I recognized some of the little changes he and the cast had made over these past few weeks to improve their dynamics onstage and heighten the comedy.

He was just so *good*.

I wanted to give him a standing ovation after only the first scene.

And, although I knew the bright lights had to make it impossible for the actors to see anyone out in the audience, I could have sworn that Dane looked directly at me in that moment when the opening scene ended.

And again, a few scenes later.

And again at a number of places during Act II. Too many times to count. It was almost unsettling.

I told myself this was probably just my imagination at work. Dane was and would always be exceptionally professional. He would never break character in an obvious way. He'd most likely worked on this "searching gaze" thing in the weeks since the dress rehearsal. Maybe the director had even suggested it? (I pondered that for a while.) I'd bet half the women in this crowded theater felt as if he could be looking right at them.

During intermission, I spoke briefly to Elsie and Shar, then slipped off to a quiet place to text Analise and to remind her that I would be up at her camp for Parents' Day tomorrow. She'd been going through one of her "down" days on this week's emotional roller coaster so, when the play ended—after much cheering and multiple curtain calls—I stood as unobtrusively as possible off to the side to check my phone again, just in case she'd sent any new messages during Act II.

There was one.

"Parents can start coming in at 10 tomorrow morning," she'd texted. "Don't be late, okay?"

I exhaled in relief. This request I could handle, unlike her last one (which involved having me hire a professional helicopter pilot to fly her out of camp before bedtime).

"Okay," I texted back, and then added a row of "XOXOX."

"Hey. How's everything?" Dane's breath tickled my neck.

I turned around to answer but was struck anew at how handsome the guy was. He'd changed quickly out of his last costume, scrubbed his face free of all stage makeup, and dressed himself in a dark suit and tie.

He was, in a word, HOT.

For a moment, I just stared at him, aware that I was gaping but unable to stop myself.

"F-Fine," I managed to say. "That was a fast change. Is there anything else you need to do here before we go?"

"Nope." He pointed vaguely in the direction of the front doors. "I just saw your friends, Shar and Elsie, heading out to the reception. Ready to join the party?"

Was I ready? Hardly. But I said, "Sure."

Before I knew it, he'd ushered me out into the parking lot—"I'll drive," he suggested—then into his rental car, and then onto the road. We were at the private Carmody Room, located in a sectioned off floor of Dane's swanky hotel, in under fifteen minutes.

After Dane gave the keys to the valet in charge, got our names checked off by the security guard manning the private elevator, and escorted me into the heart of the reception, I thought, "Now it's *really* showtime."

The VIP party, for want of a better description, was like an office holiday party on steroids. Everyone was dressed beautifully and, initially, they were on their very best behavior. As the first half hour turned into the second half hour, guests began to drop their guard, the alcohol began to flow more freely, and the dancing started, which signaled the beginning of the end of most formalities and proprieties.

We chitchatted with my friends, of course, but it was

obvious—to me, at least—that Shar and Elsie had made a pact to leave me alone in the company of Dane Tyler as much as possible. Before they could come up with an excuse to rush off, though, Rosemary, the stage manager, spotted all of us talking together, and she and her husband joined our merry group for a little while.

"Wonderful Closing Night performance," Rosemary said to Dane. "I thought it was your best show yet."

"Thank you," he said graciously. "It seemed...almost electric out there tonight."

Shar glanced at me and raised her eyebrows.

A few more theater folks sidled up to us, and we all ended up chatting about the appreciative crowd, while the various cast and crew members said many times over how glad they were to have gotten to work with Dane and each other and how it would be so exciting if they were able to join forces for another show again. Yadda, yadda.

Shar and Elsie excused themselves at this point and went off to meet other members of the production. Shar was soon flirting with the director of the play—the famous Zachary Leeward. (Although, when I pulled her aside for a moment, she confessed it was all in good fun. "The guy's been married *five* times!" Shar hissed in my ear. "Seriously, this won't go anywhere. I read his IMDb bio. My brothers would dismember him if he showed up at a family gathering and said he was my date.")

Rosemary's husband Thomas was nice—some sort of building contractor—but she and Thomas were mix-n-minglers. They reminded me of one of those teacup rides at an amusement park, just spinning around from one side of the room to another, in a seemingly endless series of circles. Rosemary looked, admittedly, rather surprised when she realized and Dane and I had come together on a date, but she was very kind and welcoming.

Aside from the people we both knew, though, Dane had some other social duties to perform, and he gave me a heads up on that.

"I'm apologizing in advance for the dry conversations ahead," he told me. "But there are some people here that have greatly supported the theater and who made a point to be very attentive to me when I arrived in June. I need to at least acknowledge everyone and thank them personally."

"Of course. Do you want me to wait for you—"

"No! No, stay with me. I just wanted to explain what was about to happen." He reached for my hand and squeezed it. "I'd much rather be having a long, private conversation with you. But it's really nice having a friend to do this with. I'm so used to always having to struggle through these things alone."

"I'm sure you've brought many dates to many parties in the past, haven't you?"

"Yeah, but it was pretty obvious early on that, in most cases, there was an agenda. Making strategic contacts. Networking with agents or directors. At least four or five times a lady I brought to a party left me within a week or less for some dude she met there." He paused. "So, maybe you want to take a few minutes to look around. Chances are high you'll find someone else here tonight that you'd like a lot better."

I rolled my eyes. "I don't think so."

"Why?" he said with a wry grin. "Because you actually like me better or because you've already checked out the men who are present and none are to your taste?"

I laughed at this. "Insecure much?"

The moment the words were out, his eyes widened in surprise. I felt almost guilty but, really? Could he actually have worries like that? Looking at his face, the answer was...maybe.

"Oooooh, okay," he said with a chuckle. "Yeah, perhaps a little."

It was my turn to take his hand. "Listen, Dane, I realized I don't know the complexities of your life, and I have no idea what's involved behind the scenes at Hollywood gatherings or entertainment industry events, but you were the one who asked me here tonight, and I came because... It's simple, really. I like you. And I like spending time with you."

There was a long, awkward pause.

Then, suddenly, he pulled me into his arms and just hugged me. "Thank you, Julia," he whispered in my ear before letting me go. "Means a lot to me to hear you say that."

We chatted with some of the VIPs he'd told me we were going to see, but he was always very inclusive of me in the conversations, even when they were focused on topics I knew little about. Funding for various arts events. Theatrical and literary causes. Filmmaking stuff.

A few more people from the cast came up to us, more small talk. Very pleasant but equally superficial. Dane brought us a couple of glasses of champagne, and a large plate heaped with very elaborate and intricately created appetizers.

I spotted Elsie and a few crew members laughing over a platter of some impossibly structured shrimp canapés. Shar, meanwhile, was on the dance floor with the director, being twirled around. She looked like she was having a blast.

"Wanna go out there for a spin?" Dane asked me.

If I'd ever been forced to explain my high-school fantasies regarding Dane Tyler, I would have to admit that most of them started with him asking me to dance (at prom or some big public event) and ended with us dancing at our wedding. Embarrassing to think about that now, as he took my hand and led me to the dance floor. But, likewise, impossible not to remember.

The DJ played Celine Dion's "The Power of Love," which made me smile. It was one of the major songs featured on the *Warriors of Warrenville High* soundtrack. I didn't mention this to Dane, of course, because it would only alert him to what a crazed fan I'd once been, but he seemed to sense my recognition of the music nevertheless.

"I always liked this one," he said, bringing his body closer to mine as we swayed to the Canadian songstress's famous hit from the nineties. I was worried he might be able to feel just how fast my heart was beating, especially when he added, "And, hey, I'm getting to dance with an official card-carrying fan club member."

"Not exactly," I said, laughing. "The card's not with me."

"But you didn't throw it in the trash or burn it so...close enough."

"True."

"Official fan club members get kisses. I told you that, remember?"

I nodded and started to make some joke when he bent down and kissed me very softly on my mouth. Not much pressure. No tongue. Just his lips lightly on my lips.

Oh, dear heaven.

It shouldn't have felt as electric as it did, but there was no way I could deny the truth. As brief as it was, it was powerful, and the current of his kiss reached all the way down to my toes.

He smiled at me, his grin growing even broader as I licked my bottom lip right after he pulled away.

"You'd better be careful, Julia Meriwether Crane, aka number 49202. Licking your lips constitutes as an invitation for *another* kiss in some circles."

I felt myself flush everywhere and glanced away from Dane's amused gaze, only to catch Shar staring right at me, her mouth agape.

"Uh, oh," I murmured.

"What?"

"My best friend just saw that. I'm never going to hear the end of it."

Dane shot a look in Shar's direction, smiled at her, and

then leaned close to me again. "Wanna give her something really good to talk about?"

"Dane, you don't know Sharlene Michaelsen Boyd. She'd do more than just want to *talk* about it. She'd probably get her brother Blake to broadcast it, too."

"Oh, that's right," he said, laughing. "I keep forgetting those two are related. I liked Blake. The radio interview with him was the most fun I've had at a press event this month."

"Yeah, he's a good guy. Hilarious to talk to and—oh!" My heel caught on something on the floor. A thick piece of black tape that had been used to cover up some wire. The tape had come unstuck, and it was just strong enough to catch my shoe and make me lose my balance for a second.

Dane caught me, but the weird angle I was moving— my body one way, my foot another—made me twist my ankle.

"Are you okay?" he asked, as I took a couple of steps forward and hobbled.

"I will be. I think." I took another step. *Ow.* "I'd better take the weight off of it, though."

He led me to a nearby circular cocktail table, which had a handful of empty chairs. "Let's take a look."

I showed him my foot and ankle. He massaged them for a moment and I winced.

"Hurts, huh? You should probably put an ice pack on that, just in case it starts to swell. I can get you one."

"No, don't do that," I said quickly. I glanced around. Already we were getting some odd stares from several of the other guests, I didn't want to draw even more attention to myself. "I don't want anyone to think I got a serious injury in the middle of your big party. It's just a little twist. I'll be fine soon."

"Okay. But do you think you can walk without too much pain to the elevator?"

I knew it was located just outside of the reception area.

Maybe thirteen or fourteen yards from where I was sitting.

"Yeah, I think so. Why?"

"Because my hotel room is almost directly above us." He pointed to the ceiling. "Well, sixteen flights up but only a few feet from the elevator."

"Oh, we don't have to go—"

"Yes, we do. C'mon. I have ice in my mini fridge."

So, without attracting much attention (other than Shar's, since she had a way of noticing everything, even when she was all the way across the room being held captive by the play's director), Dane helped me get to the elevator and up to his suite.

"Nice digs," I said when we entered. The hotel room was just as he'd described—spacious, clean, and lovely— but, obviously, it was very different from the coziness of his childhood apartment. "And, wow. Planning to construct a float for the next Rose Parade in here?" There were dozens of flowers in vases of all sizes on every available surface.

He looked a tad embarrassed. "I still get some 'break a leg' bouquets from fans."

"Apparently."

He helped me get comfortable on the sofa and set to work creating an ice pack from ice cubes in his mini-fridge and a plush hand towel. Then he propped me up with a couple of extra pillows and asked what I'd like him to bring me to drink.

"I could get used to this," I told him. "Thank you. You've already done plenty. You don't have to bring me anything else, although—" I sunk deep into the sofa. "This is almost *too* relaxing. I could fall asleep right here."

He shrugged. "I wouldn't stop you. It's after midnight already. Why don't you stay?"

"Here? With—uh, with you in the hotel room?"

"Are you worried I'm going to jump your injured bones?" He eyed my reclined body comically, lingering on my twisted ankle with his makeshift ice pack.

I couldn't help but laugh. "No, it's not that." I told him about my daughter's Camp Willowgreen event the next morning and how I'd promised her I'd be there by ten. "It's a two-hour drive up to the camp, so—"

"So get some rest now. When do you need to wake up? I can set an alarm for you."

Theoretically, this should have been a very bad idea. I mean, there I was, lounging on Dane Tyler's hotel-room sofa, after having spent the night as his "date." Forget the possibility of curious paparazzi or my own longstanding fantasies, the idea of staying over when I knew I would need to go home to shower and change clothes before driving up to see Analise should have been enough for me to just say no.

And, yet...

It was a sign of how tired I was that I was considering this so seriously.

"It would be tough to drive when your ankle is still bothering you," he reasoned.

"And I know it's late, but I'm more drained than usual," I admitted.

"I bored you to exhaustion?" Dane suggested.

I laughed. "No, that's not it. I think it has more to do with the champagne I drank at the party and the fact that I haven't been in heels for almost a year."

"You did have a couple of glasses, didn't you? You definitely shouldn't be driving then. Wait here."

Dane disappeared for a few minutes but returned armed with a bunch of stuff I could only partially identify. He handed me a sealed plastic packet and explained, "The hotel has a complimentary toiletry pack, so you'll find a mini toothbrush, some toothpaste, facial cleansing pads, Q-tips, and God knows what else in here. But wait, there's more!" he said, like a game-show host. He put a couple of folded items into my hands. "The t-shirt is brand new. Got it this week from the gift shop, but I can grab another. It'll be long on you, but I think it'll look way better on you than me." It was a pretty light blue, featuring the Windy City's skyline etched across the front and the words "Sweet Home Chicago" in scripty lettering at the top. "And here's a fresh robe from the bathroom to warm you up after your shower or bath, whichever you'd like." He pointed toward his bathroom. "Get yourself ready for bed, and I'll fix up this pull-out sofa, all right?"

He had it all so well planned out. "All right," I heard myself agreeing. "Thanks, Dane."

"No problem."

After taking a quick but hot shower, changing into the t-shirt Dane gave me, and brushing my teeth, not only my ankle but all of me felt about three-hundred percent better. I emerged from the steamy bathroom to find him waiting for me—pillows, sheets, and a blanket already on the sofa bed.

"Wow. That was fast," I said, patting my hand on the mattress and reaching over to pull down the covers.

"Get your hands off my bed, young lady," Dane said.

"What?"

"You're not sleeping here. This is my spot for the night. I've got you set up in the master bedroom." He nudged me toward the private room.

"Oh, no, no. Don't be silly. That's your—"

"The sheets were changed by the staff this morning," he interrupted, "and I didn't even snitch the mint on the pillow. Come, I'll show you to your room."

It had been so long since anyone had taken care of *me* that his kind gesture nearly brought tears to my tired eyes.

"Thank you, Dane—once again," I said, as he turned down the covers for me, hung up my fluffy robe and, finally, tucked me in.

As I looked up at him from the pillow, he brushed the hair off my forehead the way someone might with a child, kissed the tender skin there, and rubbed the tip of his nose against mine, but only for a second. Still, time expanded in that instant, and it felt as though life itself were on pause as he hovered above me. I held my breath.

"My pleasure," he murmured.

And then, like the gentleman he was, he pulled away, flicked off the lights, and left the room.

I exhaled, long and slow, fighting sleep for as long as I was able and reliving the fairy-tale sweetness of the evening in my mind, like my own personal motion picture. But the darkness eventually claimed me and I knew nothing more of the night until a smell I recognized roused me hours later.

Bacon?

I got out of bed, pushed the door open, and saw Dane, wearing another of the white robes, sitting up on the sofa bed and arranging items on a food cart that must have recently arrived.

He saw me peeking and grinned. "Good morning, sunshine. The alarm is set to go off in about five minutes, but I thought this would be a more pleasant way to wake up." He pointed to a silver pot on the cart. "Hot coffee? There's also bacon, scrambled eggs, English muffins with butter and jam, and a bowl of mixed fruit. Help yourself."

I had to stop myself from running over there, flinging my arms around him, and kissing him senseless.

Instead, I said, "Yum. This is wonderful."

"Good." He handed me a plate. "Eat something. How's your ankle this morning?"

"I can still feel a few twinges, but it's a lot better. Shouldn't be a problem walking or driving today."

He nodded and loaded up his plate with eggs, bacon and a few spoonfuls of fruit. "So, what do the organizers have the parents do at this camp thing today?"

I scrunched my nose up. "I'm not entirely sure. I'm afraid they might make us row across the lake in canoes or construct birdhouses or something. Hopefully, the kids will just show the parents around and we can all admire what *they've* done in the past two weeks."

"Sounds fun, actually. Kids have an energy that can't be contained. Their enthusiasm is contagious."

"Yes, and it'll be so nice to see Analise again. I've missed her like crazy."

He nodded as if he knew exactly what I meant. However, the expression he wore was an odd one, so I could sense he was wrestling with wanting to ask or tell me something. I hadn't expected the words he said when they finally came out, though.

"Want some company?"

"At Camp Willowgreen?" I asked. "Today?"

"Yeah. I mean, I don't have to go into the actual event with you, especially if it's something you'd like to do alone with your daughter. But if you wanted to have somebody else along for the ride—I know it's a long drive—I'm free. We're striking the set tonight at seven, but I don't have anything else on my schedule until then."

It was strange. Necessity had made me the sole parent this year, so I'd gotten used to being the only one who went to my daughter's events. The only one who did the grocery shopping. The only one who ran errands. The thought of having someone do something like this with me was so welcome, such a gift, that I was rendered speechless for a moment. Like last night, Dane's kindness almost brought tears to my eyes. And I realized that, more than anything, I wanted to spend the day with my daughter. But, also, when I was no longer able to do that, I wanted to be in Dane's company for the rest of it.

"Are you sure you'd want to spend your free day that way?" I asked him.

"Yes."

"Why?"

His handsome face broke in to a grin so breathtaking that I nearly dropped my coffee mug. "Because I like you," he said, mimicking my words from the night before. "And I like spending time with you."

That made me laugh, as I was sure he knew it would. So, I feigned a bored shrug. "Well, that's not a very *original* reason, but okay."

He crumpled up his cloth breakfast napkin and pitched it at me. "Smart ass. I suppose I'd better get ready then." And, true to his word, after he finished his eggs, he pulled off his robe and tossed it on the sofa bed.

My mouth ran dry as I watched him paddle around the suite without a shirt and wearing just a thin pair of navy boxers. A perfectly respectable ensemble if, perhaps, we were in Southern California. At a beach. And this were a "Hot Men of the Entertainment World" photo shoot for *Sports Illustrated* or something.

As it was, in the confines of the hotel room, I felt the air temperature spiking around us. It burned all the warmer to me because I was so aware of my desires coming back to life after such a long hibernation. I couldn't believe how much I wanted to run my fingertips across Dane's shoulder muscles. Then down the length of his strong, smooth back. Then around his waist. And then...

I watched him slip a black vee-neck t-shirt over his head. And, as he started to pull on a pair of blue jeans, he glanced over at me and caught me staring. For a second, he was motionless. Then he flashed another one of his incredible movie-star grins and I knew, with bone-deep certainty, that he was well aware of the effect his body had on the opposite sex.

On me.

But the fact that he didn't in any way act on this knowledge was what made me breathless. If he hadn't been across the room, I knew it would have been nearly impossible for me to stop myself from touching him.

I licked my lips without thinking about it and his eyes darkened as he gazed at me.

"That's dangerous, Julia." They were whispered words, but I could still hear him clearly.

I didn't say anything.

He swallowed and finished pulling on his jeans. "We probably need to stop at your place, right? So you can drop off your car and change clothes?"

Clothes... I took one last gulp of coffee and gobbled up the rest of my bacon slice. "Yes. I'll hurry up," I said, but it was hard to tear my gaze away from him.

CHAPTER FOURTEEN

Change was a funny thing.

As soon as I saw my daughter, I realized that a lot could happen that might significantly alter a person in a relatively short period of time. This was especially true if the person in question wanted, on some deep level, to change.

Analise had wanted to change. To get over her depression. To stop grieving quite so much. I knew she'd prayed for the pain to lessen. Kept her fingers crossed for it. Wished on shooting stars, fallen eyelashes, and birthday candles. And, after just two weeks at Camp Willowgreen, I could tell she was getting closer to having her wish granted.

I knew this time away wasn't long enough to heal the past, but it was, perhaps, long enough to show her that a bad spell could be broken, even for a short while. It was long enough to create hope.

And while I also knew that her new sparkle of happiness would have been immediately apparent to any adult who'd known her over this past and very difficult year, I sensed it wasn't quite apparent to *her* yet.

"Mommy!" she squealed when I walked into the camp's giant rec room. She threw her tanned arms around my body and squeezed.

I enfolded myself around her. She was too big to cradle in my arms anymore, but a part of me kept wanting to try.

"Oh, my sweet girl. I think you've grown an inch at least since I last saw you. And you're so tan! You must have been spending hours out in the sun."

She nodded. "I'm not as tan as some of the other girls, but Ms. Watkins, the camp director, makes us put on sunscreen every single day—morning *and* afternoon."

"Your dermatologist will love Ms. Watkins for that later."

"My derma-what?"

"Never mind," I said, unable to stop hugging her. "Just tell me what we get to do together today."

"Okay," she replied, her eyes bright.

She produced a folded sheet of orange-colored paper from her back shorts pocket with the words **PARENTS' DAY: 10AM - 3PM** bolded and in all caps across the top. "First thing, I get to show you our cabin and how we decorated it. Then," she read from the sheet, "is a visit to the art studio, so you can see my projects. Then there are games by the lake. *Then* it's finally lunch!" She paused to take a breath and I laughed.

"Do you know what they're serving?" I asked.

"Yes. It's Sunday, so we'll get cheesy pizza burgers, which are really good here. Tater tots. Milk. A salad, I think. And chocolate pudding."

"That sounds delicious," I told her, but the truth that I'd happily sit through a meal of roasted crickets and dried celery sticks if it meant I'd get to spend that precious hour with my daughter.

"Yeah," Analise said. "But then there's the afternoon skit, which is gonna be bad, but after that it'll be time for the awards cerem—"

"Why will the skit be bad?"

She shrugged. "There's this boy in our group—Justin—

and he's really bossy. If I don't say my lines fast enough, he says them for me in this high-pitched voice, like he's pretending to be me. Then he says his next line." She sighed. "I wish I was in Lindsay's group or even Brooke's. They have nicer people."

I felt myself frowning and tried to force my lips into a neutral position.

"So, what would make you feel more ready for the skit? To have one of the camp counselors—maybe Shannon—pull Justin aside and tell him to stop jumping in so fast? Or to practice your lines a bit more beforehand, so you'll know them better? How can I help you, sweetheart?"

She looked up at me, hopeful. "I don't want to tell on Justin. I just want to show him that I can do it."

"Okay. Shall we practice?"

She nodded. "But first let me show you our cabin and my art projects. I don't care if we skip the games, and I don't need the whole hour for lunch."

An idea began to form in my mind, but I wasn't sure I should act on it. There I was, up at this camp with an incredibly skilled actor not more than a fifteen-minute drive away, and I had a daughter who needed help with a skit. It wouldn't take a MENSA member to put those two people together.

And yet...

I neither wanted to inflict another new man on my daughter (especially after her negative reaction to Kristopher) nor did I want to infringe upon what little privacy and time off Dane had. For all I knew, the idea of serving as an acting coach to a ten-year-old could be right up there for him with getting difficult dental work done...or dealing with the most obnoxious members of the paparazzi.

So I said nothing to Analise about Dane through the cabin visit and the art exhibition. But after chatting with Shannon and a group of her fellow counselors and seeing Analise's face get all pinched with worry when one of them mentioned the skit this afternoon, I decided to take a chance.

The ace actor was, I knew, currently wandering around the next town in his baseball cap and dark sunglasses. ("My disguise," he'd joked.) I was supposed to text him when I was done at camp. Something told me that he'd respond quickly if I sent him a message a little early.

"We don't have to do this unless you want to," I told Analise, "but do you remember the friend who sent me those flowers a few weeks ago?"

She nodded. "D.T."

I laughed. "Right. The initials stand for Dane Tyler. He was a very famous actor when I was in school, and he's in the area right now. So I was thinking—"

"How famous? Like on TV?"

"Oh, yeah. TV, movies, theater. He just finished being in a play in Chicago. I went to see it with Ms. Sharlene at the end of June, remember?"

Her eyebrows shot up. "So, why did he send you flowers?"

"Um, that's a long story, and I can explain it later, but what I wanted to know is if you'd like to meet him. He's just over in the next town today. Maybe he's busy—I can't be sure—but if he's not and you're interested in this, I could ask if he'd be able to come to camp for a little while and give you some advice on remembering your lines. But we totally don't have—"

"Oh, *cool!*" Analise looked impressed. All right. Good sign. "You think he'd really help me? A guy who's been on TV?"

I fished out my cell phone, praying I wasn't getting her hopes up for nothing or greatly overstepping with Dane. But he *had* offered to drive me up here. He couldn't be entirely opposed to meeting my daughter and visiting the camp for a half hour, could he?

I inhaled deeply and then texted him. "I have a HUGE

favor to ask. Could you please text me when you get this?"

Literally ten seconds later, my cell phone buzzed. Dane wrote, "A bigger favor than letting you sleep in my bed last night? LOL."

I blushed and held the phone's screen away from Analise's inquiring eyes. "Significantly bigger, actually," I messaged back. "It's about my daughter. She's in a skit this afternoon and could use some expert advice on her lines. Any chance you could come over here, for just a little while, and help us practice?"

The pause before his reply was longer this time. Much longer. Twenty seconds went by. Then a minute. Then two minutes. Still no answer.

I swallowed when I thought of all the requests Dane must have gotten over the years from acting hopefuls. All the favors mere acquaintances must have asked him, not necessarily realizing—or caring—that it was a grave imposition.

I fought the embarrassment I was feeling only because I'd asked on behalf of Analise. I would do a million things for her that I would never dream of doing just for myself.

My daughter sat on a tree stump in the middle of a grassy field and looked up at me anxiously. "Did he say yes, Mommy?"

"Honestly, I just don't know yet. He hasn't—" My phone finally buzzed, and I held my breath as I read his short message.

"Already in the car," Dane wrote. "See you at the front gate of the camp in ten minutes."

And at that moment, I knew just how easy it might be to fall in love with Dane Tyler.

Analise and I took a pass on playing games by the lake

and, instead, found a quiet spot behind the rec center to bring Dane for "skit practice."

When my daughter first laid eyes on him, she looked at him with interest, but the moment he took off his baseball cap and sunglasses, her small jaw dropped open.

"I've seen *pictures* of you," she stated, awestruck.

He grinned at her and reached his hand out to shake hers. "Online or in magazines?"

"Both," she whispered, taking his hand.

He leaned closer to her. "I've seen pictures of you, too."

"Really? Where?"

"On your mom's keychain," Dane said solemnly. "You've got to be *really* important to somebody to make it onto their keychain."

I smiled and silently blessed him for being so sweet, but I was also surprised. I'd kept photos of Analise on my keychain ever since she was a baby, updating them with newer ones each year. I knew Dane was observant, but I hadn't realized he'd noticed the little photos I'd carried with me. He hadn't commented on them, so I wasn't sure when, exactly, they'd caught his eye.

Analise took in this information and just nodded. "How long have you known my mom?"

"A little less than a month," he replied.

"Why'd you send her all those flowers?"

"Sweetheart—" I started to say, hoping to cut off the inquisition, but Dane laughed and held up his hand to stop me.

"That's okay, Julia. She should know." Then, turning to my daughter, he said, "Because the night I met your mom, I made a big mistake. I thought she was someone else, and I said something insulting to her. And when a person makes a mistake like that, they need to apologize, right?"

Analise nodded. "Right."

"Thus, the flowers." Then he added, "Were they

pretty?"

"They were beautiful," my daughter said. "And there were, like, a million of them."

"Good."

Analise smiled at him, accepting his explanation with ease, probably because it was the truth. She had a great built-in B.S. detector and Dane wasn't trying to snow her or talk down to her.

Yet another thing I admired about him. Maybe he'd had so much experience with his legions of female fans that he knew just what to say to girls and women. I couldn't rule out that possibility. But I didn't think his choice to be honest or his ability to come across as so natural with my little girl was for that reason alone.

His behavior was in sharp contrast to Kristopher's that day at the coffee shop. Dane had much more of an excuse to be guarded than my old high-school boyfriend did, but he elected not to be. The only thing I could figure was that it was simply a character issue. Dane was just more willing to be authentic than Kristopher was.

Analise had picked up her copy of the skit's script from the cabin before Dane arrived, and she set about explaining the different roles to him.

"There are five characters," she told him. "I'm Clara. But there's also Tommy, Alice, Pam and, finally, Bobby—that's Justin's part," she added, and I caught her rolling her eyes.

"Hmm," Dane said. "Is he one of those difficult actors to work with?"

"Oh, yeah."

"They're out there, kiddo. Don't let 'em get to you." He paused. "Okay, I'll take the two boy roles, your mom can take the other two girl roles, and you can be Clara. Let's do a read-through all together first, then we'll go from there. Sound like a plan?"

She nodded.

And so, splitting up the parts as Dane had suggested, we read through the short skit, which was some kind of modern take on the fairy tale "Beauty and the Beast." Although, in this case, the "beast" was a semi-demented Sasquatch-like woodland creature (Justin's role) and Analise's character was a forest dweller who came upon him and protected him from the hunters.

"Now," Dane said to her, "let's you and I do it again without the script. We'll let your mom hang onto it for the two parts she's reading and, also, to make sure we get our lines right. And when—"

"Wait! You memorized the other parts already?" my daughter asked in shock. "You only read it *once*."

He shrugged. "But, see, I know some tricks. Wanna learn a few?"

I almost laughed aloud when I saw Analise's expression. She was completely enthralled. "Yes, please, Mr. Tyler."

"Call me Dane."

She glanced at me to check if this was okay. I nodded.

"Yes, please, *Dane*."

He smiled warmly at her, and I knew that there was no one—no one of any age—who would be immune to the power of Dane Tyler's charisma when he turned it on. He was a master, and I could only watch what he was doing with heartfelt gratitude.

Having been an English major, the feeling reminded me of something Jane Austen had written about in her novel *Pride and Prejudice*. The way the main character, Elizabeth Bennet, felt her feelings change for Mr. Darcy, a man she'd initially despised. He was wealthy and attractive, but she'd ignored those attributes and settled into a firm dislike of the man until she'd gotten to know him. Gotten some insight into his real character, not just her negative first impressions of it. And then, to a large extent because of the gratitude she'd felt toward him for the good things he'd done on her behalf, her appreciation and respect for the man transformed into love.

For the first time, I truly understood how this wasn't just a clever literary device in a classic 19th-century British novel. How it could really happen.

"The biggest trick is to step into the body of the character you're playing," Dane instructed Analise. "Don't just say the lines. Understand the viewpoint of the person who's saying them. If the words make sense in the character's point of view, they'll be a lot easier for you to remember. And if you make a mistake and change a word or two, that'll be okay, as long as you manage to convey the meaning and can get the majority of the phrases right."

The two of them tried the first half of the skit this way, as I read the lines of the two other female characters. I could see Analise's growing confidence in her part. And Dane was just remarkable. Full stop. He was encouraging, attentive, helpful to her, and he took the task seriously.

When we reached the second half, though, Analise slipped up. There was a line that she kept accidentally omitting.

"This is where a different trick comes in," Dane said. "For tougher lines, you might try using what I like to call 'the ridiculous connection.' You think about the line that's said right before the problematic one and the line after it, and you come up with the weirdest thing you can imagine to bind all three lines together in your head. That way, when you think of the first line, you'll remember the second one and your thoughts will flow right to the third line."

He helped her come up with an absolutely absurd mental image to connect her lines about the hunters arriving with the sentence she kept forgetting—something about the Sasquatch's matted fur—with her next line that involved an escape plan for the duo.

"The only hard part now is gonna be to not laugh when

I say it!" she said, giggling.

"I have every confidence you'll get through it perfectly," he replied. "Let's take it from the top, just one more time."

It had been over an hour since Dane had gotten to the camp and, because we were in a serene section of the property, we hadn't been interrupted by anyone else.

But chatter was now coming from the rec center and a stream of people were passing near us to go in for lunch.

"All right, honey," I said when we finished that last run through. "I think we've kept Dane long enough." I looked at him and hoped he could see my boundless appreciation. "You are amazing. Thank you."

He shrugged off the compliment. "It was no problem at all. Glad to help."

My daughter shook her head. "No. You're not leaving, are you, Dane?"

"Well, I—" he began.

"Please stay," she begged. "You can have lunch with us. Can't he, Mommy?"

"Of course he can, if he'd like to," I said, "but Dane may have some plans, Analise. We don't want to trespass upon—"

He winked at me. "What's for lunch, kiddo?" he asked my daughter.

She recited the menu.

"Tater tots! I haven't had those in forever," he confided. "Or cheesy pizza burgers, for that matter. And I'm starving. But I should warn you. When I'm around a large group of people, sometimes I get interrupted. I doesn't happen as much as it used to, but it's still pretty often. And I don't know how you'll feel about that if it happens. Would it be too distracting for you if some of the adults and, maybe, a few other campers recognized me? They might come up to talk to me or ask for an autograph or a selfie during lunch."

"Really?" she said.

He nodded. "Really. So, it's your call, Analise. 'Cause I could just take my tater tots and zip out." He thumbed in the direction of the parking lot.

To my daughter's credit—and maybe, again, because Dane wasn't talking down to her but leveling with her, like he might an adult—she didn't seem remotely conflicted about this decision. "I hope you'll stay *all* afternoon," she told him. "But if *you* don't want to be bothered by other people, it's okay. Sometimes I like to just be alone without anyone talking to me."

An expression crossed his face that I couldn't read. "That's very considerate of you to think of me," he said to her. "You're even better at getting into someone else's point of view than I thought." He took a deep breath and exhaled, slowly, then smiled. "But I don't want to be alone this afternoon. So, I'll tag along with you two, if that's okay."

"Yay!" Analise said, pumping her fist in the air.

He laughed then looked at me. "Okay with you, too?"

"If you're willing to chance it, Dane, I certainly am."

"Good," he said. "Then let's get us some hot tater tots."

The rest of the afternoon had a touch of magic about it.

Dane wore his cap, though not the sunglasses, into the rec center. And while many of the campers were too young to have recognized him right away from his movies, their parents were not.

I heard whispers around us all throughout lunch, a couple of audible gasps, some giggles, and a few people who came up to us directly. One of them said to him, "You know, you look so much like Dane Tyler."

"I get that a lot," he said with a good-natured laugh and

then introduced himself.

By the time we started on our chocolate pudding cups, word had spread around the entire camp that a famous actor was in the house.

Fortunately, most everyone was on their best behavior. Once lunch ended, Dane got about two dozen people who came up to him asking for autographs or for selfies to post on their social media sites. But they were courteous. And when it was time for Analise's performance to begin, he politely excused the three of us and said, "We have a skit to get to. You all should come watch."

Analise blanched, but he leaned down and whispered in her ear, "You're gonna be great. Break a leg." Once again, I wanted to throw my arms around the man and hug him.

Dane and I sat together as my daughter's group did their little play. She got through every line on cue and without so much as a hiccup. Dane gave her a thumbs up from the crowd while they were all taking their bows, and she couldn't have looked more proud of herself than if it had been Broadway.

While the other skits were being performed, Yvette motioned me over to her. I told Dane I'd be back in a moment and went to say hello.

"Hey," I said to her and her husband Andy. "How was your week in Door County?"

"Seriously?" my sweet neighbor hissed at me. "You're asking about our vacation?" She laughed. "You're here with *Dane Tyler*. I clearly missed some very important news, Julia."

Andy nudged me and added, "All my wife could say for the past half hour was, 'That'll teach us to leave Mirabelle Harbor' for nine days.'"

Yvette and Andy had been away since the weekend before Dane's radio interview. Their plan had been to drive directly from the quaint Wisconsin resort town they'd been staying in to come to Camp Willowgreen for Parents' Day.

And though my friends were joking with me, I suddenly realized just how much had gone on in my life in only the past week.

"Kind of an involved story." I smiled at Yvette, who looked at me with the sort of exasperation I usually only got from Shar. "But I'll fill you in when we're all back home. I promise. And," I added, "I also have your mail."

"Bring it over tomorrow," Yvette said. "Early. Plan to stay for breakfast and lunch. I might hold you hostage through dinner if you don't give me enough details."

I laughed, waved at them, and wandered back to Dane, who whispered, "Analise said there's an awards ceremony next."

"Yes, last thing on the schedule, from what I was told."

"Excellent," he replied, turning his attention back to the penultimate skit and seamlessly transitioning to the final event of the afternoon.

When it was time for all of the parents to leave after the awards ceremony, the pang of missing Analise was almost as strong for me as when we'd had to part two weeks ago.

This time, though, she was flanked by quite a few more kids than just Lindsay and Brooke. Even Justin from the skit was hanging nearby, watching her say goodbye to me and to Dane.

I hugged her tight. "I love you, my beautiful girl," I whispered in her ear.

"Love you, too, Mommy."

Then she thrust her hand out at Dane. "Thanks for showing me how to remember my lines," she told him sincerely. "I couldn't have done it without you."

"I think you could have, but I was glad to help. You were brilliant up there, kiddo," he said.

And, somehow, I managed to tear myself away from her and make it to Dane's car before I started to cry and before a horde of his admirers could awaken from their awed trance and descend upon him.

We rode the first twenty minutes in silence before he broke in. "It's hard to leave her, isn't it?"

I nodded. "It was just a tiny bit easier this time, though, knowing she'd had such a great day. I can't thank you enough for that. Truly, you were wonderf—"

"It was nothing." And, as was his usual reaction to praise, he brushed it away and fiddled with the radio instead.

I reached out and touched his hand. "No, Dane. It *was* something. What you did meant a lot to me, and to Analise, too."

He grasped my fingers in a quick squeeze then, just as quickly, pulled away.

"You're welcome, Julia. Now," he pointed to the radio of his rental car, "choose a station and let's get out on the open highway." He pushed the button for the window to roll down and let a gust of wind blow in. Then he hit the gas pedal and smiled. "God, I miss driving in the Midwest."

"You do? Why?"

"Ever visit New York or L.A.?"

"No. Neither."

"Both coasts are a traffic nightmare. This, though—this is fun."

As he turned onto the Interstate and increased his speed, I found a radio station that was playing Roxette's "Dangerous" and settled into the return drive. Just listening to music. Enjoying the wind whistling through the car. And chatting with Dane about nothing and, yet, everything.

When we arrived back at my house, I immediately invited him inside.

"Look," I said, "after all of the things you did this weekend, the least I can do is make you dinner before you have to go to the theater to strike the set. Are you a lasagna fan?"

"Homemade lasagna? You may not have leftovers

tomorrow."

"Good," I said. "I'll throw it together."

And, somehow, the magic that had swirled around us up at the camp followed us into the early evening. I opened up a bottle of wine. We drank half of it while the lasagna baked. We nibbled on crackers and cut-up veggies. And we kept talking. It was as if we hadn't already spent more than twenty-four hours together. We should have been sick of each other. I should have been looking forward to finally having a bit of quiet time. He should have been itching to leave.

Instead, I found myself wishing he didn't have to go at quarter to seven, and not just because I missed my daughter and didn't want to be alone in the house. I wanted to be *with him*.

He sighed. "I think I'm gonna go into a carb coma if I eat another bite. They'll have to roll me into Hotel Royale tonight."

I laughed and we both glanced at the clock. 6:46. Damn.

"I know you have to leave now," I said, "but thanks again for the party yesterday and for today. Every bit of it."

I walked him to the door.

He paused before pulling it open. Took a step closer to me...and then another. Put his arms around my shoulders and waited until I raised my gaze to meet his.

Then he said, "I can be a few minutes late to the theater."

I swallowed and licked my lips.

He grinned. "I warned you about that, Julia."

"I know," I whispered.

And he brought his mouth down on mine.

It wasn't a peck this time. No little brush across my lips. It was fully engrossing. Utterly transporting. Dane had pulled me so far out of myself that I was all but levitating. Even in my most imaginative state as a teen, I could never have fantasized *this* kiss. It wasn't a sensation I would have known could exist when I was that age.

When he stepped back, he shook his head and said, "I'm not leaving until you tell me when we can see each other again."

"Tomorrow night?"

"How about tomorrow afternoon *and* night?" he countered.

"Deal," I said, and he kissed me again. Then he slipped away.

In a zombie-like haze, I wandered back to the kitchen, finished putting everything away, and then meandered through the rooms of the house, one by one, until, at last, I came to a stop in front of my bedroom dresser. I stood and stared at it for the longest time.

On one side, there was a family photo of the three of us, taken about two years ago when Analise was in third grade. On the other side, there was a picture of just Adam and me, taken on our wedding day. I picked that one up, kissed the smiling face of my late husband, and set it down again.

Oh, my heart. I still missed him. I'd *always* miss him, and I knew it. But it seemed our daughter wasn't the only one who had changed significantly in a relatively short period of time. I just hadn't realized until this very moment that I had, too.

I reached for my gold wedding band, twisted it on my finger a few times and then, finally, pulled it off.

CHAPTER FIFTEEN

The next several days were, as I tried to explain to Shar on the phone at the end of the week, the kind that a person would always look back on and remember in chunks, rather than as distinctly individual days.

I'd felt this way even while they were happening.

That they were grouped as a set.

That one day blended into the next like watercolors on wet paper.

That certain themes echoed for me over and over again within those merging twenty-four-hour periods until I didn't know when or where the ideas originated anymore.

It was like living within a romance film montage—those joyous moments in every movie where the characters were shown interacting in a bunch of different scene snippets, all set to music. Viewers watched the onscreen couple talking, laughing, ice skating, feeding each other pasta, or whatever, but the only words that were heard were those of the lyrics to the song playing loudly.

For Dane and me, it was like having the soundtrack of LOVE FM ballads on high in the background as we chatted, ate meals together, and made out behind closed doors.

Dane and I spent so much time together—but in very few locations—that, later, I could no longer disentangle where, exactly, we were when one conversation began or another one ended. All I could say for certain was that, from the moment he picked me up on Monday afternoon (the day following our camp visit) until Friday (when all hell broke loose), he and I were almost constantly together. Conversationally, we were as intimate as two people could get, but physically, we'd self-imposed some limits.

Dane had been quick to remind me that he was leaving Chicago at the end of July, and that he knew I was still processing the death of my husband. He said it didn't feel right to push our relationship too far, too fast. Logically, this made sense to me, of course, so we only gazed at each other on the rare occasions that we were out in public. We held hands in elevators and other semi-private spaces. And, in the privacy of his hotel or my house, we kissed. We didn't go much beyond that—at least not initially—but there was lots of deeply enchanted kissing.

"Back up," Shar said to me. "You need to explain what you mean by the 'deeply enchanted kissing' bit because I don't know what you're talking about."

"You know how when you kiss someone and you're not only enjoying what's happening in that moment but, also, there's a part of you that's daydreaming—simultaneously and spectacularly—about what your future with this person would be like? When you project all kinds of fantasies onto someone else that are totally fictional, but you don't realize it at first because, for a while, the fantasies feel just as real as what's actually going on?"

"No," my best friend said.

I tried to think of another way to explain it.

"Take the Cinderella Story as an example," I said. "Every little girl wants to be Cinderella at the end of the fairy tale. She gets whisked away from the meanies, her sad life of drudgery is over, she's going to be a rich princess with a handsome prince, and she's even got a fairy godmother waiting in the wings, looking out for her best interests, right?"

"Yeah, okay. I follow you that far. But what does this have to do with enchanted kissing?"

"When people in the real world look at life as if it's a fairy tale, we might find ourselves projecting that happily-ever-after ending in any kind of Cinderella/Prince situation we're in and not even bother to question the daydream. If the guy looks like a prince and acts like a prince—"

"And kisses like a prince?" Shar interjected.

"Yes. If all of that is true, it makes it so easy to buy into the enchantment. Too easy. But something very important is missing when we do that."

"A glass slipper?" she suggested. "Is this your sneaky way of saying you need to go shoe shopping?"

"No, Shar." I paused. "We're missing the Prince's perspective. The Cinderella Story is told entirely from her point of view. It focuses on her struggles, her attitudes, her motives and needs. But what about the Prince's viewpoint? How well do we ever get to know *him* and what he wants, aside from hooking up with that mysterious woman from the ball? What motivates a wealthy, powerful man like him to find that one elusive young lady whose foot fits the slipper? How much of the Prince's interest in Cinderella has to do with her actual personality, rather than his *projections* about her? What does he really know about her, anyway, beyond the most superficial details? Or is his attraction really just a reflection of him falling in love with his own self image? Is he, maybe, captivated by the idea of himself as a hero? A man who can solve a mystery, successfully pursue an attractive woman, rescue her, and then earn her gratitude forevermore because, after all, he took her away from a hard life and handed her riches and a royal title?"

"You may be over-thinking the fairy tale, Julia."

"I doubt it. But, even if I am, that's the power of enchantment. And the danger of it. When *both* people are projecting fantasies onto each other and no one is seeing the relationship clearly. I might second guess myself and my own motives when it comes to Dane Tyler because, let's face it, I've been infatuated with the public image of the guy since I was a teenager. But what I'd completely overlooked was that he'd been infatuated with the *idea of me* since he was a teenager. *The Girl Next Door.* And that's just as fake—just as much of an illusion—as my enchantment with him."

There was a long moment of silence on the line. "What did he do to you?" my best friend asked. "Julia, did he hurt you in some way?"

But I couldn't tell her a quick "yes" or "no." It was much more complicated than that. I needed to start explaining from the start of last week, not just its fiery conclusion.

The more I discovered about Dane, the more I realized just how much there was that we didn't know about each other. So much private history we had yet to discuss.

And, yet, like a paradox within a paradox, I had the strangest sense of certainty that I knew the essentials about him. Many of his core values. Some of his fondest wishes and longstanding dreams.

In a way, it was as if the most amazing part of my teen fantasy had come to fruition. Not just the fact that Dane Tyler and I had met—or even kissed—but that we were truly similar and we genuinely had important things in common. That he really *did* like me, once he'd gotten to know me, as I'd always suspected he would. My adolescent self would have felt so vindicated by this.

He likes me. He really likes me.

Monday afternoon, the day after our Camp Willowgreen adventure, he picked me up and took me to dinner at this little hideaway Lebanese restaurant in neighborhood Chicago. In a corner booth, we gazed at each other over shish-kabob skewers, saffron rice, and hummus, and then we went back to his hotel and made out like teenagers until midnight. Because it was late, he suggested that I stay over again, and he tucked me into his bed, just like he did after the VIP party.

Unlike last Sunday morning, however, when I had to rush up to camp, we arose to a Tuesday morning that was completely devoid of all plans. With no pressing need to go anywhere, we lingered over our room-service breakfast, which turned into lunch. We watched old music videos together on TV and laughed about the hairstyles from the nineties. We shared more high-school stories. He told me about all of the girls he'd had crushes on who wouldn't date him because he was "offbeat." I told him about Kristopher and my circle of teen friends back in those days of Mirabelle Harbor High.

It was early evening before he drove me home, but I invited him in for pizza.

"Pizza Palacio delivers," I said. "If I call them now, they can be here in twenty minutes."

Dane laughed. "How could I refuse? As long as we get sausage on it. And how do you feel about mushrooms?"

So we had sausage and mushroom pizza and transitioned into watching an action flick together in the living room. It was completely comfortable and relaxing and, when he kissed me goodnight, it was utterly sensual. I collapsed into my own bed after he left, dreaming of him.

But I scarcely had time to miss him. Wednesday morning, we'd already made plans to return to Highbury Park, visit Samuel at The Lovin' Spoonful Bakery, and go for another fairly inconspicuous walk around the park. We checked in on his brother's apartment, picked up local carryout, and somehow ended up back at Dane's suite, laughing and talking until nearly two a.m.

"This is becoming a bad habit," I said, as he tucked me into his bed for the third time in a week.

"Nah. I don't think I'd call it *bad*," he whispered, bending down to kiss my forehead, my nose, and then my lips. "I kinda like waking up and finding you wandering around my hotel room."

I didn't want to admit it aloud, but I kinda liked it, too.

Thursday, we made an adventure out of a mostly incognito trip to IKEA, since I needed to get a new bookshelf for Analise's bedroom. (Her novels were overflowing onto the floor.) While in the store, we pretended Dane was a visiting Swede who spoke no English.

Very few customers even glanced our way, but one of the workers did a double take when we were checking out. He said, "Hey, aren't you—"

"Johannes," Dane said brightly and with a heavy accent, pointing to his chest.

"Oh. Um..." the guy said, squinting to see Dane's face better from under his baseball cap.

Dane ducked his head a little more and plastered a weird grin on his face that made him look positively demonic. *"Hej! Hur går det?"* he added with feeling.

The man looked at me with growing concern.

I just shrugged. "I think it's a greeting."

"Right," the guy said, hurrying to ring us up so we'd leave.

We barely made it to the car before we burst out laughing. I was holding my sides, doubled over in the passenger seat, wondering when the last time was that I'd laughed this hard. Before meeting Dane, it had been a long time.

"Oh, God," he said, wiping the corners of his eyes. "I never realized how valuable learning to say, 'Hi! How goes it?' on the set of *Scandinavian Knights* would be. Dreadful director, but the dialect coach was awesome."

"So, *Johannes*, you can actually speak some Swedish?"

"Only a handful of phrases," he said. "Most of them filthy."

"Well, you'd better brush up just in case I got the wrong size bookshelf and we need to go back."

"Det finns ingen chans."

"What's that mean?"

"There's no chance," he translated with a grin. "I'll drive you if you need to return, but you'll be going in by yourself. That's a role I should probably retire. Plus, the real world is wearing me down today."

I knew the reason for that. He'd been stopped countless times in the hotel lobby for autographs as we were trying to leave this morning. And some newspaper person had been pestering him with phone messages at the hotel. He wasn't sure how she'd figured out his room number, and I didn't know all that had been said between them, but it set him on edge.

Even so, he'd been unfailingly polite to everyone. Still, I could tell he was getting irritated with all of the intrusions.

"Yeah, I don't blame you," I told him. "It's got to get old, not being able to go out without always having to be on guard in case you're recognized."

"You don't know the half of it," he murmured.

We got back to my house that afternoon and Dane helped me assemble the bookshelf for Analise in the middle of the living room. It wasn't a difficult task, but the finished piece was heavier than I thought. We both ended up a little sweaty after lugging it into her bedroom and filling it with her books.

Dane sniffed his shirt. "I should probably head back to

my hotel, take a shower, and change clothes."

I laughed. "Well, you know you're welcome to shower here, although I don't have those fluffy white robes like the ones you have waiting for you at your suite."

"True, but you have other inducements." He pulled me close to him and gave me a parting kiss that left me with nothing but pure wanting.

When he stepped away, he grabbed his car keys and walked to my door. Deep within me, a knot filled with longing—one that had been building in my stomach all week—tightened.

I exhaled slowly in an attempt to relax and loosen the tension. But, truly, it was useless.

Dane spun abruptly toward me. "Why did you do that?"

"Do what?"

"Sigh like that."

"Oh...I was just, um, I had too much carbon dioxide in my lungs," I joked.

"But why so deep? So much like you were trying to rid yourself of something else that was mixed with it? Is it annoyance at me? Relief at getting to be alone for a while?"

I wasn't sure what came over me. A bolt of honesty? Momentary insanity? Maybe I was just drained from fighting the strength of my attraction toward him. Fighting two decades of fantasy.

So, I said, "No. Neither. I just—I just *want* you to this crazy degree, Dane. But I know you're leaving town soon, and my daughter will be coming back home in no time. And I don't know. My body and my head are at war, both trying to deal with the reality of you." I shrugged. "That's all."

His expression froze and he betrayed no emotion, at least none I could read. "What makes you so sure I'm leaving?"

I squinted at him then pointed at his hand. "Well, right now you're holding your car keys and standing at the front door. I thought it was a logical deduction. Plus, you told me so."

"No, I mean, what makes you so sure I'm leaving town?"

"Because you told me that, too, Dane. Remember? You're planning to go to New York City for a few days and then back to L.A. in August to shoot a film."

"Well, plans can change." He tossed his keys to the floor and strode back to where I was standing. "I want you to a crazy degree, too."

"I...really? I mean, earlier you'd told me that you didn't think we should—"

"Seriously, Julia? I'm an actor. I lied."

I got as far as saying, "Oh," before he started kissing me again. Passionately kissing me, in a way that signaled he wouldn't be stopping until we weren't wearing anything and it was tomorrow morning.

I broke away for a breath. Also, I suddenly needed to think. Switching gears like this threw me. It was one thing to fantasize in the privacy of my mind about stripping off Dane's clothes and getting down to business. It was another to realize it could begin happening in, like, under a minute.

I hadn't slept with anyone but Adam in over twelve years. What if, when we got to the big moment, I wasn't ready after all? What if I disappointed Dane?

"What's wrong?" he asked.

"What else did you lie about?"

He grinned. "I was worried admitting that fib to you would bite me in the ass."

"Then why did you tell it?"

"Because it was the right thing to say. You know it was."

I pondered his words. "What else would you lie about just because it sounded like a better line than the truth?"

"Julia, I know you know I'm an actor, but you don't understand it, do you? Acting isn't just a profession. It's a way of being. Most actors don't *choose* this. We *are* this."

"Meaning?"

"Meaning that playing a role becomes a way of life. We're aware of ourselves as characters in any given situation and at any time. Switching between parts is instinctive. But that doesn't mean it's impossible to tap into our real selves or be honest about our genuine motivations in the midst of a world of potential roles. It just takes concentration and a good reason to do it."

I nodded at him and took a few steps back. I was in way over my head with this guy, and I knew it. "I just realized I'm very thirsty and need a drink. Want one?"

"Sure," he said, but he didn't move from his spot. He crossed his arms and trained his blue eyes on me with a half contemplative, half amused look—like the military sniper he'd played in that one indie film, *Dead Man's Will*.

"Great," I said. "Mine's going to have alcohol in it." A lot of alcohol. "I can go lighter on yours, though. Since you'll be driving...later."

"You're adorable." He flashed one of his trademark grins at me. "I won't be driving anytime soon. Unless you kick me out." He paused. "Are you planning to kick me out?"

"No," I said. "But plans can change."

He laughed. "Touché." Then he walked with me into the kitchen, put his arms around my shoulders, and whispered, "Relax. I know we just did a 180. Fast enough to make us both a little lightheaded. Let's have a drink. We can slow it down a bit."

I grabbed a bottle of vodka from the cabinet and orange juice from the fridge and made screwdrivers that were one part juice, three parts lighter fluid.

Dane took a sip of his and then cough-laughed. "You reversed the proportions there, eh?" He took another sip and shook his head.

"Maybe." I downed about half of mine, hoping the

increased quantity would made the potion take effect faster.

Dane studied me. "Where's your bedroom?"

I guzzled a little more of my slightly orange-flavored vodka. "I don't want to go in there."

"Okay. Where *do* you want to go?"

"Almost anywhere else in the house."

He ventured another sip of his drink then pointed toward the Persian rug in the middle of the living room.

I considered this. "Nice tight weave, but carpet burn is a real possibility."

He pointed to the top of the polished mahogany dining-room table.

I considered this, too. "Surprisingly spacious, but clearly not a soft surface. If you have any back issues at all, well..."

He laughed openly at that. "Any guest bedrooms? Sofa sleepers?"

"There is a guest room, but the walls are this really nauseatingly ugly apricot color."

He raised his eyebrows and waited for me to continue.

"Um...and there's a pullout sofa bed in the house. It's in the basement, though. There might be some stuff on it. Old blankets. Maybe a spider or two."

Dane set his drink down on the counter, reached for mine, and placed it deliberately in the spot next to his. Then he held out his hand to me. "Take me to it. I'm not afraid of a few spiders, but I am afraid I'll combust if I don't get to finally lay down beside you."

I put my hand in his and silently led him down a flight of stairs and to our mostly finished basement.

Sure enough, there were a stack of ratty old blankets on one side of the sofa. A couple of Milton-Bradley board games were on the other. And though I couldn't immediately locate any arachnids, I knew there had to be a bunch nearby.

Dane surveyed the space. It was cluttered with bags

filled with Analise's old toys, a few boxes of Adam's medical-school textbooks, and a handful of infrequently used houseware items.

"Oh, that's where I'd stashed the crock pot," I murmured.

"Did you want to stop everything and throw together a quick stew? We'll probably be starving when it's ready...in about six hours," Dane said, smirking.

"Watch it, or I'll actually go back upstairs and do it."

"I am watching," he said, his gaze undressing me, one article of clothing at a time.

I swallowed and struggled to get a full breath. The odor in the basement was vaguely musty. I should have tried to air it out somehow, I supposed, but we'd never spent much time down here as a family. Right now, that was a very good thing. The place didn't hold the jumble of bittersweet memories that the rest of the house did.

"You okay here?" he whispered.

I nodded.

"Good. How about we move these things off the cushions and open up the sofa? I promise I'll crush any rogue spiders before I throw your sexy body on the mattress."

I felt myself smiling, remembering something I'd seen when I was seventeen. "Like the way you threw Kendra Leigh down on the sofa bed in the frat house in *Dorm Daze*?"

He looked fleetingly amused. "Maybe. Maybe not." He paused. "Did you know she hated me? I mean *really* hated. She told me that I was the worst actor she'd ever worked with on a film. During the press junket, she insisted that we always had to have someone else from the cast sitting between us or she wouldn't do any of the interviews."

"What?" I had to admit, I was stunned. "I remember how all the tabloids were full of speculation about you two, and how you were secretly a hot real-life couple, and—"

"I loathed her." He ran his thumb down the side of my face, his expression totally serious. "Julia, I'm an *actor*," he said once again.

"Are you acting now?"

"No." And he moved in to kiss me.

I had that levitation feeling again. It happened every time our lips met. I pulled away and gasped for some air and, perhaps, a little sanity.

"Are you sure?" I asked him.

"Am I sure of what?"

"That you're not acting now. Because, unlike stupid Kendra Leigh, I know you're not a terrible actor. I mean, in addition to your award-worthy performance as Johannes of Stockholm today, you got an actual Oscar nomination for your portrayal of that mountain hiker, and you won two Golden Globes for your work in—"

"What are you, Ms. Wikipedia?" He stared at me.

"I read your IMDb page, Dane. Memorized it, in fact. And you said yourself that acting wasn't just a profession, it was a way of being. So how could you honestly *stop* playing a part just because you're not currently being filmed?"

He pulled back abruptly and shot a sudden nervous glance around the room. "Are you sure we're not being filmed? For all I know, you might've been contacted by *TMZ* or *Access Hollywood* or another show." He snaked around the sofa, eyeing the bookshelves and the storage cabinets. "Did you set up a few hidden cameras down here? Promise the producers they'd get 'Dane Tyler's Scandalous Suburban Sex Tapes' or something? One clip like that and it would go viral in minutes."

I gaped at him, thinking he had to be kidding at first. But then I realized in horror that he looked more serious than I'd ever seen him. "You can't possibly think I'd—"

He angrily shoved the blankets and games from the sofa and tossed one cushion on the floor, then lifted up the second one and scrutinized it. "Spiders, huh? Are you sure you don't mean *bugs* of another kind? *Testing one, two, three*," he said into the corner of the cushion.

"C'mon, Dane, I would never, ever...I can't even believe you'd suggest I'd do something like that."

"I *know* you wouldn't," he roared, tossing the second cushion on the floor, throwing the third one on top of the other two, and yanking open the sofa bed with one infuriated motion.

"Well, then why—" I began.

He stopped all movement, rolled his eyes at me, and broke into a sly grin. "Now, see? That was acting. I'm trained to do it on command." He marched back over to me, lifted me up, and plunked me down onto the middle of the mattress. "And that was me being just a wee bit dramatic." Then he laid down next to me and kissed me. Kissed me until I was floating again and had forgotten my original question. "And *that*," he said gently, "was real. Okay?"

"Okay," I whispered.

"First time, right?" he asked. "Since your husband...?"

I reached for him and unbuttoned the entire row of buttons down the front of his dress shirt before I answered. "Yeah."

He shrugged out of his shirt and then pulled mine off in a well-practiced maneuver. I shot him a questioning look.

"It's been a little over six months since my last time. With Emily. And, between you and me, I can tell you that it was more often lousy than not."

"Sorry," I told him, although I didn't mean it. I'd never liked Emily Brennan. Or her movies. Or the thought of her touching Dane.

He shrugged.

"Well, look on the bright side," I added. "At least she didn't die by crashing her sports car into a street light on an icy highway."

"True," he said. "There's a decided absence of ice in southern California and, also, she lacked the sports car. She always prefers being chauffeured in a white Caddy."

"Ah."

"I realize our situations aren't the same, Julia. I just wanted you to know that it's been a while for me, too. I'm not the manwhore that the media and my publicists at the studio like to portray."

"I didn't think you were." Although, if I were being truthful with myself, I'd have to confess that I'd only just realized it. For all of our talking, there was still so much I didn't know about him.

He glanced between his still-clothed lower body and mine, and said, "Your move."

I could have stopped here, if I'd wanted to. Dane was making that clear. But unless he'd been not only acting but blatantly lying about his desires, he didn't want us to stop any more than I did. It may have taken my mind a few minutes to catch up, but it had quickly come to realize what my body had already decided.

I reached for his belt and unfastened it. I undid the top button of his jeans and unzipped them.

He studied me for a long moment before rolling onto his back, kicking off his shoes, and sliding the denim off his legs and onto the floor. He rolled back—only in his boxers and socks now—and smiled at me. It was like when he'd undressed in his suite last Sunday. Only, this time, neither of us had to go anywhere.

In my bra and black yoga pants, I shivered beside him despite the summer's heat. He was so beautiful. I ran my fingertips underneath the waistband of his boxers and pulled myself closer. There was a small tattoo on his hip that read, "CATS." I traced it with my index finger as he watched, his eyes darkening. I'd ask him about that later.

"Your move," I whispered.

He drew me completely into his arms, bringing my

body flush up against his, with only a few thin slips of fabric between us. He unlatched my bra and removed it. Then he kissed his way down from my lips to my neck to my collarbone to each of my nipples. And that was where he stayed until I began to moan and arch against him.

I could feel his lips curve into a smile as he kissed further down—to my belly. Then, with a fluid but unrushed motion, he slid my stretchy yoga slacks, along with my panties beneath them, off of my body. He slipped his head in between my knees, kissing the soft skin of my upper thighs. First the left side, then the right.

"Um, Dane?"

"Mmm." He began to do something very swirly with his tongue, suckling his way to the juncture of my legs. And I, like a spider's unsuspecting prey—one that had been immobilized by the clever arachnid's special venom—was paralyzed on that sofa bed. Caught up in the silken web that was Dane Tyler and the profound hold he had on me.

"I want to touch you," I finally managed to say.

"You'll get to. Soon."

But it wasn't *that* soon. He didn't stop his delicious torture until I was panting and crying out his name. Only then, did he finally raise his head up, look me in the eye, and grin with an expression that was nothing short of triumphant.

He pointed at me. "Don't move." Then he sprang off the mattress, dug through his jeans, and opened his wallet.

I did as he instructed, although, truth was, I couldn't have moved if I'd wanted to. My bones had dissolved and I was just a heap of warm flesh and pounding blood. But he retrieved the foil packet, ditched his boxers, and put the condom on before covering my body with his like a quilt. He entered me—hard, fast, and completely—and I was quickly proven wrong about being unable to move.

As it turned out, Dane was quite capable of *making* me move. And gasp. And scream his name all over again. But I could touch him now. And I did. Until I heard him groan. Until I felt him come apart in my arms.

I'd loved Adam. I would forever. But I wasn't delusional, and there was nothing wrong with my memory. Adam had been a kind, loving, and devoted man. He'd been *good* in bed.

But Dane...he was *stellar*. Making love with him was in a different category. At least for me. Maybe this kind of intensity was commonplace for him, though—his experience with Emily Brennan notwithstanding. The mere thought flooded me with unexpected insecurity. Maybe this was what he was used to. What he expected. Maybe, for him, this was just an average hour of screwing.

The fact that I didn't know what he was thinking bothered me more than I wanted to admit. So I tried to ask. "Was it, uh...I mean, when you're with someone new, are you typically, um..."

"What are you getting at, Julia? Are you asking whether it was good for me, too? If so, short answer—yes. Or are you wondering if it meant anything to me?" He gestured in the space between us. "Or if I thought this was just a hook up?"

"Did you?"

"Think it was a hook up? No. Think it meant something?" He paused. "That depends. What do you want it to mean?"

"Look, Dane, I'm not an actor. I don't want to play games—"

"I'm not asking because I'm playing a game. I need to know what you *want* it to mean. Maybe you're just looking for some fun out of real time, fulfilling an adolescent fantasy that's bound to be disappointing once you get to know the real me a little better. I've been trying to show you who I really am—unmasked, unwrapped, uncensored. I'm not saying that's a great gift or anything, just one that not a lot of people have gotten to see."

He reached down to the floor, snatched up his boxers, and pulled them on.

I watched him, still unsure how to answer his question. *What did I want this to mean?*

He sighed. "Julia, we just slept together for the first time, and I have no idea why you wanted me beyond sheer chemistry. Were you trying to rid your mind of your late husband's memory? Have sex with your first movie star? Do something more aerobic than Wii Fit?"

His expression was solemn. Was he acting or was he genuine? I couldn't be positive, of course, but his words rang true. "Are those my only choices?" I asked.

He smiled slightly and shook his head. "There may be a few other possibilities out there."

"I'm sorry," I whispered. "My mind is still trying to wrap its head around the fact that I even know you, let alone—" I motioned in the space between us. "This."

"You know, I'm just a normal guy in a lot of ways, trying to have some decent after-sex talk with a woman I really like and figure out if, maybe, she likes me, too, and wants to see me again."

"Is this like *Notting Hill*? When Julia Roberts's character says to Hugh Grant's character that she's just a girl asking a boy to love her, or something like that?"

"Kinda. But I wasn't in that film."

"Hmm. You seem a little defensive about it, though," I teased. "Bad audition?"

He cleared his throat and leveled an incisive look at me. "Am I understanding this right—that you're making fun of me now? That you're actually *mocking* me?"

I tried to smother a laugh. I was unsuccessful. "Maybe."

The corners of his mouth twitched upward. "You know what else I wasn't cast in? *Fifty Shades of Grey*. But I read the script, and there's a punishment for people like you."

I was sort of snickering until he grabbed me, effectively trapping my arms against his broad chest. He wrapped his right leg around both of mine, so I couldn't move any of my limbs. Then he pulled me half on top of him, cackled wickedly in my ear, and gave me a playful spank.

I squealed, and he swatted me again.

"Dane!" I cried out, laughing and squirming in his arms, though it didn't even sting. "There's no Red Room of Pain anywhere in this house."

"No," he said, feigning a serious and slightly regretful tone. "Apparently, there's just an Apricot Guest Room of Ugliness."

He laid me back down on the mattress and rose above me, gazing into my eyes and waiting for me to stop laughing. When I did, his brushed his lips against mine, kissing me so tenderly that it hurt. Drawing me so deeply into the enchanting wonder of him that I questioned everything I was feeling all over again.

What was I getting myself into? I'd been falling for this guy for half of my life. How could any of these emotions be anything but a fairy tale, even if they felt real in this moment?

No. It had to just be some kind of powerful infatuation—on both our parts.

I searched his face for a response to something I hadn't asked him, but I couldn't decipher what I most wanted to know. Finally, I just came out with it. "So, what's it feel like for *you* to be with a regular, non-famous, Midwestern suburban woman?"

He smiled. "To, at long last, get to sleep with The Girl Next Door, you mean?"

I nodded.

He exhaled slowly. "It feels like coming home."

CHAPTER SIXTEEN

"**Y**ou slept with him?" Shar cried on the phone. "Oh, my God, Julia. I'd been wondering. That's...massive news. It changes everything!"

"Yeah, I know."

Only, I couldn't bring myself to tell her how much I wished we hadn't done it, wonderful as it was. How there was no stuffing back into a box the emotions Dane had dredged out of me. How I no longer had the tight grip on reality that I'd worked so hard to accept, and I'd lost the comfort of the fantasy, too.

"So, wait," my friend said, incredulity, wonder, and dawning comprehension in her voice. "Does that mean there are *other* things you haven't told me about this week? That 'news article' was—"

"Oh, Shar. It's such a disaster. Dane's so upset."

For a long, long moment, there was no sound on the other end of the phone line.

"Where's he now?" she asked finally.

I squeezed my eyes shut. "I have no idea."

As I later explained to Shar, Friday had started out well enough. In fact, I thought it was pretty damned marvelous at the time.

We'd been awakened initially by the ringing of the house phone, but the number on the Caller ID wasn't one I'd recognized (Analise and the camp counselors always called my cell phone; I knew it wasn't them), so I just let it go to voicemail. No messages were left, and we fell back asleep.

Dane and I snoozed on the sofa bed in the basement and, when I woke up later that morning, he trailed a line of butterfly kisses down my bare neck and shoulder.

I shivered under his touch, grabbed him to me, and we made love. Again.

And, again, it was spectacular.

He'd barely entered me when I started moaning, pushing him deeper, craving more. Everything about our connection had happened too fast, in my opinion, but I didn't have many other sexual experiences with which to compare this one. I'd only slept with Ben a handful of times when we were dating in college, and with Adam, of course. Dane was my third.

"So, what was it like for you, once you hit it big, having all of these women throwing themselves at you?" I asked him. "Since, as you claimed, you couldn't get any dates with girls during high school. The attention must have been...overwhelming?"

He was lying on his stomach next to me with his arm across my belly. A thin sheen of sweat covered his body, and I could hear that his breathing was still a little labored in the afterglow of the moments before.

He raised his head and squinted at me. "What's this leading to?"

I smiled. "Just one of those post-sex discussion questions. I mean, we can talk about sports instead, if you'd rather. Chicago has a lot of sports teams."

He laughed. "Fine. Yes, it was overwhelming. Difficult to figure out who likes you for you and who just wants a conquest." He flipped to his side, facing me. "You know in the film *Dirty Dancing*, when Patrick Swayze's character is talking to 'Baby' in bed about when he started to be known for his dance skills, how women suddenly wanted him? How they smelled so nice and were throwing cash his way, and he thought at first that they really liked him, but they were just using him?"

"Yeah."

"It was like that."

"I'm sorry."

"Don't be," he said. "When I was eighteen, I thought it was the greatest acting perk in the universe."

"When did that change?"

"It took a few years, Julia." He rubbed my belly with the pads of his fingers and then began to slide them upward, circling my breasts. I could feel myself wanting him again. Already. The unnerving intensity of that desire had me asking another question.

"So, did you keep track, um, of all of those women? Like a...tally? Or a chart or something?"

He pulled his hand away from my chest and tilted his head at me. "A chart?" Then he collapsed onto the pillow and started convulsing with laughter. "God, you're funny." He shook his head. "No. There were no graphs, no charts, no tally marks on my wall or notches in my bedpost. And, before you ask, the answer is 'no idea.' I have absolutely no idea how many women I've slept with. These last few years have been different. I could tell you exactly when and with whom. But there's a good decade-long period where those details are pretty fuzzy."

"Huh. Not even a range? Like one hundred to two hundred? Or seven hundred and fifty to a thousand?"

He stared at me, astonishment etched on his handsome

face. "We are so not having this conversation."

"But other women you've slept with must have asked you about it, too, right? I can't be the first one who's ever wondered—"

He groaned comically, cradling his head in his hands for a second and then covering his ears. "La, la, la, *laaaaa!*" he sang. "This topic. *Never*. Ends. *Wellll*."

I giggled and poked him in the ribs. "Wimp."

He pulled his hands off his ears. "You have five seconds to ask something else, or I'll find us a new conversation."

"Be that way." I ran my fingertip down his body until I reached his hip. "Tell me about your tattoo, then. 'CATS.' I don't remember reading anything about your having been in the show on Broadway or anywhere else but, apparently, you have secrets, so..."

He grinned. "Yeah, a few." He paused. "The letters don't stand for the Andrew Lloyd Webber musical, although I've often wished I were a 'Jellical Cat,' so I could sleep all day, play around all night, and go to a big ball. The nine lives would be nice, too."

"Are they initials, then?" I guessed.

He nodded.

"A woman's?"

"Yeah."

"Someone you had a relationship with?"

"Someone I'm *trying* to have a relationship with," he countered.

I pulled back a little. "Oh. I'm—I'm sorry. In that case, I must be prying. I shouldn't have—"

He reached between us and lightly tapped my lips, stopping me from saying more. "Julia, please listen to me. I have some real feelings for you. Actually—" he paused. "If I'm being completely honest, I'd have to admit outright that I'm starting to fall in love with you." He paused again and studied my reaction to this statement.

I'd felt my mouth fall open as he said it, but my brain was so locked on the words "I'm starting to fall in love with you" that I had a damn near impossible time trying to process anything else. I couldn't come close to speaking.

Dane Tyler was falling in love with *me?* No. That couldn't be true.

"It's okay," he said. "You don't have to say anything about that yet. But, because I want to be open with you, I'm going to tell you a few private things. Only, you have to promise me you won't talk about this with anyone else, all right?"

"I...um..."

"Please *promise* me, Julia."

I managed to nod. "I promise."

"Good. CATS stands for Cathleen Aria Tyler Stanton," he said. "My daughter."

Somehow, my brain managed to process that. "W-What? You're a father? But when? I mean, how old is she—Cathleen?"

"She goes by Cat and she's sixteen now. She lives with her mother in New York. She's who I'm going to see at the end of the month."

"I've never read a word about this. As far as I know, there's never been anything written on...on you with a daughter."

"No, there wouldn't be. At least, we've worked really hard to keep it out of the press. Cat's mother, Marissa Stanton, is a classically trained singer, and she's been in a bunch of musicals, on and off Broadway. She got pregnant when we were both twenty-three, and Cat was born when I was twenty-four. Marissa wouldn't let me give her my last name, let me acknowledge her publicly, or even let me be listed as the father on her birth certificate. She insisted that line be left blank."

His jaw tightened as he told me this. All these years later, I could tell he was still hurt and angry about it.

"But she did, at least, include Tyler as part of Cat's name," he said. "And we had a lawyer discreetly draw up the papers for a special trust for her. Marissa wanted me to sign away rights to see her in exchange for no child support payments, but I insisted on both. Cat and I Skype every week and we get together every few months. No set dates, just whenever we can. Always out East, though. Marissa won't let her come to California."

"Oh, Dane. That's got to be really hard."

"It is. But I don't regret her. Not for a second. The risky behavior, yes, but not the baby. My little girl, who's not so little anymore." He stared off into the distance for a long moment. "The hardest part is that Marissa has convinced Cat that she shouldn't tell anyone I'm her dad because my 'reputation' isn't the best. And there have been so many times when she's tried to turn Cat against me. The woman keeps clippings of every bad thing the press has ever written about me, whether it's true or not, so I have to be pretty careful. Once Cat is eighteen, though, she can decide for herself if she wants to acknowledge our relationship openly. But, legally, I can't say anything about it in public until she does."

The magnitude of what he'd just told me slowly began to sink in.

Dane's ability to relate to my daughter with such ease made sense now. He had a daughter of his own. And his understanding of the difficulty I had in separating from Analise made sense, too. He'd experienced similar pangs of separation pain and more.

I also recognized these days of insularity for what they must be to him: Not just the two of us simply being caught up in each other, as might be typical of couples who were actually falling in love, but as an exercise in extreme discretion.

With the notable exception of the camp visit, which I was still hearing about from Yvette and other more casual acquaintances (most who'd heard through the Mirabelle Harbor grapevine and the gossip of social media that Dane and I were there together), we hadn't interacted much in public at all.

Yes, there was that quick stop at IKEA.

And, yes, we'd dined out a couple of times.

But, for the majority of the hours we'd spent together since Sunday, we stayed in and traveled a path of triangulation between private residences—namely, his brother's apartment, his hotel suite, and my house. It gave the illusion of movement without much real travel.

Funny thing was, I was never big into going out on the town. I appreciated our quiet fun. But it was one thing to personally select introverted behavior and another to have so many consecutive days of seclusion chosen for me. I hadn't even realized it was happening, and I didn't know whether I should be upset by that or not.

"Your daughter is very lucky to have you in her life, despite her mother's resistance," I told Dane, and I meant it sincerely. "You're doing your best to be there for her."

"Thanks—" he began.

The house phone rang. I wrapped myself up one of the sheets and picked up the line in the basement. Shar.

I cleared my throat. "Hey, how are you?"

"Haven't talked to you in a couple of days, girlfriend. What's up?"

"Oh, I've been in and out..."

"Alone?"

"Well, not exactly."

"So, by these brief, vague responses, do I guess correctly that you have company?"

"That would be true," I said.

"The *same* company that you've apparently been keeping all week? People have been talking, you know. Facebook. Twitter. Instagram."

Damn that social media.

I sighed. "Anything I should worry about?" I asked her. A few feet away, Dane raised a curious brow at my words.

"Hmm. Not that I know of," Shar said. "But I'll keep my eyes and ears open. And when your *company* goes home, you need to give me a call and fill me in. On everything. Got it?"

I smiled. "Yeah, yeah. Talk to you later, Shar."

"You'd better," she said and then clicked off.

"Your friend Sharlene?" Dane guessed.

"The very one."

"She's rather well known in town, right? The center of Mirabelle Harbor society?"

"Uh, sure, I suppose." I hadn't really thought about that but, yes, Shar was a popular person in town. "Why?"

Dane opened his mouth to explain, but the house line rang again. Weird.

I checked the number on the Caller ID display. Didn't recognize it.

"I don't know who that is," I told Dane. "Probably just some telemarketer. I'll let voicemail pick it up."

But the caller didn't leave a message.

Whoever it was immediately tried calling a second time, though. Then a third. Freaking persistent.

I rolled my eyes at Dane.

Then my personal cell phone rang and I felt a momentary panic. Very few people had my cell number. Maybe it was someone I knew after all? Maybe it was an emergency?

"Sorry," I said to him. "Guess I'd better get it or they'll keep interrupting us." I answered the phone. "Hello?"

"Julia Crane?" a woman with a very matter of fact voice replied.

"Yes. Who's calling?"

"I'm with the *Tinseltown Buzz*, and we had a few questions for you about Dane Ty—"

"The *Tinseltown Buzz*?" I said, unable to hide my

surprise.

Dane shot me an alarmed looked and started to get dressed at once.

Was it that same lady from the play's Opening Night? I couldn't tell. In any case, the woman on the line said, "A number of guests at the Knightsbridge Theater reported that you were Dane's companion for the show's Closing Night and that the two of you left the After Party together. Can you confirm that the two of you spent the night in his hotel room?"

My pulse went into minor shock and stopped mid-beat. "What did you just ask me?"

"Mrs. Crane, we have pictures of you and Dane Tyler that were taken in a number of locations. It's pretty clear from the photos that you two are an item. Especially the Camp Willowgreen pictures where, we've heard, your daughter is spending the summer. How much does she know about your relationship with—"

"Who *is* this?"

"I told you, ma'am, I'm with the *Tinseltown Buzz*. Would you say Dane is as good of a lover in real life as he is on the big scree—"

"How did you get this number? What's your *name?*"

"And, of course, it's rumored that the two of you secretly met before he came to Chicago this summer. Can you respond to—"

I clicked off the phone.

Sitting up on the sofa bed fully dressed now, Dane looked an unhealthy shade of ashen. He didn't immediately speak, but I saw him swallow more than once, as if trying to prepare for the words that were to come.

"I hate the *Tinseltown Buzz*," he whispered, his voice a low hiss. "They're vicious."

"Our home phone number and street address are listed," I told him. "You found my address, so you know that. Sometimes we get robocalls or telemarketers, but my cell number is private. Adam insisted on it. Just friends and family have that. So, I don't know how this woman got ahold of that number."

"From one of your friends, perhaps? Shar?" His voice was cold with an edge of accusation that couldn't be ignored.

I shook my head and pulled on the clothes I'd thrown to the floor earlier. "Shar's my *best friend*. She'd never betray my trust or violate my privacy. And she wouldn't say anything that might get you in trouble either."

"What about that neighbor of yours? The one we saw up at the camp?"

"Yvette?" I shook my head again. "She's so sweet. I've known her since high school, and there's never been a time when—"

"Well, somebody, at some point, wasn't acting like a *friend*, Julia. I realize this is my fault, okay? We weren't as discreet as we should have been. I asked you to the VIP party. I went with you up to the camp. But if your cell number isn't widely known, somebody had to be the source of that information."

"Maybe the reporter managed to get my number from one of the Camp Willowgreen staff members, although they have a firm confidentiality policy, so—"

There was a loud knock on the front door upstairs.

Dane closed his eyes, and I could hear him murmur, "Oh, shit."

I couldn't see who it was without going up to the first floor. I looked at Dane.

"Don't do it," he said.

I heard a male voice calling my name from outside the house. "Mrs. Crane?" More knocking.

"I'll just look out of the peephole," I whispered to him. "It might only be the UPS guy with a delivery or something."

He shrugged. "Suit yourself. But I wouldn't get too

close to a window, and I definitely wouldn't open the door."

I tiptoed upstairs and peered through the tiny hole. I'd expected there to be a mail truck at the end of the driveway or the gas meter reader nearby. I'd expected wrong.

Oh, my God.

I ran back down to the basement. "There's a news crew out there! With cameras and recording equipment." I quickly zipped around the entire downstairs, looking for any open window wells. Anything that might make the basement visible to someone standing on our lawn. I breathed a deep sigh of relief when I realized all of the windows were shaded. That no one could see in from the outside.

Dane, however, did not look remotely mollified by this. "You do realize they're going to make it impossible for either of us to get out of the house, right? I drove here in a rental car. I parked in your driveway. Bet they blocked that with their van, huh?"

I couldn't remember the exact position of the news van or the few other cars out front, but Dane was probably right.

There was more loud knocking on the front door.

The house phone rang again, and so did my cell phone.

"It's not good," Dane said with a heavy sigh, reaching for his own phone. "Trust me, I know."

CHAPTER SEVENTEEN

"**H**e actually thought I'd call the tabloids on you two?" Shar asked on the phone, indignant. "That's crazy! I used to like that guy, but now—"

"Don't take it personally, Shar," I told her. "He was suspicious of everybody. Besides, I'm really the one he was most angry with."

"Why would he be angry with *you?* He knew you didn't contact any reporters, and the two of you had just finished a marathon shagging session. He said he was 'starting to fall in love' with you, Julia. I don't get his behavior at all. He seems so moody and insecure."

"Maybe, he is—a little," I said.

Or maybe he's not...

I couldn't tell Shar everything Dane and I had been talking about on Friday morning. I'd promised utter secrecy when it came to information about his daughter, and I wouldn't go back on my word to him, not even to share it with my most trusted friend.

Because of that, I knew Shar wouldn't be able to understand why Dane was so tense and worried about what the reporters might say or what the consequences their public insinuations might have on his relationship with his daughter. Why he was probably feeling especially vulnerable that day—trapped, as he was, in my basement after he'd just shared all of this personal information about himself with me. Why he'd tried so hard to warn me, even though I hadn't been listening closely enough then.

Within twenty-four hours, though, I came to understand that the *Tinseltown Buzz* story wasn't something we could easily brush away. It wasn't a slow, containable leak, dribbling out a few rumors and lies about us.

It was more like a flash flood, with the intent to drown.

After the first set of ceaseless telephone calls on Friday, I turned off the ringer on my home phone and muted my cell. Then I watched Dane as he rapid-fire texted a series of messages on his own cell phone.

"I need to let my agent and the PR people know about this," he explained wearily to me. "To prepare for whatever ends up in tomorrow's paper. You know when media people say things like 'Representatives for the actor declined to comment on recent allegations that he did such and such' and they go on to tell their readers or viewers whatever heinous things the actor reportedly did?"

I nodded.

"The people I'm calling now are the ones who'll need to either comment or decline to comment on my behalf," he added.

Although I didn't have to listen to my two phones ringing anymore, I couldn't do anything about the intermittent knocking on the door, short of calling the police and reporting the paparazzi on our lawn for harassment.

Don't think I didn't consider this. Seriously.

But somehow I doubted that a squad car in the neighborhood would lessen the migraine I was getting. Besides, I had to know what Dane wanted me to do before I acted impulsively and contacted *anyone*. I didn't want to make matters worse for him.

Dane finished up his first set of texts and sighed. "In a few minutes I'll have to give Marissa and Cat a call. They'll need a heads up so they don't get blindsided. I can't tell you how much I'm not looking forward to *that* conversation."

I rubbed my pounding head. This situation seemed ridiculous. So unnecessarily complicated. "Dane, we haven't done anything wrong—legally or morally. We're single, consenting adults. Just tell them that if they hear anything about you and me, it means nothing. That we're friends and we were just hanging out together during the time you were here. That the press was pestering us and they jumped to conclusions."

His face turned from pale to a surprising shade of red. "No," he said loudly. "For one thing, this is *not* 'nothing.' Do you really think I'd put myself in this kind of position for something *insignificant?*" He streaked his fingers through his hair, and then crossed his arms and glared at me. "Dammit, Julia. I don't care what the public thinks of me, but I *never* lie to my daughter. And I don't lie to anyone else I care about either." He shot me a pointed look. "The tabloids are a pain in the ass, but the biggest problem we have here is that *you* don't trust me. *You* don't believe what I've been telling you. *You* don't think what I feel can be real."

I blinked at him. I wanted to tell him that I believed every word he'd said, but I couldn't. I couldn't deny my skepticism. Not with everything I knew about infatuation and enchantments.

"Maybe you're right," I said. "Maybe I don't completely trust whatever this thing is between us because it's happening too fast and feels too much like a schoolgirl fantasy to me to be real. But let's face it, Dane. Say what you will, but you don't entirely trust me either. When those reporters came calling, the first thing you did was accuse me of blabbing information about you to my friends. You pay lip service to the idea that you *know* me, that you've watched my behavior and believe I wouldn't betray you, but the instant that notion is challenged, you change your story."

"Look, I'm angry about our privacy being violated. About whatever pictures of us they're going to dig up. About the incredibly deceptive piece of fiction they're going to print tomorrow as if it were truth, and how fast their slanderous words will go viral. But it was a mistake if anything I said made you think I was accusing you."

I shrugged. "I didn't contact any reporters. I didn't tell my friends a single thing about you that wasn't common knowledge or that they couldn't see firsthand when they met you. But you realize that trust and love don't happen on command, right? Some things can't be rushed. Some things take time, even when they're the *right* things. Like...grapes. You can choose the right grapes for a wine, but you still need to give the grapes the time to ripen. If they get pressed too early, they'll be bitter."

"Wow." He shook his head. "That's a terrible metaphor." But I could see a small smile tugging up the corner of one side of his mouth.

"Perhaps, but that doesn't make it less true."

"Julia, there's more to all of this than you realize. I've gotten slammed by the *Tinseltown Buzz* before, and they'll include just enough truth in their bundle of lies to keep people guessing. To get people who've known you all your life to doubt what you say. The wild card in all of this is what they'll have uncovered about *you*. And what that'll do to this thing we've begun. This *right* thing. Which, for the record, I think has a shot at lasting if we don't screw it up.

Do you agree?"

This much I couldn't deny—Dane and I did have things in common, and we were genuinely attracted to each other. We'd developed a real friendship, however newly formed. If he hadn't been a celebrity, I would have been much more hopeful of anything between us lasting for a little while.

But that particular element of his life wasn't just *one small part* of his existence; it nearly defined him. His fame wasn't just a deterrent to our personal privacy and our time alone together, but it was practically an entity in itself that would stalk our lives together. Adam's "popularity" in town had been bad enough. Everywhere we went in Mirabelle Harbor, people would recognize him and, frequently, they came up to us to chat. I immediately noticed the absence of that interference whenever we went on vacation together, and I was always relieved to be away.

How could I sign up for a life that would have a thousand times more scrutiny—maybe a million times more—and not just for myself but for Analise, too?

"I don't know," I murmured. "And I don't know how you think you can know either."

His light-blue eyes turned dark. "Maybe you're right," he snapped. "This," he motioned between us, "might have all just been some hallucination of mine." He nodded abruptly at his phone. "May I have a few minutes alone please?"

"Of course." I went upstairs, careful to avoid walking in front of any open windows. The news people were still milling around outside but, eventually, they'd have to leave, right?

I could hear Dane's voice downstairs. Not his actual words but his intonation. He was stressed out. Frustrated. Angry.

It took almost an hour before he emerged from the basement and joined me in the kitchen.

"Coffee?" I asked him.

He shook his head. "I'm going to be leaving in a few minutes."

"You're going outside? Driving away?" I looked doubtfully toward the front door.

"No. I called Samuel. He's going to pick me up in the cul-de-sac behind your house." He pointed toward our backyard and the tree-lined area that divided our lawn from our neighbors' garden. Beyond that was their little paved circle.

"That's not a bad spot," I acknowledged. "It's very low traffic. As long as you can get over there without any of the press people out front seeing you."

"I'm counting on it. I just need to wait for a distraction."

A distraction? I could only think of one thing that would bring everyone around to the front. I swallowed. "Do you want me to go out there? If I open the door and talk to—"

"God, no. Samuel's eldest son is going to help me with that. And either he or Samuel will come back later for my car. " Dane suddenly pulled me into his arms and crushed me to him. "I'm sorry for all of this. The sooner I get out of your house, the sooner your life has a chance to go back to normal. I just wish...I don't know. I wish you could have seen what I saw in us, and that it would have been enough to make all this trouble worth it."

He gazed at me sadly and kissed my forehead before stepping away.

"Dane—" I began.

There was a weird clattering sound out front, like a motor scooter had just rammed into a couple of metal garbage cans or something and was dragging them by our house.

"That's my cue," Dane said, grabbing his things and quietly unlocking the sliding glass door to the back patio. "Take care of yourself, Julia. I'll talk with you, um...later."

He poked his head outside to look around. The coast must have been clear in the backyard because he slipped away. As I locked the sliding door behind him, I saw him make a clean dash to the cul-de-sac in the distance and hop into a silver sedan that was idling in wait.

Thanks, Samuel. Take good care of him, will you?

I turned my attention back to the front of my house, just in time to see a jeep with a man and woman in it, driving away. It had tons of metal cans attached to the back, as if the couple were newlyweds. Was that Samuel's son with his wife or, maybe, his girlfriend? Either way, I mentally thanked them, too.

With Dane gone, I decided to check all of the messages I'd gotten since I'd clicked off the phones. Between the home line and my cell, there were so many voicemails and texts that I had to sit down.

The same "unknown" number—which I now knew belonged to that obnoxious *Tinseltown Buzz* reporter, Caryn-something—had shown up over twenty times.

Shar had texted, saying, "Are you okay?! Yvette said there was a news crew in front of your house..."

Speaking of Yvette, she'd left two voicemails—one on my home line and another on my cell—the gist of which was, "What is going on over there? Do you need any help, Julia? Let me know. I can be right over if you need me!"

Kristopher had sent a text, too. "Hey! Sorry I lost my temper the last time we were together. Can we just let bygones be bygones? Wanna grab some coffee this week?"

Analise hadn't left a message, but there was an odd, cryptic voicemail from her counselor Shannon. "Mrs. Crane, sorry to bother you. Analise is fine, but there's this woman who keeps calling the camp and asking questions about her and your family..."

Oh, good heavens.

I called Shannon back first, thanked her for letting me know about this, and told her that this woman was big trouble.

"Don't worry, Mrs. Crane. We didn't give her any information," Shannon assured me, "and we won't. I just thought you should be aware of her questions."

After being promised several times that my daughter was perfectly fine and safe, I finished my conversation with the camp counselor and gave Yvette a quick call back.

"The news people have been asking the neighbors questions about you and Dane," she said. "I told Mrs. Lancaster to zip it when she started blabbing to them about how you'd always been a fan of his movies. But, Julia, I don't know if anybody said anything they shouldn't have when I wasn't around. The reporters have been like ants swarming around an ice cream spill on the sidewalk."

"I know." I sighed. "Thanks for trying to keep the lid on my personal life."

"Is there, um...anything actually newsworthy going on over there?" Yvette asked.

"No," I said quickly. "Dane and I are friends. We were just hanging out at my house."

"Okay," she replied. But I could hear the doubt in her voice, and I knew even sweet Yvette didn't completely believe my story.

I read through the text messages I'd gotten, deleted Kristopher's immediately, but I did send a short response back to Shar.

"I'm okay," I texted her. "But from what Dane said, there will probably be some kind of story in the *Tinseltown Buzz* tomorrow. In print, online, or maybe both. If you see it before I do, give me a call. Otherwise, we'll talk for sure in the morning."

She replied within thirty seconds. "I'm here for you, girlfriend. Don't forget that. No matter what happens. I don't care about any stinkin' news crew stalking your place either. If you need someone to keep you company, I can be on your front doorstep in ten minutes."

I loved my best friend.

"You're the BEST, Shar," I texted. "But stay home for now. I may need you even more tomorrow..."

I didn't have to wait until it was Saturday morning in the Chicagoland area before the shit officially hit the fan.

Nope. I got a text from Dane just after eleven p.m., which would have been after midnight on the East Coast but only nine at night in Hollywood. Guess the reporters didn't want to delay their attempt to ruin our lives for even an hour longer than necessary.

"You have no idea how sorry I am about all this," Dane wrote in his message, which included a link to the *Tinseltown Buzz* website. "I'd understand if you wanted me to stay away from you now and forevermore. Far away."

I didn't reply to him at first—not for a couple of hours, in fact—because I was too busy reading the "article" (such that it was) and trying to recover from my shock. On the tabloid's homepage, in huge letters across the screen, it said:

FADING ACTOR & MERRY WIDOW'S SECRET LOVE TRYST!

Oh, shit.

And in smaller letters, a byline with a name I knew: Caryn Dizinger.

I hadn't recognized her voice on the phone, but she may have been trying to disguise it. After all, I'd done my best to get away from her at both the theater and the radio station. She was clearly mean-spirited, but she wasn't stupid. She knew I didn't want to talk to her. And with good reason.

I held my breath as I scanned the opening paragraph. It went from bad to worse to truly appalling:

> *Aging actor Dane Tyler—on the verge of hitting forty-something status—has bounced back from the crushing blow of being dumped by America's sweetheart, Emily Brennan. He's now got an unexpected new girlfriend that has set everyone's Tinseltown tongues wagging! He and a recent widow— prim schoolteacher and mother, Julia Crane—have been playing house in the upscale northern Chicago suburb of Mirabelle Harbor. It's reportedly a torrid affair that began in secret months ago. Some suggest that their relationship even preceded the death of Crane's late husband. Was that, perhaps, what pushed the poor man to an early grave?*

I wanted to kill that Dizinger bitch.

Really and truly.

I imagined dismembering her, limb by limb. I didn't want to read on, but I knew I had to. It would be worse not to know. But, oh God. How many people were going to see this piece of trash and believe it?

> *One friend of Crane's, who spoke to us on condition of anonymity, stated adamantly that Crane and Tyler had been involved for years. "Julia has been obsessed with him since high school," Crane's friend claimed. "I'm not surprised they ended up together. She'd literally do anything to win his affection."*

Who the hell was this supposed "friend" of mine? He or she would be on the executioner's block, too, if I had anything to say about it.

Sources close to the actor assured us that this month's tryst with the widow was merely a fling for him, though. "Dane's known for always having quick rebound action after a relationship ends. But he's still hurting badly over Emily's abandonment," said an actor pal.

Of course, maybe, these revelations about Tyler's Midwestern and (until recently) married love interest succeed in shedding more light on Brennan's departure from his life. "Dane has a pattern of infidelity," another member of the acting community confided, "He's charming but rarely sincere. Emily knew she couldn't stick around for more of his bad-boy behavior."

For however long it lasts, it's certainly looking as though the fading actor and the merry widow have been enjoying themselves in the Windy City and the surrounding areas. Just look at these exclusive photos below and tell us that you don't agree that this is a couple who can barely keep their hands off each other.

What followed were a dozen snapshots taken from a variety of angles and in nearly every location Dane and I had been together. Not only did they have candid shots of us together at the theater and slow dancing during the VIP party, but someone had snapped photos of us talking in the hallway of the radio station and also in the lobby of Dane's hotel—even before he'd started signing autographs. There was one of us by the elevators, too, taken from the back. We were holding hands and leaning in to whisper to each other. I hadn't realized anyone had been there watching.

And, oh, there were camp photos as well, which looked like they were pulled directly off of Facebook or Instagram and printed without permission. I doubted the people who'd originally took these photos even knew they'd been purloined for this purpose. But, worst of all, there were some long-lens shots of Dane and me in front of my house. Getting out of his rental car. Going inside. Even one fuzzy photo of Dane kissing me by the door. These bastards must have been stalking us for days.

Tyler has spent the past month in the city playing a wild ladies' man who juggles relationships with multiple women simultaneously in the Knightsbridge Theater production of "The Bachelor Pad." His performance onstage earned him only tepid praise, but he really seemed to take the show's lead character to heart. Method acting, anyone?

"It's a case of life imitating art...or vice versa," said an observant member of the stage crew. "We all saw Julia at several of the performances, and she was Dane's personal escort during the Closing Night party. They were very lovey-dovey." But when asked what Tyler was like when Crane wasn't around, the crew member laughed. "When she wasn't there, he was really flirty with lots of other women, especially the many attractive actresses in the cast. He was

perfect for the role he played in the show."

Who knows what's up next for this unlikely couple? Crane's emotionally fragile daughter has been conveniently squirreled away at summer camp while Crane has been traipsing around Chicagoland with Tyler. Maybe the young girl will return to a quiet house, though, since the actor is set to return to L.A. soon to begin shooting the film The Scorpius Project *with director Stan Henley Miles. The upcoming sci-fi/thriller, slated for release next year, also stars Brazilian beauty Cassandra Inigo, a woman that a man like Tyler will be hard pressed to resist. Even the actress herself was reportedly overheard saying to one of her costars, "I'm prepared to be propositioned by him daily."*

Representatives for Tyler refused to comment on the actor's latest antics, but the Tinseltown Buzz *feels that a slideshow of revealing pictures more than speaks for itself.*

Look for The Scorpius Project *to open in theaters next November.*

I felt positively ill. My "emotionally fragile" daughter? How dare they write that. Please, dear God, do not let Analise read this. Ever.

This whole piece was too atrocious for me to even speak to anyone about yet. Not even Dane. Not even Shar.

How did reporters get away with writing lies like these? Making insinuations that were downright slanderous? Not to mention posting photographs without any consent from the subjects?

I slumped down on the sofa, clutching my churning stomach. I was too stunned to even cry. For half an hour at least, the only thing I could do was stare at the wall and reread the defamatory lines that witch wrote, again and again in my mind. I didn't even have to look at the screen.

"...a torrid affair..."

"...what pushed the poor man to an early grave..."

"...charming but rarely sincere..."

"...he was really flirty with lots of other women..."

"...emotionally fragile daughter has been conveniently squirreled away..."

Finally, I texted Dane back. "You were right. Completely right," I wrote. "It's not good."

Then I ran to the bathroom and threw up.

CHAPTER EIGHTEEN

Sleep had a weird way of helping.

Even in wretched situations like this one, just being able to close my eyes and block out the present dreadfulness and misery for a few hours was beneficial.

I had nightmares, of course, but they weren't about tabloids or brutal gossip.

No. They were all about Adam. About his car crash. About the police officers coming to the door to give me the horrific news that my husband had been pronounced dead on the scene. About his funeral.

In a bizarre respect, this reminded me to keep my priorities in check. Reminded me that there were, in fact, worse things that could happen.

I talked to Shar first thing, which also helped. I had no doubt she was on my side, even though there were details about my relationship with Dane that I couldn't tell her. And, after I sent her the link to the website, her fury at the reporter approached levels that were almost dangerous.

"We're going to talk to a lawyer about that tabloid tramp, Julia. Soon. Very soon," she said with a low, enraged hiss. "I'll call someone I know. Today. Just to find out what kind of recourse private citizens have in cases like these."

But I'd spoken briefly with Dane about the press and privacy during one of our conversation this past week. Once someone was seen to be "dating a celebrity," all bets were off. We became "public figures" in that situation and, thus, there was very little legal recourse available. Besides, in my case, the damage had already been done. The story—complete with pictures—was "out there," and there was no pulling it back.

I'd left a message with the director at Camp Willowgreen to let me talk with my daughter as soon as possible this morning. If there was going to be any sort of media deluge that might reach her, I wanted to prepare Analise as best as I could...without telling her the exact phrases used in that damning article. For once, I was very relieved that she and her fellow campers weren't allowed to use the Internet for most of the day.

So, when the phone rang, I reached for it on the first ring.

"Julia?" said a voice I hadn't heard on the phone for months. Not since Easter Sunday, in fact.

"Um, hi, Katia," I said to my older sister. "Everything okay in Ann Arbor? How are Paul and the kids?"

There was an odd, cold laugh on the other end of the line. "Did you expect your family not to find out about you and that actor?"

I sighed. "You read the *Tinseltown Buzz* article online?"

"*I* didn't, no. I don't read trash like that. But just because I don't live in Mirabelle Harbor anymore doesn't mean that I don't still have friends there. *Several* people sent me emails about you this week, and one person forwarded the website link to me last night. That was the last straw."

"The last straw?" I parroted.

"Yeah. I wanted to stay out of it—like I need any sordid

drama in my life right now—but you have to knock it off with that guy, Julia. You're making us all look bad."

This was classic Katia. She didn't care about my feelings...or the truth, for that matter. She wasn't calling to be a supportive sister. She just didn't want anything I did to reflect poorly on *her*.

I inhaled and exhaled deeply before I responded. "It's a good thing we don't have the same last name anymore, huh? That has to cut down on most people making a quick connection between us. Except, of course, for those good 'friends' of yours who felt it was necessary to immediately spread gossip about me." I wasn't trying to disguise my sarcasm, but if she heard it, she didn't react to it.

"When did you even meet him?" she asked, a weird kind of disdain-slash-jealousy in her voice. She was four years older than me—Dane's age exactly—and had been a fan of his movies as well.

"We were introduced at the Knightsbridge Theater last month, during the dress rehearsal of his play."

"Not before that? Not when Adam was still alive then?"

"Jeez, Katia. Really? You believed that part of the article?"

I could almost see her shrug through the telephone line. Again, she didn't care about *truth*, just public perception. It didn't much matter what had actually happened between Dane and me. She'd continue to think whatever she wanted.

"Look," I told her. "I'm not planning to tell Mom and Dad about this just yet because it's still so early in the day and I need to see—"

"Too late," she snapped. "I called them first. You can't hide things like this from your family."

Oh, shit. Now they were probably worried out of their minds.

Damn Katia for being such an interfering, self-centered little snot. She'd done exactly the worst thing possible, and

I'd now have to spend an hour or more trying to soothe Mom and Dad's anxiety, when I really needed to save my patience and time for other more urgent matters...like my daughter's wellbeing.

"Well, then I'd better talk to them at once," I told her, glad to have a good and immediate excuse to hang up on her.

"Wait," she commanded. "People have been asking me if you and Dane—"

"Bye, Katia. Talk to you later." Much, much later, I thought as I clicked off.

My parents, living a thousand miles away in South Carolina and not being especially Internet savvy, had still managed to work themselves into a frenzy over this. They, at least, were focused on how I was feeling and if I was all right, rather than on what other people might be thinking about them.

But, still. It was incredibly hard to focus on comforting them when I was in need of so much comfort myself.

I spent most of the day responding to messages—voicemails, emails, a couple of in-person visits, too, from Shar and Yvette, even though I'd told them both on the phone not to stop by.

Yvette said, "I could tell there weren't any reporters on the block this morning, so I just wanted to visit real quick." She came across as sincere, but her eyes darted around my living room for the whole ten minutes she was at my house. Looking for Dane, no doubt, or at least some evidence of him.

I mentally reviewed everything I'd ever told Yvette about Dane Tyler—both when we were teens and just this past week, after he showed up at Camp Willowgreen with me.

And when she asked gently, "Have you talked to him about all of this?" I lied and said, "No. Not yet." I didn't know if she believed me, but no one seemed to believe what I said anyway today, and I'd had it with being grilled.

One of the worst side effects of that nasty story was that it made me question the motives of my friends. Had Yvette, wittingly or unwittingly, been the one who gave that interview to the *Tinseltown Buzz*? Or was it someone else? Maybe another person I'd known since high school, like Kristopher? Or other classmates that I hadn't kept up with in recent years? Perhaps the "anonymous source" was a member of the Quest group who'd overheard me talking about being an ardent fan of Dane's. Someone like Bill or Vicky or Elsie.

I flat-out refused to suspect Shar. (She had a healthy sense of distrust when it came to the press, and I just *knew* she wouldn't say anything.) Although, aside from her, it could have been *anyone* in town. A teaching colleague. Someone I'd chatted with at the radio station that day. A nosy neighbor. Or even some thoughtless friend of my sister's. Whomever it was, though, I knew I needed to be extra careful.

"Well, if you need anything, just let me know," Yvette said sweetly.

I thanked her, hating that I had to second guess her earnestness, and ushered her out the door.

A half hour later, Shar showed up.

"I won't stay unless you want me to," she told me, "but I needed to give you a hug, girlfriend."

After the coldness and insensitivity of my witchy sister, Shar's warmth and kindness made me cry. She let me sob on her shoulder for fifteen minutes, handed me tissues, and made me a cup of hot coffee before she left. Even after I told her that there were details I couldn't share with her, she just smiled at me. "I'm not here for juicy gossip, Julia. I'm here for *you*." And she assured me that, whenever I was ready to talk out all the questions that would arise once the eye of the storm had passed, she'd be waiting.

"Thank you," I said, wishing she could stay with me all

weekend, just so I wouldn't feel so alone. But there was too much thinking I needed to do by myself. Too many messages that needed answering, and I still hadn't heard back from Analise. What was taking so long?

I composed a standard text/email message that I used to respond to people who'd contacted me to offer words of support, whether they meant them or not.

"Thanks for your concern. The tabloid story was, of course, not true, but it's upsetting nonetheless. Will look forward to talking with you when things calm down..."

Kristopher, who'd texted me several times, expressed surprise at the turn of events and, while he didn't come right out and say, "I told you so, Jules," he did imply that Dane's character had revealed itself. He also suggested that he hoped things would soon get back to normal and that we'd see each other again before too long.

Not. Likely.

Dane or no Dane, I still couldn't get over Kristopher's weird sense of possessiveness. But, even if he wasn't the right man for me, someone *like* him probably was. Someone who wasn't famous. Someone who was my male equivalent. The Boy Next Door, if you will.

Which was why, when my inbox dinged with an email from Ben Saintsbury that afternoon, I paused and considered it carefully. Had I been too hasty in dismissing him from my life?

Ben wrote, "Just caught one of the Hollywood news shows and was surprised to hear your name... I'm sure you've got a lot of people jumping to conclusions about what happened, but I'm not one of them. I know the kind of person you are, Julia. And I was serious about getting together. Let me know if you ever want to talk, okay?"

It was nicely written and, hopefully, kindly meant. But I wouldn't be sure of his intentions unless I saw him in person again. And I wouldn't be able to figure out until then if what had driven him to reach out to me was genuine supportiveness and interest in my life. Or, perhaps, if it was merely curiosity combined with a desire to have less than six degrees of separation between himself and the ritzy kind of fame he'd always admired.

He'd also let me know—in quite possibly the gentlest way imaginable—that I'd made the entertainment industry news. That this stupid story had spread beyond the *Tinseltown Buzz* website.

Dammit.

I searched online until I found the TV clip that had just aired. I watched with numbed dismay as that arsenal of snapshots of Dane and me together were flashed on the screen, and a truncated version of the article was reported by a too-cheery chick in mini clothing (a mini skirt, a shrink-wrapped tank top, short fashion boots, etc.).

It was funny. They repeated the part about Dane's upcoming fortieth birthday. It was a week from today, on August first. I hadn't needed their reminder, though. I remembered the date from his "Star Profile," and it was burned into my memory, along with all sorts of other things that I knew about him.

Then again, as my so-called "friend" had told Caryn Dizinger, I'd been "obsessed with Dane Tyler" for years. Of course I knew these things.

Just a few days ago, which seemed like a lifetime ago now, I'd been imagining how fun it would be to surprise Dane with a homemade birthday cake next Saturday. But then I totally blew the surprise by asking him what his favorite flavor was.

He'd laughed and said, "Anything made with kindness...and topped with ice cream. With the notable exception of Samuel, no one's baked anything for me in ages. And I haven't had a homemade birthday cake in two decades at least."

To me, his comments felt bittersweet. How heartbreaking that he hadn't had such a simple pleasure in so long and, yet, I was elated at the thought of getting to do this little thing for him. Now, though, it was highly unlikely that I'd even *see* him on his birthday, let alone get to bake him a cake.

It was sad. And I had no idea even where he was. He'd replied to my "you were right" text with just a brief message this morning. "Again, I'm sorry," he wrote. "I'll disappear from your life for awhile." And, true to his word, he did.

Along with the sadness, though, another side of me was furious about Dane's professions of love and affection this week. The guy had to be on the brink of insanity to think I'd be willing to bring my daughter into the madness and maliciousness of the Hollywood scene, especially after witnessing paparazzi crap like this firsthand. He'd *known* what it was like, even though I hadn't. And, sure, he'd *warned* me, but he also had to realize that I didn't understand the situation the way he did.

Being a parent as well, it was hard to forgive him for that oversight. As unintentional as it may have been, he'd let me put my daughter into a position that he'd worked so hard to prevent with his own.

Speaking of daughters, I finally got to talk with mine in the early evening.

Ms. Watkins, the director, opened the conversation and explained that there was an absolute zero tolerance policy for harassment at the camp. And, yes, there had been an incident or two that day as a result of the news story. "However, I'll let you talk with Analise, and she can tell you what happened and how it was handled," the woman said calmly. "I'm here if you have any questions afterward."

"Hey, honey," I said when Analise came on the line. "How are you doing?"

"Oh, Mommy," she said on a sigh. "I'm okay."

Her voice sounded strange to my ears. Subdued and

resigned. Drained, perhaps, but not depressed. I didn't know whether or not I should consider that a hopeful sign, given the bizarreness of this situation, or if I should be more worried than usual.

"I'm not sure what you heard about me today or what was said to you," I told her, "but I want you to know that nothing bad has happened. That sometimes media people don't tell the whole truth because they want to be popular and have others pay attention to them."

"I know," she said quietly. "Not just media people do that."

Out of the mouths of babes.

I fought back a groan. "What did the other kids say to you today, sweetheart?"

"Just that you were Dane Tyler's girlfriend, and that you weren't very smart to go out with a jerk like him. Shannon and Ms. Watkins told them to hold their tongues or their parents would get called."

"Did anyone say anything else to you after that?"

"No. Some kids have looked at me kinda funny," she admitted. "But they did that before."

My heart clenched up at the thought of anyone trying to hurt my little girl. She'd already been through so damn much.

I tried to keep the sound of tears out of my voice. "Well, they're probably just jealous of you. You're such an amazing kid."

"I don't know," she said. "But it doesn't matter. My *real* friends said they thought it was cool that you were going out with a movie star. And I know that you're not dumb and that he's not a bad guy. I mean, I *met* him. And he was nice to me. He helped me."

"That's right, Analise. He did. Dane wanted you to do well on your skit, and you did beautifully."

"Yeah," she said, and I could hear her pride in just that one word. "I'm okay," she repeated before she handed the phone back to the camp director, and this time I could gauge her meaning better. She was still my Analise. She was still the sensitive kind of kid who worried about life changes and other people gossiping about her and the unnerving unpredictability of the future.

But, as I'd also discovered about myself, she could keep this latest blow in perspective. She knew there had already been much bigger calamities and much harder adversities...and she'd managed to live through them. She'd be able to live through this one, too.

The afternoon and early evening entertainment shows were nothing compared to the ones at night. The all-male hosts of "late-nite comedy" showed no self-restraint whatsoever when it came to using material from my life for their opening monologues.

"Hey, guys, is it just Dane Tyler and me who think so, or are widows getting younger and hotter all the time?" said that balding asshole Gregory Carrington.

I'd never liked his brand of humor much. Now, I felt justified in despising him forevermore.

"I mean, you hit forty and a whole new demographic opens up," he added with an idiotic laugh. The live audience smirked and snickered right along with him as he riffed on the aging actor/merry widow theme before finally moving on to another victim.

I curled into a ball of mortification on my bed, just imagining my parents watching that clip. And I realized that Dane's family had been forced to tolerate this kind of crap for over twenty years. His mom and his brother must have felt as powerless and humiliated as I did. Time and time again. Not to mention how it must have affected Dane himself.

To make the night even *more* fun, right after that segment aired, I got an email from my boss, Principal Jack Richardson at Mirabelle Harbor Junior High.

"Sorry to bother you during vacation, Julia, but could you please give me a call at home tomorrow?" Jack wrote. "Personally, I know better than to believe what the tabloids print, but you and I may need to work together to do a little PR damage control before the new school year starts. I got a number of messages from 'concerned' parents today..."

Terrific.

At least Jack wasn't calling for my immediate resignation, although I was sure there were parents of incoming seventh and eighth graders who'd be proclaiming in hushed whispers to anyone who'd listen that I was "morally unfit" to be teaching their innocent children this fall.

And sometime after two a.m. I finally gave up my internal fight and just called Dane's cell phone.

"Hey," he whispered when he answered, his voice raspy.

"Did I wake you?"

He sort of laughed. "Not even close to sleep."

"Where are you? Still in Illinois?"

"I don't want to say, Julia. For your sake. Just in case someone's listening in or tapping my phone or hacking my emails or whatever. I don't want to involve you in this mess anymore."

"I'm already pretty deeply involved. I'm the 'Merry Widow' after all."

"Fuck them."

"Yeah, well." I swallowed. What I could say? "How, um, are Cat and Marissa taking the news?"

"Okay and rather badly, respectively," he replied. "You don't want to know the details, and I shouldn't talk about it on this line anyway. Just in case."

"I understand that. But we are friends, Dane. If you

need to—"

"We're *friends*, huh?"

"Yes," I said. But, of course, a part of me knew we were more than that, too. Whether or not we should be.

Dane let me marinate in those unspoken words for a long while before he said, "It doesn't matter anyway, though, does it? You're still convinced that what I feel isn't 'real,' right? That it's just a fantasy?"

"I wouldn't claim these past two days were *fantasy*-like," I said, trying to lighten the mood, but I knew what he was trying to say. And he knew I was purposely pretending to misconstrue his question.

He sighed heavily.

"What's that sigh mean?" I asked.

"Just too much carbon dioxide in my lungs," he murmured, mimicking my words from Thursday afternoon. From just before we made love for the first time.

I held the phone in silence, remembering.

He cleared his throat. "Truth is, I know you're entitled to run away from me, especially after all of this media shrapnel was fired at you. I have no right to try to hold onto you. But make no mistake, you *are* running. This tabloid shit is an excuse—a very convenient and very understandable excuse—but all the same, I know it's not the entire reason. And I can't blame you, but I'd hoped for better for us."

After having had the thin layer of hard-won peace ripped away from my life this weekend, I just couldn't see any other alternative but to let go of whatever this thing with him was.

"I'm so sorry, Dane," I whispered. "The price...the risk to my daughter and to me...it's just too high."

Maybe I'd expected him to argue back, or at least keep talking to me for a while longer, but he didn't. He must have guessed that I wasn't changing my mind.

After a lengthy pause, he just said softly, "Understood.

You've dealt with a lot and, unfortunately, my presence in your life isn't doing you any good. I wish it weren't true, but I know the best thing I can do for you, Julia, is to say goodbye." And he hung up.

CHAPTER NINETEEN

Four and a half days later, on the last day of July, Shar called for an emergency meeting of the Quest group.

It had been a hellacious week, with media people calling and stopping by uninvited, speculating about me and my relationship with Dane in their print and digital publications. But I couldn't give them much, even if I wanted to. There wasn't anything to say—he was gone. And I thought, under the circumstances, that I'd been working through the ordeal reasonably well.

My best friend, however, felt otherwise.

"You've been trying your best to sort through everything that's happened, Julia, I know," she told me gently. "But this situation is creating a major life change for you. A huge disruption after you've already had a serious life trauma. You're smart and you're grounded, but you can't be expected to think clearly when your world is so messed up."

I tried to shrug this off. "It's so comforting to know that no one has very high expectations of me. Really takes the pressure off."

She squeezed me in a side hug. "Given everything

you've had to endure since December, I think you have the mental and emotional fortitude of a saint, girlfriend. But some of the things you've been telling me this week have me worried. You need a broader perspective than just what I can give you. And that's where other friends come in. Other people that I feel confident you can trust."

She sent me a significant look, and I knew why. One of the most common refrains of our conversations over the past few days was how hard it was to know who I could confide in. Who wouldn't betray me or gossip about me. That fear had made my already very private world even more insular.

"While you've been dealing with the press this week," Shar said, "I've been doing a little investigative reporting of my own, and a few people you know have helped." She led me to her car. "C'mon. We need to get you over to Elsie's house for a little gathering with just the inner circle of the Quest crowd. A few of us have some interesting information to share with you."

When we arrived, Elsie had a teapot filled with steaming Earl Grey waiting on the table for us, a platter of lemon bars, and a room with carefully closed blinds and dim lighting.

She hugged me. "You won't have to worry about *anyone* pestering you here. And anything that's said in this room will stay here. I promise."

"Thanks, Elsie," I whispered.

Then, to Shar, she said, "The others are on their way."

The "others," in this case, included Vicky, who slipped in the door a few minutes later; Nia and Olivia, who came together (neither were members of the Quest group, of course, but they were women Shar obviously felt confident confiding in); and to my utter surprise, Rosemary, who was Elsie's longtime friend, although I'd always think of her as Dane's stage manager at the Knightsbridge.

I glanced sharply at Shar. Was this really a good idea?

In response to my silent question, she nodded and mouthed, "Trust me."

Once we were all gathered together and had gotten comfortable in Elsie's living room, I had to admit that I felt surrounded by a cocoon of pure friendship. Every single woman present, Rosemary included, radiated a vibe of acceptance and helpfulness. Shar most of all.

Which was why I was a little surprised by her conversation opener.

"Remember the hockey movie Dane was in with that redheaded actress—"

"Amy Coleridge," I supplied.

"That's the one," Shar said. "They were the main characters in *Center Ice Draw*. He was an up-and-coming local hockey player and she wasn't really a fan of the sport, until she met him. Then he got that big pro contract. She thought he'd be too busy for her and he thought his lifestyle would be holding her back from her own dreams. You know the story, right?"

"Right," I said. I knew the plots to ALL of Dane's movies, a fact that my best friend was more than aware of...which made me suspicious.

"So, they broke up," Shar continued, "but it really wasn't about the contract or the temporary separation that would cause. It was all about them both being afraid to face their fears. Each of them really wanted to be with the other one but they were scared to go after the relationship."

All of the women in the room were nodding in unison.

I narrowed my eyes at Shar. "So? Stuff like that happens in movies. It's called dramatic conflict."

"I know, I know," she said. "But the point is that the characters made a mistake and, eventually, they realized it.

The only thing that was keeping them apart was fear, and once they finally admitted that, they could figure out a way to move forward. He was all worried about wrecking her life, and she used the fact that he was becoming famous as an excuse to avoid him. But it wasn't the fame that was the problem, it was the fear that he was one of the few people in the world who had the power to break her heart." Shar crossed her arms and gazed steadily at me. "Sound familiar?"

I crossed my arms, too, and cleared my throat. "Amy Coleridge's character didn't have a ten-year-old child to consider. Someone whose life would get swallowed up by the hockey player's fame." I shook my head. "I'm telling you, it's not that I'm afraid of dating anyone ever again, it's just that it should probably be someone...*normal*. A guy from the area. Like, maybe, my college boyfriend, Ben—"

Vicky shot me a dubious glance.

"—or somebody like Kristopher."

Elsie's eyebrows shot up and she actually scowled at me.

"I don't mean him specifically," I said. "He's been acting strange and getting on my nerves. I just mean somebody *like* him. You know, like Bill from the Quest group."

Shar squinted at me. "Were you ever remotely attracted to Bill?"

"Well, no," I had to admit. "But he's nice and lives in the area and is normal—"

"I'm not sure any guy is actually normal," Nia interjected. She glanced between Shar and Olivia and blushed. "Please don't get me wrong, Chance is an amazing man. But just because he isn't internationally famous doesn't mean it was easier for us to find a middle ground than when I was dating a well-known CEO."

"Which CEO?" Olivia asked.

"Oh—Grant Jordan," Nia said.

"Of the Jordan-Luccio Corporation?" Rosemary asked, looking impressed.

Nia nodded.

Shar, who I knew already considered Nia to be her sister-in-law, despite the fact that Chance hadn't yet popped the question officially, studied the young woman with heightened curiosity. "I haven't heard this story..."

Nia waved her off. "It's not really worth telling beyond the fact that it proved to me that 'trusting your instincts' and 'following your heart' aren't just clichés. We need to do both when it comes to love."

She sent me a warm, kind look. She might be younger than I was by a decade, but she was a wise young woman.

Shar's attention was still on her, though. "Wait, are you saying you went out with Grant Jordan before you met my brother...or, um, simultaneously?"

Nia laughed. "We're here to help *Julia* tonight," she replied in a classic evasion maneuver that made me grin for the first time in hours. "But let's just say that your brother wasn't exempt from relationship fear or any less difficult to deal with just because he wasn't a celebrity."

Olivia and Rosemary, the only two in our group who were currently married, both nodded with vigor, muttering something to each other about their husbands. It was too low for me to hear, though.

Shar's lips twisted in amusement. She pointed at Nia. "We're not done with this conversation, but you're right. Tonight is about Julia." She turned to me. "I've been listening to you talk about Ben, Kristopher, and Dane in private all month. And all of us here have heard the public stuff, too. The late-night jokes about you and 'the movie star.' The tabloid insinuations."

I cringed, but Shar and the other women around us looked at me with nothing but understanding and compassion.

"Every single one of us here knows that was unfair and

had to suck," Vicky said.

"It was complete sensationalistic trash," Rosemary added. "I don't even know you very well, Julia, but I know that."

"And I know who's to blame for it," Elsie said with steel in her usually gentle voice.

This got my attention. "Who?" I asked.

"Bill from the Quest group is an extremely nice guy," Elsie began. "He also spent fourteen years as a prosecuting attorney. He knows how to get confessions out of people." She paused and took a deep breath. "He and I are friends from way back, and when I had my suspicions about the source of that witchy reporter's information, I put him on the case. Turns out that your feelings of irritation toward Kristopher are justified. He was the one who contacted that Caryn woman from the *Tinseltown Buzz*. The one who gave her your personal cell number. The one who told her those things about Analise, among other details."

Honestly, given Kristopher's bizarre actions, I couldn't say I was shocked, but a murderous red flooded my internal vision all the same. "Did he have any idea how much damage—"

"He did," Elsie said quietly. "That's the really troubling part. Kristopher told Bill how jealous he'd been when he saw you drive off with Dane after the radio station interview. He wanted Dane Tyler out of your life. The reporter had given out her card to practically everyone in the place, so he had an easy way of reaching her."

"That bastard," Shar breathed. But I could tell this wasn't news to her. It was why she'd insisted I come to Elsie's tonight.

Elsie leaned forward. "I learned some other things about Kristopher from Bill, too. Apparently, he and his sister came from a very unhappy home. His dad wasn't physically abusive, but he was verbally so. Bill found out that there had been some neighborhood complaints about yelling, even as recently as a few years ago. Did you know about that, Julia?"

"No. Although, looking back, it makes sense to me now, given how Kristopher always avoided talking about his parents or having me in the same place as them. Both he and his sister Tricia left home as soon as they could. And his father died three years ago. I'd already suspected that might be why he'd waited until well after the funeral to return to Mirabelle Harbor."

"I'm sure that was a part of it, but it was more than that, too," Elsie told us. "In Tulsa, Kristopher had a girlfriend. Bill was able to draw that information out of him, but it took him a few days to piece together the rest. It seemed Kristopher had begun to replicate his dad's behavior in his own relationships but, unlike his mom, his girlfriend didn't put up with it and wouldn't just 'forgive him' when he apologized. She broke up with him, and he responded by hounding her. Constant texts and phone calls. Stopping by unannounced. Showing up unexpectedly in public places where he knew she'd be. She finally got a restraining order on him. He told Bill he was 'embarrassed by the fuss she made,' and that's why he left Oklahoma. He still doesn't acknowledge his culpability in that situation."

This, too, made sense. I thought of that weird, unexpected visit he'd made to my house. His possessiveness and argumentativeness that day. His contempt toward Dane and toward me, too. And, yet, the bizarre way he expected me to just "let bygones be bygones" after he'd intentionally tried to destroy my reputation—it was as if he thought he could then swoop in and be my "rescuer." The guy needed some serious therapy.

"Elsie, thank you," I said. "It's a lot to take in, and I'm not happy about it, but it makes several things that happened seem clearer to me. Please thank Bill for me, too. I will as well when I see him next."

The older woman came over to me and hugged me tight. "We all thought you should know."

"I appreciate it." The other women in the room were looking at me with empathy, but I got the distinct sense there was more that they wanted to tell me. "What else?" I asked.

Vicky cleared her throat. "You know how you mentioned your college boyfriend Ben earlier?"

I remembered. I also remembered that she hadn't looked pleased when I said his name. "Yeah. Dare I ask, what did he do?"

"I dug a little into his background for you," Vicky said. "Once Shar told me that you'd heard from him in the middle of all the crazy press stuff this week and were thinking of, maybe, meeting him for drinks or something, I contacted several friends of mine from the college."

"Is he a possessive stalker-type, too?"

She shook her head. "Not that, but he's hardly as perfectly put together as he tried to appear during the reunion. I found out from one friend that Ben's wife divorced him five years ago for allegations of multiple acts of infidelity. That he has two young sons who actively avoid him. And that he was tangled in a dicey scandal last year that the school district tried to hush up, involving a former student, who's barely nineteen now. Someone other than the young blond woman, incidentally, who was hanging all over him at the reunion downtown."

"Oh, great."

Vicky sighed. "Maybe Ben would be upfront with you about all of this if the two of you got together in person. I don't know. Or maybe there's an explanation for the student scandal, but the divorce is a verified fact. And, unfortunately, so is the infidelity. One of my college friends was someone he'd slept with while he was still married. His wife was a detail he'd avoided telling my friend until after the fact."

I buried my head in my palms. "I am obviously a terrible judge of character. You guys have proven your point—I shouldn't be allowed to date *anyone*."

"Now, that's where you're wrong," Rosemary said. "I worked with Dane Tyler almost every day for over a month. He is as kind, as trustworthy, and as professional as they come. He's very protective of his privacy, yes, but he's been honest from the first about what he needed and why. He didn't ask for much when he came into town to do this production, but he did insist upon excellent hotel security. So the breach at the hotel last week, particularly as it related to you, Julia, hit him very hard. He feels responsible for the pictures that were taken by the elevators and any information from the staff that may have been leaked, but I know for a fact it wasn't his fault. Once the play ended, the Knightsbridge relaxed the security detail we'd had on him, which unfortunately opened the door to that tabloid reporter and her buddies."

I glanced up at the stage manager and tried to form the question that had been haunting me ever since Caryn Dizinger's article had been posted online. "I know the *Tinseltown Buzz* lied outright about a lot of things, but they also quoted 'sources' from the Knightbridge crew. Someone who said Dane was flirting with all of the actresses in the cast and—"

Rosemary cut me off with a loud laugh. "Listen to me when I say this, I *know* actors. I've worked with them for decades. They can put on a spectacular front for hours at a time, but they can't keep up an act indefinitely. Dane was nice to everyone, cast and crew alike. Lots of women, including a number of the actresses in the play and more than a few theater donors, flirted with the poor guy. A few women threw themselves at him in a way that was embarrassing to watch. He wasn't rude to them, but he also didn't encouraged them. Except for you, I never saw him invite anyone back to his hotel room. Except for you, I never even saw him entertaining someone else in his private dressing room. He was unfailingly professional. The only woman he so much as looked at with longing was you, Julia. *You.* And that's the truth. His relationship with you wasn't a game, at least not to him. I'd stake my career on it."

"It wasn't a game to me either," I whispered.

"Then maybe you need to reassure him of that," Rosemary said. "I talked with him on the phone early this morning, and he's depressed as hell."

I swallowed. I had a million unanswered questions. About where he was now. About what he was doing next. About anything else he may have said to Rosemary. Did she know about his daughter in New York? If she did, she hadn't let on, although I got the sense that he trusted her more than most people. And, yet...I couldn't help but believe that Dane had trusted me even more than that.

"What about Analise, though?" I asked the group. "She's coming home from camp tomorrow. Even if Dane and I could work out some sort of long-distance relationship—which still just seems like an adolescent fantasy—nothing changes the fact that I'm a mom and can't drag my daughter into such a chaotic lifestyle."

"You know I have three boys at home," Olivia piped up. "And I love them with my whole heart. I'd never do anything that might hurt them if I could prevent it." She paused, bit her lip, and then smiled sweetly at me. "But children are more resilient than you and I might think. They usually can adapt to changes in the world around them faster than their parents. They just have to be assured that they're loved, that their needs will be met, and that they can count on their mom or dad to help them work through whatever unknowns the future holds. A happy, well-adjusted, and emotionally healthy parent is the best advocate and best role model for his or her child. So, I think it's our responsibility to show our kids that we value happiness, healthiness, and balance in our lives. You've shown Analise tremendous courage in the face of tragedy and loss, sweetie. Now you have the chance to show her the same courage in the face of love and hope."

Tears filled my eyes. "I don't know..." I murmured. "What if I try it, and it all falls apart?"

"What if you try it, and it *doesn't?*" Shar said, reaching for my hand and grasping it tight. "You know better than anybody that there are no guarantees in life. But I know you wouldn't wish away your wonderful years with Adam just because they ended too soon, would you?"

I shook my head.

"Then," she said, "if you find happiness—no matter how unexpected the source—you need to grab ahold of it for however long you can. And, girlfriend, once you've got it, don't let go."

CHAPTER TWENTY

My daughter rocketed herself into my arms the next afternoon, clinging to me the way a koala clings to a eucalyptus branch. For a long, long moment, we just held each other—time suspended—and let ourselves feel the reunion. Mother. Daughter. Our little family of two.

"I missed you so much, Mommy," she whispered into my shoulder. Then Analise let go, stepped back, and smiled at me. "But camp was awesome," she said. "You know, overall. Promise me I can go back next summer, okay?"

I swallowed back the lump in my throat and nodded. "Okay. You can go back. Are Brooke and Lindsay planning to go next summer, too?"

"Yeah! We talked about it on the drive home."

Yvette, who'd been trying in earnest to be of help to me, had insisted that she and her husband could pick up all of the girls from Camp Willowgreen this morning. And I, admittedly, hadn't wanted to be around a crowd of curious onlookers after all of the press intrusions of the past week. So I agreed, and thanked her profusely.

"Oh, Julia," my neighbor had said. "Honestly, it's the least I can do after the craziness you've been dealing with."

She squeezed my arm quick and blew me an air kiss before driving away.

And, with that simple exchange, I felt as though I'd reclaimed just a tiny bit of my trust in humanity again. I didn't want to live in a world where I perpetually worried that someone sweet like Yvette would turn on me. Where a publication like the *Tinseltown Buzz* could strip me of my ability to have confidence in my own perceptions about people I'd known for years.

"I'm glad the three of you had so much fun together," I said to my daughter now.

"It was great but—" Analise paused and my heart paused with her. "I didn't *just* hang out with Lindsay and Brooke, you know. I made other friends, too. And they didn't...I mean...they weren't, um... Everyone I go to school with here knows all the details about Daddy dying. Most of the kids at camp didn't know anything at all about it, unless I told them. So, it was really different being there."

"You felt that they were seeing *you*, not just your family's story," I said.

She nodded. "At least until the Dane Tyler thing."

I winced. "Oh, honey, I'm so sorry about—"

"It's okay, Mommy. *Mom,*" she said, testing out the shortened form of endearment. It made her sound suddenly stronger, surer, more grown up. And I more than suspected she knew it. She immediately smiled as though she liked what she'd heard. "It didn't bother me that much and, two days later, almost everyone had forgotten about it." She shot me a curious glance. "How is Dane doing anyway?"

It was my turn to trip over words. "I, um...I don't actually know."

Her thin eyebrows rose. "Did he have to go back to Hollywood to make more movies?"

"Probably."

"But you have his phone number, right?"

"Well, yes, but—"

"So, call him," my daughter said, as if this were the easiest and most obvious thing on the planet. "Or text him. If he's still in Chicago, maybe you could invite him over. He's nice." She paused. "And he's pretty cute, too. Don't you think?"

"Uh, yeah...I do think that. But it's rare that he visits this area. Most of the time he lives far away."

She rolled her eyes at me, the way only a ten-year-old could. "You've heard of Skype, haven't you? And there are phone calls and emails. It's easy to keep in touch with people—if you want to."

She pulled out her own cell phone, checked for texts, and smothered a giggle while reading through them. "I've got messages from some of my camp friends," she informed me. "I'm gonna text them back and then go for a bike ride. Okay, Mom?"

"Yes, that's fine." I hesitated asking this next thing, but I had to know. "Analise, let's say I were to invite Dane over to our house, as you suggested, and some press people start snooping around, taking pictures, or posting articles about all of us—"

She shrugged. "Yeah, so? They did that already."

"But they might do it again. I don't know what they'll post on the Internet or what they'll say about me on some entertainment show. I'm worried that it might be upsetting to you, though, sweetheart."

She squinted at me. "You know how I said the kids at camp mostly forgot about you and Dane two days later? This one boy, Frazer Jamison, got the stomach flu that same week and threw up in the middle of the rec hall. The other kids talked about it for, like, another two days. And then one of the counselors—not mine, but my friend Lesha's—fell asleep during movie night and started snoring!" She laughed, remembering, and all at once I caught a glimpse of the beautiful, radiant, and confident woman she would grow up to be. Just a hint, but that lightning flash of illumination was enough for me to realize the changes I'd sensed in her during Parents' Day were taking hold. "Most people have a pretty bad memory," she added. "Unless it's about something really important."

"All right," I said. "Maybe I'll try to call him."

She grinned at me. "Good. You looked happy when you guys were talking at camp. He was funny and cool. You should stay in touch with him."

And with that, she meandered away from me and down the hall to her room where, a moment later, I heard a squeal of delight. "Thanks for the new bookshelf, Mom!" she called out.

"You're welcome," I called back.

And, of course, I was unable to think about that bookshelf without also thinking about when I got it, with whom, and what happened afterward...on the sofa...downstairs.

Either I had an unusually good memory, or my relationship with Dane Tyler was, as my daughter would say, "something really important."

Analise closed her bedroom door and, apparently, lost herself in the wonderful world of texting.

I sat at the kitchen table, closed my eyes and lost myself in the memories I had of Dane from the past month.

I also thought of Shar's words from last night, when we were all at Elsie's house. And, for the first time in years, I had the urge to do something at least vaguely poetic. I shuffled the phrase Shar had used around in my head until the words formed a haiku:

Finding happiness
is an unexpected gift.
Never let it go.

Then I picked up my phone and texted Dane.

"So...Happy Birthday," I wrote because it was August first and today was the big day—his fortieth. Funny. I'd fantasized about personally sending him birthday greetings almost every year since I'd first seen him on the silver screen. I only wished the reality could have been less bittersweet now.

"I don't know where you are," I continued typing, "but I still owe you a homemade birthday cake. Any chance you're within driving distance and want to collect on that?"

No response came. Not after five minutes. Or ten. Or even twenty. An eternity of silence.

I got up to make myself some coffee—something, anything, to distract me from the despair I felt, not just at losing Dane as a lover but, even worse, for being so stupid as to let our friendship slip away because of my fear. I'd pretended it was all because of wanting to protect Analise, but the truth was that it was equally about protecting my heart. My friends saw through my charade in an instant, and my daughter had just proven that she was more courageous than I was. More open to change.

The coffee maker had just begun to gurgle and drip when my phone finally buzzed.

He didn't bother with preliminaries. He wrote only, "*Warm* cake? With ice cream?"

I did a quick scan of the pantry. Flour, sugar, baking soda, powdered sugar, cocoa? Check.

And then the fridge. Eggs and butter? Check.

And finally the freezer. Rocky Road... Check.

"Yes," I texted back.

"I can be there in an hour," he replied. "Too soon?"

"Not soon enough," I wrote. "But drive the speed limit, okay?"

"Fine. Maybe just a *little* above it?"

"No. And no texting on the road either."

I got back a weird emoticon that looked like a grimacing face. Then: "All of these rules. You sure you want to see me?"

"Yes. But I want you in one piece."

"You *want* me?"

I smiled and just typed, "Yes."

There was a long pause before he responded. "Already in the car," he wrote, which was exactly what he'd said that day at camp. It made me hopeful.

No. That was a colossal understatement.

It made my heart soar like a feather-light kite on a breezy afternoon.

I was just finishing up Dane's homemade chocolate birthday cake when I heard voices out in the front yard. Analise had her bike leaning up against the garage door. She was putting on her helmet while talking with Dane, who'd pulled into the driveway with his rental car. Still dark blue in color, but a different model than he'd driven before. So, maybe, he *had* gone somewhere else this week? Hmm.

I watched the two of them through the front window, surprised at the funny, warm, natural way they interacted. Their body language was so relaxed, so unaffected, so without tension, as if they'd known each other for ages. I knew Analise had hit it off with Dane but, until I saw them chatting like old pals in the middle of our driveway, I hadn't fully understood what my daughter had been trying to tell me today. Yes, he was nice. And he was cute. And he was funny and cool. But the important thing, I realized, that she'd been trying to convey was that he was trustworthy. That, in fact, independent of whatever I might think, *she* trusted him.

I tiptoed back from the window so they wouldn't see me, but I cracked the front door open in order to hear a little more of their conversation.

"...and I ended up having to do two more skits after that one when you and my mom were there," Analise was telling him.

"But the techniques I showed you carried over to those performances as well?" he asked.

"Yeah, it was awesome, Dane. I mean, I had to practice

my lines a bunch of times before I could remember them. I still don't know how you memorized your parts that quickly. But the ridiculous connections trick *really* helped."

He nodded. "That's one of my favorites." He pointed to the bike. "So, where are you off to?"

"Just riding around the neighborhood. I feel like I've been away forever."

"Ah, you wanna see what's changed, huh?"

"Exactly!"

"Your mom inside?"

"Yeah. She made you a cake." Then Analise clapped her palm across her mouth. "Oh, no. Maybe I shouldn't have told you that. Was it a surprise?"

Dane laughed and shook his head. "She already gave me the heads up on it. But I don't know the flavor."

"Well, I won't tell you that, then," my daughter said, "but I think you'll like it."

"I know I will."

There was more to their conversation, but I had to step away. Tears had been pooling in my eyes as I eavesdropped, not because the two of them had said anything especially touching or poignant, just because their driveway discussion was so beautifully, hauntingly *normal*. Like the conversations Analise used to have with her dad.

Dane eventually knocked on the door, and I motioned him inside.

"Hey," he said.

"Hey."

"You've, um, got a very cool daughter." He thumbed in the direction of the street, where I could see Analise already halfway down the block on her bike.

"She thinks you're cool, too."

"Really?"

"Oh, yeah. She told me. And you're nice and funny and even cute."

"Wow. Glad I made a good first impression on

someone, which is more than I can say for our first meeting, eh?"

"Well," I said, "you kind of grew on me." I paused. "I missed you so much, Dane. I'm sorry I panicked like that. I just—"

And before I knew it, he had his arms wrapped around me. Another koala hug, and I buried myself in his embrace.

"Julia," he murmured. "*I'm* sorry. I knew what could happen. I should've prepared you better. Told you sooner. But damn them all. I'm not letting anyone wreck this. Wreck *us*. No one gets to come between us again."

He kissed my forehead, my right temple, my cheek, before pressing his lips to my mouth and pulling me even closer to him. Every part of me followed along. Every fiber of my body and soul was drawn to wherever he would lead.

It didn't seem possible that, after everything that had happened over the past year, especially Adam's death, that I could feel such a surge of joy. I may have spent most of the month doubting the realness of my own emotions (not to mention Dane's), but after his absence over the past week, I couldn't deny the feeling of pure happiness on his return.

It's a gift. Never let it go.

Those words echoed in my head until I surrendered to the power of Dane's mouth on mine and let myself get completely pulled in.

When we finally came up for air, he whispered, "You said you wanted me. Is that still true?"

"It's true." I met his gaze and held it. "But I don't know much more than that. I don't know where we go from here. What's next for all of us—you, me, my daughter and yours. How to work out the details. If what we're feeling will last forever. But, yes. Yes, I want you. I...I'm falling in love with you. It was foolish of me to try so hard to fight it."

I watched him take this in, swallowing several times after I spoke. His eyes were suspiciously moist, but he swiped the back of his hand across them before speaking. "This doesn't have to be a 'life in the fast lane' thing," he whispered. "We can take everything slow. It's best that way. But I'll warn you. You'll find me a very hard man to get rid of."

"Why's that?"

"Because I love you, which you already know. And you sure as hell better believe me this time." He smiled slightly. "And because you're the one that I want." He stared at me for a long moment. Until I knew that he was sure I'd taken his words seriously.

I nodded. "Okay."

"Good." Then he sighed. "Unfortunately, Julia, I leave for New York tomorrow. After I see Cat, I'm immediately off to L.A. for seven or eight straight weeks of shooting. So right now I'm feeling a desperate desire to hold you and to make love to you one more time before I have to go." He tugged me toward the stairs to the basement. To our sofa.

"But my daughter—"

"Is on a long bike ride," he finished for me. "We've got a few minutes. And, trust me, I've been aching for you for over a week. This will be quick."

I laughed. "Then come to my bedroom," I said, tugging him in a different direction. "That door at least has a lock."

"Wise plan." He sniffed the air suddenly, as if finally noticing the scent. "Hey, smells delicious in here. Chocolate?"

"Yes. Oh, your cake!" I stopped mid step. "I promised you a *warm* piece with ice cream and—"

"Seriously? You actually think I'd choose cake over you?" He grinned. "Maybe cake on top of you, but..."

"Well, it *is* your birthday."

"Damn right. And, Julia Meriwether Crane, I thought I made this clear—you're the only gift I want."

❁❀❁

Eventually, we did eat the cake (warmed up in the microwave) and topped with Rocky Road. Dane confessed that it was the best birthday cake he'd ever tasted.

"No way you could possibly remember," I said with a laugh. "You told me the last time you'd had a homemade birthday cake was about twenty years ago."

"I have a good memory," he claimed. "Especially for important things."

Ah, yes. *Important things.*

He reached across the table and squeezed my hand. "We'll work out the details. Don't worry. Plus, I don't want to have to wait another two decades to meet somebody who cares enough about me to make me a special birthday cake. I'll be *sixty* then."

"Bet you'll still be cool and cute at sixty."

"Don't know," he said with a shrug and a sly smile. "Let me stick around that long, and maybe you'll find out."

Analise returned from her bike ride in the middle of our dessert discussion and joined us for a piece.

"So, tell us about the movie you're making this month?" my daughter asked Dane.

He raised his eyebrows at me, asking silently for permission.

I bobbed my head. I wasn't sure how my daughter would react to our idea, but it was worth asking. And, having it come from Dane almost guaranteed success, given the respect Analise was showing him. Then again, he'd earned that respect from her.

"It's called *The Scorpius Project*." he explained. "It's a science fiction film that takes place on Earth in the year 2424 and in another galaxy as well. The plot includes lot of suspense and action, so they call it a sci-fi/thriller. I have the script in the car, actually, if you'd like to see what it looks like."

"Sure." She looked mesmerized. Dane knew just how to set up a story.

"All right. I'll get it in a sec. And also, Analise, your mom and I were talking this afternoon. Got any interest in maybe visiting California sometime this year? If you and your mom came out in the next month or two, I could show you the set where I'm filming the movie, or you could see—"

"*YES!* They'd really let me go in there to watch? Could I see you shoot a scene?"

"Definitely." He gave my daughter two thumbs up as he stood and stepped away from the table. "I'm gonna grab the script. When I come back in, we'll compare schedules. So tell your mom to pull out the school calendar. That way we can block off a good date." Then he glanced over at me and winked.

"I will," she said.

Mission accomplished.

The instant he was out of the house, Analise turned to me with the hugest, most triumphant grin on her face. "See? Aren't you glad you invited him over?"

"I am," I admitted. "And you, my sweet girl, were absolutely right to insist on it."

Then I kissed the top of her head and waited, my eyes on the door, for the second love of my life to walk back into the room.

EPILOGUE

Tinseltown Buzz ~ September 7th Edition
BREAKING NEWS!

Labor Day in L.A. just got a little steamier for Oscar-nominated actor Dane Tyler, who was reportedly hosting visitors from the Windy City over the long holiday weekend.

The romance is apparently still going strong between Tyler and his Midwestern lady love from the summer—Julia Crane. He'd been in Chicago for several weeks, starring in a live production of "The Bachelor Pad" at the Knightsbridge Theater, where they supposedly met. But from the looks of things, Tyler may not be a bachelor himself for much longer. Sorry, ladies!

Just take a peek at these candid and oh-so-cozy shots we snapped of the actor and his guests at Disneyland, Universal Studios, the

Hollywood Walk of Fame, and Madame Tussauds! We even have a few exclusive behind-the-scenes photos at the ReelMax Pictures set where Tyler's upcoming film, The Scorpius Project, *is currently shooting. (It's not slated for release until November of NEXT year, folks, so don't get too excited yet.)*

Tyler's famous costar—Brazilian actress and fashion model Cassandra Inigo, who's still recovering from her recent battle with yoga addiction—confided her jealousy over the Tyler-Crane love match to a source close to both actors. "Cassandra thought she and Dane had a special spark between them ever since they were introduced at the spring auditions. Their screen-test chemistry was off the charts," Inigo's good friend claimed. "She's done everything to try to reclaim his attention since filming began last month, but he's been freezing her out."

However, another source hinted that Inigo hasn't been kept in the cold—at least not when it comes to time spent with Golden Globe-winning director Stan Henley Miles.

"All I'm sayin' is that Stan's wife would be SO pissed if she knew what was going on between takes..." said a buddy of the director's, who spoke to us only on condition of anonymity. Hmm. Could this mean one tall glass of Marriage on the Rocks for Mr. Miles?

Who knows what's in store next for the hot Hollywood pairing of Dane Tyler and Cassandra Inigo? Much as we love what we've seen of their onscreen sizzle, it appears their offscreen romantic paths may be headed in different directions. We'll be the first to let you know, though, if the changing winds of love blow them back together in the near future... Stay tuned!

~END~

STORY EXCERPT: TAKE A CHANCE ON ME (MIRABELLE HARBOR, BOOK 1 – OUT NOW!)

If you enjoyed THE ONE THAT I WANT (Book 2) from Marilyn's new *Mirabelle Harbor* series, check out this short excerpt below from the novella TAKE A CHANCE ON ME (Book 1), which is available now, and keep an eye out for the next stand-alone novel in the series, YOU GIVE LOVE A BAD NAME (Book 3), coming soon!

Description and an Excerpt from TAKE A CHANCE ON ME (July 2015)

Welcome to Mirabelle Harbor! In this scenic suburb on Chicago's North Shore, overlooking the sparkling waters of Lake Michigan, the Michaelsen family has made their home for generations. Although their parents and grandparents are now gone, siblings Derek, Blake, Sharlene, and the twins—Chandler and Chance—all have fond memories of growing up in town, and most still live there.

Chance Michaelsen, the youngest member of the family (by two minutes) and the quietest (by far), is a dedicated twenty-eight-year-old personal trainer at the local gym. While he might not say much, Chance has made it clear that he's not a fan of toxic people, unhealthy habits, or sharing too many of his emotions. With anybody.

Enter Antonia "Nia" Pappayiannis—the prettiest member of the loudest and most overly demonstrative family in town. They're also the owners of The Gala, a Greek restaurant and bakery known for its decadent pastries and located just a few steps from Chance's gym. He considers their entire family business to be the enemy of good health, but he can't quite shake his attraction to Nia, who doesn't seem nearly as impressed with him or his sculpted physique as most of the women around Mirabelle Harbor.

Unfortunately, between her doctor's orders and the interfering ways of Chance's crazy-making ex-girlfriend, who just happens to be one of Nia's long-time friends, Chance gets assigned to be Nia's fitness coach for the month. Pure torture. And if his ex weren't already causing enough problems, he also has to deal with Nia's current boyfriend—some hotshot Chicago CEO who talks big but, in Chance's opinion, is as fake as a Styrofoam barbell.

The road to romance is going to be a rocky one, and though Nia has her doubts about getting involved, Chance has a well-developed competitive streak and might just be willing to give it a shot...if he can convince her to do the same.

In matters of the heart, would you risk it all? TAKE A CHANCE ON ME, a Mirabelle Harbor story.

From the Novel:

"Nia?" I extended my hand out to her because I was a *professional* and that's what we did when we met a new client. It didn't have anything to do with my desire to touch her. Much.

She looked at me oddly. Hesitant. Like she was afraid I'd try to out muscle her or something. So I added a slight smile.

If anything, she looked even more worried then, but she finally took my hand and shook it.

God, her skin was *so* soft.

"Chance." She stated my name rather than asked. How insane was it that I was proud of this? That she knew who I was already? Then I looked down and realized I was wearing my trainer nametag.

Oh.

"Yes," I said. "Nice to meet you." This was such a freakin' understatement it was almost a lie. I was usually only attracted to very athletic women, but Nia Pappayiannis had a different style and body type than the typical crowd of single twenty-somethings I ran into at the gym. She was all softness and curves, dressed in her very conservative white t-shirt and her stretchy blue yoga pants. Other women might appear frumpy in such a plain outfit. Nia rocked the look.

"Likewise," she said.

A long, awkward silence followed. I wasn't used to that either. Most of my clients talked my ear off from the second of introduction on. Not her.

I cleared my throat and flashed the clipboard I was holding at her. "On your questionnaire, you mentioned that your doctor prescribed at least ten half-hour fitness sessions to work on core strength. Correct?"

She nodded.

"Okay." I pointed toward the treadmill. "Why don't we do an easy five-minute walking warm up, just to get your muscles moving, before we head over to the weights?"

"All right."

I helped her set the treadmill to a moderate walking speed of 3.3 miles/hour and showed her how to adjust the incline. It looked as though she'd never stepped on one of these pieces of equipment in her life.

"Have you belonged to a gym before?" I asked.

She shook her head. "It's not really my scene."

I was suddenly very interested to know what *was* her scene, but I didn't make a habit out of asking clients personal questions, and I wasn't gonna start now. No matter how sexy her ass looked as she walked on that treadmill.

Man, five minutes lasted a long time.

Check out the Mirabelle Harbor page on Marilyn's website for more information on the series: www.marilynbrant.com/books/the-mirabelle-harbor-series

COMING SOON: YOU GIVE LOVE A BAD NAME (MIRABELLE HARBOR, BOOK 3)

About the Book:

"Nothing but love, 24/7" is the slogan of Mirabelle Harbor's only radio station, 102.5 "LOVE" FM. At age thirty-four, local DJ Blake Michaelsen is well-known for several reasons: his very sexy on-air voice, his omnipresent family, his eligible bachelor status, and his reputation as one of the most impulsive men in Chicago's northern suburbs.

High-school French teacher and lifelong romantic Vicky Bernier is not at all wild about reckless conduct. Or men with gigantic egos. Or grownups who still act like teenagers. She deals with enough adolescent behavior during the school day. Unfortunately, she's the staff advisor to the Homecoming Committee, and they've chosen Blake as their DJ for the big fall dance.

What happens when a man whose job it is to play love songs for a living is forced to admit his deepest secret—that he doesn't believe in true love—only to discover that the one woman who might capture his heart is the same woman who distrusts him the most?

No matter what you call it, with love there's an exception to every rule. YOU GIVE LOVE A BAD NAME, a Mirabelle Harbor story.

ABOUT THE AUTHOR

Marilyn Brant has been told she writes with honesty, liveliness and wit (descriptors she's grown terribly fond of) about complex, intelligent women—like her friends—and their significant personal relationships. Although her favorite pursuits undoubtedly involve books, she proves she's not just a literary snob by confessing her lifelong fascination (read: obsession) with popular music, especially from the '70s and '80s, most flavors of ice cream and a variety of sensuous body lotions/oils.

As a former teacher, library staff member, freelance magazine writer and national book reviewer, Marilyn has spent much of her life lost in literature. She is the *New York Times* and *USA Today* bestselling and award-winning author of nine novels to date, and a lifetime member of the Jane Austen Society of North America. The Illinois Association of Teachers of English (IATE) selected her as their 2013 Author of the Year.

Her debut coming-of-age novel, *ACCORDING TO JANE* (Kensington, 2009), featuring the ghost of Jane Austen giving a young woman dating advice, won the Romance Writers of America's prestigious Golden Heart® Award and the Booksellers' Best, and it was named one of the "Top 100 Romance Novels of All Time" by Buzzle.com. Her second novel, *FRIDAY MORNINGS AT NINE* (Kensington, 2010), was a Doubleday and Book-of-the-Month Club pick in women's fiction. *A SUMMER IN EUROPE* (Kensington, 2011) was featured in the Literary Guild and BOMC2, and it became a Top 20 Bestseller in Fiction and Literature for the Rhapsody Book Club. The Polish translation of the novel was released in June 2013.

She's also a #1 Kindle and #1 Nook bestseller, who writes fun and flirty romantic comedies, like her stories in *THE SWEET TEMPTATIONS COLLECTION*, that involve sweet treats, unexpected love and large doses of humor. *THE ROAD TO YOU*—a coming-of-age romantic mystery—was selected as one of the Top 20 Best Books of the Year (December 2013) by The Reading Frenzy. Several of her novels will soon be available in audio CD/download from Post Hypnotic Press. Look for them in 2015 and beyond, and be sure to keep an eye out for more romances in the "Mirabelle Harbor" series, coming soon!

Marilyn currently lives in the Chicago suburbs with her family. When she isn't reading her friends' books or watching old movies, she's working on her next novel, eating chocolate indiscriminately and hiding from the laundry. Please visit her website: www.MarilynBrant.com.

www.ingramcontent.com/pod-product-compliance
Lightning Source LLC
Chambersburg PA
CBHW020554180626
46810CB00007B/2505